SHADOW LANDS OF MEMORY

A TIM STRANGE NOVEL

JONATHAN M. NIELSON

Macauley-Ritter Publishing, Ltd.
El Dorado, CA USA

Library of Congress Cataloging in Publication Data

Nielson, Jonathan M.
Shadow Lands of Memory

1. Mystery
2. Historical Fiction
3. Thriller

ISBN 978-1-6-4945-542-0

FIRST PRINTING 2020

SECOND PRINTING 2021

Printed in the United States of America

‘Twilight, even remembered twilight, is better than no light at all.’

China Mieville

CHAPTER ONE

"Be at peace cousin. Secrecy will conceal all but history is forever in the shadow lands of memory…"

CHAPTER TWO

"Abby, hand me the baby sledge would you?" She reached-up on her well-worn Reeboks to hand Tim the tool he was using to demo sheetrock so old and brittle it had yellowed to the color of wheat and fell off the studs in large chunks pulling right through the nails as it fell in clouds of dust and patches of old wallpaper. "Thanks babe."

"Good thing we're wearing masks and safety glasses," she said, her voice muffled by the white cotton cup over her mouth and nose. Tim took the sledge looking down at her from the 8-foot ladder through his slightly fogged face shield appreciating the view, again acknowledging his good fortune. Timothy Strange, tenured professor of history, knew that past and present sometimes aligned in unpredictable, fortuitous ways at this moment he loved the serendipity of it all.

Abeline Davis, Abby, his twenty-two years-younger wife for just over a year now had come into his life two years before like a hurricane, blowing away all his preconceived notions about propriety and age difference and testing his professional ethics. He'd weathered both challenges discarding his reservations and, except in his strained rationale, not crossing the line his position demanded he respect.

Once his irrepressible student she had become his irreplaceable partner, their relationship forged in extremes of harrowing, life-threatening adversity both exhilarating and terrifying in equal measure, he reflected. No amount of raised eyebrow, eye-shifting, whispered disapproval by the morally indignant sufficed to weaken the deepening attraction between them defying convention and expectation. To the contrary they found the opprobrium weirdly amatory.

Thrown together by the murder of her mother and younger brother by her dirty-cop father, they'd fled Prescott, Arizona seeking refuge in Montana only to become ensnared in Big Sky country by Barry Seal's High Line' drug operation. The multi-state chase that unfolded ended back in Prescott in a deadly cartel shoot-out on Thumb Butte, leaving both battered and bruised but committed to an unlikely, conflicted romantic relationship neither had sought but both needed for their own reasons. A senseless auto accident had recently killed his wife, Karen, and Abby provided solace and emotional safety when he most needed it. Mutual desperation, he'd once made light but it wasn't far from the truth of it.

That following summer his sabbatical took them to London where his high profile research into the Armenian Genocide nearly got them both killed. Abby's abduction by Turkish agents following a horrific bombing in London was the beginning of Tim's desperate attempts to rescue her. The trail led to the Armenian capital of Yerevan and the ancient city of Ani where her captors entombed her to assure Tim's compliance with their plot to use him to assassinate pro-Armenian scholars and prevent the release of evidence that would finally prove Turkish guilt in the atrocity following the First World War.

The region then engulfed in Cold War era Soviet-Armenian-Turkish intrigue amplified both the dangers and the sacrifices both had to endure amidst the devastation and human catastrophe of the great Armenian earthquake that killed tens of thousands and leveled entire cities. They had survived but the scars, emotional and psychological, cut more deeply than physical wounds. But if anything, their ordeal had brought them even closer. Staring down death at every turn led to life's affirming if finite clarity. Marriage with all its complications and uncertainties seemed out of the question for both of them ...until it didn't.

On a Saturday afternoon in August, surrounded by the towering red rock cathedral of Sedona's canyon country, with monsoon lightening arching far off in the Verde Valley, they exchanged simple vows with one of Tim's 'ordained' colleagues officiating. It was secluded, unpretentious and just them, a shared moment of intimacy in the quiet grandeur of nature's unspoiled beauty, accompanied only by the twitter of Kingfishers and Tanagers and the shrill chwirk of a goshawk circling high above as a soaring, solitary witness. Theirs was a throw caution to the wind leap into the dark…an act of faith. Isn't everything?

"So how much longer do you figure?" she asked as she swept debris into a large dustpan and from it onto a tarp, blew a wisp of bond hair off her forehead.

Good question Tim thought. They'd been at it now for two days, 'it' being the remodel of the cabin in Show Low, the commercial and tourism hub of the White Mountain resort area south of Interstate 40, along a stretch of Arizona Hwy 260. Show Low was a winter paradise with weather similar to Flagstaff's and milder summers than endured in Prescott or Phoenix-Scottsdale.

The cabin had belonged to a cousin, Justin, who'd inherited it. He'd left the area and offered it to Tim years before as a get-away haven from the academic grind. He and Karen had used it often…ski trips, summers on Fool Hollow Lake. Fond memories…

The cousin lost interest and sold the place to Tim. He called it 'ranch rustic'. She called it a dump. So here they were with plans in hand and DIY renovation underway. The hewn log exterior was cedar and although needing restaining was in good shape as was the roof thankfully. This was their third weekend and the interior demolition was nearly behind them except for this last interior wall. There was no electrical wiring in this section which included a small pantry, merely dividing the small kitchen from the living room, so the work had gone quickly.

"Unless we get into something unexpected I think by cocktail hour," Tim checked his watch, "we should be done with the worst part. Tomorrow we'll hang the new rock," he indicated the ten sheets of new wallboard stacked in the living room. It goes up a lot cleaner than it comes down," he assured her. We should have it knocked out by noon if we get an early start."

"How early is early? All work and no play you know," she winked. "Besides my back and shoulders hurt like hell."

"Not to worry. Steaks on the grill, beers in the fridge…and there's the hot tub for your aches and pains," he shot her a 'what's not to like' grin. "As for play…"

"Tim, what's that?" she asked abruptly. He followed her finger to where the shallow pantry recessed into the 2x6 wall. They'd emptied the space of its few canned foods, dry goods and paper products leaving its few wooden shelves bare. The pantry would be relocated to the attached garage opening-up more space in the redesigned pass-through living space.

Examining the panty more closely now, Tim could see a barely visible vertical line behind one the shelves. All the constant pounding, he surmised, must have exposed this previously hidden seam. It was clearly man-made not a crack or flaw. "Well I'll be damned. Abby there's some sort of compartment built into the wall here that we've knocked open." She moved closer "Here, hand me that pry bar." She passed it up examining more closely now what had caught her attention. "Good eyes, Babe."

"What do you think it is exactly?"

"No clue but we're about to find out." With a protesting creak a 6x12-inch panel opened. Abby had taken off her gear as had Tim and both were now staring into the dark void.

"There's something in here," Tim announced inching the ladder closer for a better look. Reaching in, he removed a heavy pouch.

"What is that?"

"It's like a canvass bag with a draw string. Here, see" he removed their discovery holding it by its leather thong.

"It looks like it's been in there for a long time," Abby offered, "but you're the historian."

"True, but historians aren't archaeologists," Tim observed as he blew-off a thin lamina of dust. Whatever this is someone put it here years…maybe even decades ago. It has weight to it," he demonstrated. "It's made of some kind of waterproof material like Burberry or Gabardine, I think."

"First question: why would your cousin hide something behind a secret panel?"

"And the second?"

"If it was important enough to hide, why didn't he tell you about it…he just forgot?"

"Both damn good questions," Tim replied as he stepped down the ladder holding the bag. "I haven't spoken to Justin since I bought the place," he shrugged. "What's say we find out what's in it? Maybe that will provide us some answers," he offered hopefully.

Walking with her to the wooden slat kitchen table Tim carefully set the bag on it. It made a muffled thud. The room at this time of day offered little natural light. "Grab the flashlight over there so we can see better. Thanks." Abby had to admit she was curious as hell but given their recent track-record she also felt a twinge of apprehension. None of their recent surprises had been good ones.

Carefully Tim pulled the thong tie and opened the pouch. Upending it he let the contents spill out onto the table. Tim starred open-mouthed. Abby gasped. What the…"

CHAPTER THREE

"What are we looking at...besides the obvious?"

Finally, after long moments: "Abby, I'd say what we have here is a mystery...and a big one."

Tim lifted the heavy revolver by its grips. Its barrel, cylinder and frame were the deep blue of case-hardening with elaborate etched gold engraving on the frame and barrel. Involuntarily she stepped back. A year ago her knowledge of firearms had been near zero. Since, of unwelcome necessity, she'd been on an accelerated learning curve. She'd killed a man in Armenia who'd tried to rape her. That education and experience, however justified, had not diminished her dislike of guns and the violence associated with them. But it was more than that: the rush of power, of righteous vengeance, she felt scared her.

Tim turned the weapon from side-to-side examining it from every angle. "Wow," of offered finally. "I haven't seen one of these in ages and the last time was in a museum."

"A museum? It looks in new and perfect condition. Is it loaded?"

"It does and is but it's far from new. This old guy has been very well cared for by someone."

"Not your cousin?"

"I have no idea but I don't think so...a gut feeling," he threw her a shrug. And no, it's not loaded. Tim released the top latch and the revolver hinged to reveal the five-shot cylinder and ingenious ejector mechanism. No," he showed her. No brass center-fire cartridges.

"How old is it...and what is it?"

"This" he said admiring the gun, "this is a Smith and Wesson Schofield 3rd Model Russian, single action. The bore's probably 44.40."

"A what? But then her recognition screwed into a question.

"Isn't Smith and Wesson an American company?"

"It is and a famous one. They were big rivals of Colt and its "peacemaker". Some think this design was superior when it was introduced in 1871."

"1871? That was just after the Civil War…over a 100-years ago!"

"You remember. I knew I gave you A's for a reason."

"You know damn well why you gave me A's," she cooed teasingly.

"That was …before," he dismissed the inference.

"And since?"

"Abby, stop already." He shrugged noncommittally. "Not bad." She slugged his shoulder playfully.

"S&W sold thousands of these to the Russian military through 1915, as I recall, in addition to thousands for the American market," he redirected. That was just before the Bolshevik Revolution, Lenin, Trotsky...all that.

"Czar Nicholas II…Anastasia…Rasputin…" Tim nodded approval.

"How do you tell a Russian from an American model?"

"OK, see this hook or spur curving down from the trigger guard? That's the real tip-off. Only Smiths for the Russian market had them. This is a single action revolver so the spur helped the shooter cock the hammer and helped with recoil as did this raised hump on the back strap here above the grips. And this," he indicated the metal ring at the frame strap below the grips. "That too is unique to this model. It's what they call a lanyard ring…cavalry used them so if a man lost his grip during a charge, the lanyard prevented him from losing his gun."

"What kind of wood is that?" Abby indicated the grips.

"It's not wood. Looks like yellowed ivory to me."

"OK. But what's a century-old Russian gun doing here in Show Low, Arizona in your cousin's shack?"

"Cabin."

"Whatever."

Instead of answering her directly Tim followed his own thoughts.

That's what I'd like to know, he ruminated. He'd only met Justin…a second cousin a few times at family functions over the years. They weren't especially close and had little in common. He was an accountant in Cheyenne, Wyoming and although he didn't get out west much he fell in love with Arizona. He was hard right Republican and religious, Tim a 'spiritual' Democrat and a 'lefty' at that and after one rip-roaring argument, their interactions thereafter were distantly superficial but civil. So given all that when Tim learned from his cousin's attorney that Justin had died suddenly of uncertain causes and left him the cabin, it came as a total surprise.

The one thing they did share was a love of history although their interpretations often clashed as sharply as their politics. Still, they enjoyed each other's enthusiasm and command of the subject each always, on the rare occasions they met over beers, managing to bring interesting perspectives and some esoteric quote or reference-or-other that kept things interesting.

But in none of those interactions had Justin ever mentioned anything about Czarist Russia, its Revolution, Bolsheviks or anything remotely related to those events. Tim had been to the cabin two-three times over the years with him and never had Justin talked about firearms of any kind, showed him any, or expressed any interest in them. Tim had never raised the subject but typically guys who collected or hunted or were seriously into home-defense talked about their guns. He didn't. And Tim had never seen so much as a BB-gun in the cabin.

As Tim thought about it now increasingly it seemed likely that Justin had no more idea of what was hidden in his pantry wall than Tim did. So…who put it there and why? Abby was right. That was the question…and the mystery.

"What's this?" Abby held-up a banded sheaf of elaborately engraved paper notes pale yellow about twice the size of a dollar bill.

"These look like banknotes or stock certificates of some kind," Tim ventured.

"They have 100 printed on them and over here in this circle is a crest of some kind with a crown above it," Abby pointed out. Who is this?" she indicated the woman."

"Not sure but it could be Catherine the Great, she's the only czarina I would recognize.

"Makes sense these are also Russian...must be paper rubles. Could be wrong but that looks like the Romanov crest to me. See the two – headed eagle-the crown. I do know that even after the Revolution 'Romanov money' as it was called was highly sought after and even the Bolsheviks used it for a few years amidst all the chaos because it was backed by gold and offered some financial stability."

"Wow! Abby suddenly exclaimed. "Gold like this?" She had uncorked a waxed paper tube and let the contents fill her palm. Tim started at the six coins. "Is that who I think it is?" she indicated the man's raised profile replete with beard and mustache wreathed by Cyrillic letters.

Tim recognized it immediately. "Czar Nicholas II. Look on the reverse," she turned the coin over.

"The two-headed eagle under a crown," Abby confirmed. "These are real? I've never even seen a gold coin before much less held six in my hand," she seemed truly impressed, Tim noted.

"I'm sure they are. I inherited two twenty-dollar Liberty Head gold coins from my grandfather minted in 1900 and nothing else looks and feels like gold.

"What are these worth do you think?"

"These are 15 ruble coins," see here," he pointed out, and here's the date: 1897. They're worth a hell of a lot more than that today. Gold is gold no matter what the face value but these also have collector-historical importance. I wouldn't even venture a guess but I'll check with my coin guy in Prescott."

"Look at this?" Abby alerted him. She held a small embroidered plush pouch with an ornate silver snap closure. "Looks like a jewelry or coin purse and it's definitely old."

Tim studied it closely. I have something like this from my grandmother. Definitely 19th-century…or a very good copy."

"Shall I?"

"Go for it."

The pouch opened with a soft tic. Abby upended it and a heavy coin slid into her hand. It was made of silver and slightly smaller than a Morgan silver dollar, Tim observed. On the face was the profile of a man surrounded by the same kind of lettering. Beneath his profile was a date: 1825. On the back, as Abby turned it over, was the same wreathed double eagle crest under a crown, the circumference edge crowded with more Cyrillic lettering. "What is it?"

Tim picked it up by thumb and finger by its edge. "It's definitely Russian like the gold coins but obviously silver…and clearly older by the date."

"Who's the guy…another czar? How is that spelled by the way?"

"Probably…some spell it with a 'T' as in 'Tsar'." Abby slid the coin back into the pouch and set it aside.

The only other item in the bag she was holding up for him to examine. Tim took it from her to get a better look. It was a round disk about the size of a half-dollar and it was made of thin bronze. On it were stamped two letters-'I.P.' "Ever see anything like that before?"

Tim flipped it over but there was nothing on the reverse side except a small spot of some kind. He handed it back to her. "Abby, I have no clue," he confessed, "but I don't think this is Russian."

"Military maybe?" Abby ventured.

Tim examined the disc again. "You could be on to something. This little dot on the back could be a solder-point for something that's broken off…like a pin. Yes! He seized on something. It's a collar insignia of some kind. These attached with a brad that fit over a pin on the inside of a uniform shirt collar. Officers wore them. I had a set in Nam…little gold- plaited oak leaves…Major, he explained. This one probably dates from early 1900s…maybe WWI…like these other things we've found.

"How can we be sure?"

"When we get back, I have some military references in my library I can check…see if I can find a photo-match or description."

"Sounds like a plan," she offered brightly. "Now can we finish this crappy teardown. I want a shower and a cold beer and a burger sounds heavenly."

Tim collected their find and put the bag in the bedroom. "Demo it is Mrs. Strange."

"I don't know if I can ever get used to being called 'strange.'"

"You are strange in a very attractive, desirable way," he shot her the lopsided grin she had come to love as he picked-up the sledge, and soon sheetrock shattered about them in pieces again….

The moon peeked over the tall pines that surrounded the cabin. They sat in deck chairs on the open porch. The smell of burgers still wafted off the BBQ and four empty Tecate bottles lie on the weathered oak boards. "Three's my limit, you know" she said as she sipped from her beer.

"I'm counting and about to cut you off. Wouldn't want you to do anything wild and crazy."

She arched an eyebrow. "You wish. What's wild and crazy is our discovery today. That was totally unexpected. I'm intrigued for us to dig a little deeper…see if we can do a bit of historical sleuthing, as you like to call it."

"That's what I do best," he toasted. "But remember what happens when we start digging into things, turning over rocks…investigating," he laughed but with an edge to it.

"Damn, you're right. On second thought…" she trailed off into reflection. "But what the hell. Whatever it is can't be all that big a deal…doesn't involve us. How could 70-year old stuff that belongs in a museum possibly affect us, right?"

However this got here and whoever put it in the wall, it's ours now. So suddenly we have a decision to make. What the hell do we do with these things? Chances of finding the original owner is about zero. Do we just keep the coins in a safe deposit box…give them to a museum? I'd like to have the Smith but…And what about this disc? It can't have much monetary value but there must be story attached to it and probably an interesting one...."

Tim sat silently also lost in thought, she presumed. Finally... "you know that little voice in my head?"

"You mean the one that usually gets us in trouble?"

"That's the one."

"What about it?"

"It's screaming at me."

"What's it...no I don't want to know."

"No, Abby- you don't."

On the desk in their bedroom the pouch of artifacts sat silently in the wan glow of the cold moon. But for how long would it secrets remain secrets and what might happen if they came out?

CHAPTER FOUR

A thick, cold mist lifted off the Neva River delta as the broad, steel-grey river sluiced its way from Lake Ladoga through the western enclaves of St. Petersburg, its 42 islands and nearly 800 bridges connecting them to the and mainland floodplain, winding west 46-miles to the Gulf of Finland, freezing solid from December thru April in a great sheet of ice. A maze of canals and tributaries transected the city and many likened it to Venice…a very frosty Venice in winter's that plunged to -40..

It could also make solid claim to be Russia's Paris. Indeed its founder Peter the Great, the first of the Romanovs, made no apologies in 1703 that he intended his Patron Saint's city to be a reflection of the grandeur of Versailles in monumental architecture, culture and opulence. He succeeded magnificently and St. Petersburg soon rivaled and even surpassed other great cities of Europe and served as Imperial Russia's capitol city for all of the 19-century and into the 20th. The monumental, 1,500 room, English Baroque style Winter Palace, the Czar's Imperial residence, awed western visitors with its splendor and scale and symbolized Mother Russia's prowess, ambition and wealth, befitting a vast country stretching from the Urals 5,000-miles to far Western Siberia.

Protected by the massive star fortification the czar had built on Zayachy Island over thirty years, Peter and Paul fortress offered a powerful deterrent to Swedes and Poles during the Great Northern War, although never seriously tested by an adversary until Germany's 900-day siege during WWII. The fortress and naval base of Kronshtadt erected on Kotlin Island protected the city from the Gulf of Finland. At the outset of WWI the city, renamed Petrograd , became a symbol of anti-German resistance. Then after the Revolution of 1917 Petrograd became Lenningrad with advent of the Soviet Union from 1924 to1991 when it reclaimed its original name.

Tim knew this much from general knowledge and his own eclectic research interests but it was a good refresher. The day after their return from Show Low he began digging deeper, intrigued by their discovery in the cabin and by instinct and professional experience, certain that a much greater story waited to be uncovered. But first he needed full historical context and some perspective on where he thought their discovery might be leading them.

In recognition of Russia's international stature, every major power established diplomatic relations with St. Petersburg and located their embassies and consulates there beginning in the mid-1700s. Most considered these diplomatic missions, through war and peace, second or third behind only Berlin, Paris or Vienna in importance to their interests.

Even before Independence and what became the United States, England's North American colonies, violating Britain's mercantile policies, traded with Catherine the Great's empire in the 1760s. During the Revolution Catherine's 'Armed Neutrality' while maintaining Russia's technically impartial position, favored the American cause and the prospect of American commerce…even refusing Britain's requests, including bribery, for Russian military intervention. During the war Francis Dana was appointed American Minister to Russia and although Catherine refused to recognize his portfolio, or even allow publication of the Declaration of Independence, his three years in St. Petersburg sustained cordial, if wary, relations between a fledgling democratic republic and a czarist autocracy.

With Independence achieved, President Jefferson, whose diplomatic posting in Paris during the war accorded him important connections with Czars Paul and Alexander I, appointed

Levett Harris as America's first Consul-General in 1801 who, though controversial, represented America's interests there for the next thirteen years.

Jefferson and Alexander struck-up a curiously intimate relationship as the Czar's liberal tendencies, serfdom notwithstanding, found approval with the slave-owning denizen of Monticello, exchanging letters and even gifts. The president's violation of the Emoluments clause of the Constitution earned a raised eyebrow. Finding common aggravation in the British Navy's suppression of free trade and neutral rights, it required a stinging defeat at the hands of Napoleon in 1807 to cause Alexander to spurn his British alliance against France and, under duress, join forces with Napoleon. It would prove to be a fateful decision. But within two years the Russia and the United States established formal diplomatic relations by exchanging ministers, William Short briefly followed by the much more consequential posting of John Quincy Adams to St. Petersburg in June of 1809.

At this time, Tim discovered as he dug deeper, the two nations were already on a collision course in a most unlikely corner of the world: the North Pacific and the vast territory of what for thirteen years had been the colony of Russian-America since its charter by Czar Paul, centered on the island of Sitka or Novo-Arkhangelesk, claiming all of what would become Alaska and waters north of the 55th Parallel. But Russia entertained grand ambitions, founding other colonies in Hawaii and Spanish California at Fort Ross in 1812 with clear intentions of pressing their claims into British Columbia and further south into the Oregon Country then occupied by both American and British commercial fur companies. In Alta California its interests clashed with those of Spain, France and England. It was a potentially explosive mix.

Alarmingly for now Secretary of State Adams, Czar Nicholas I issued an Imperial Ukase, or pronouncement in rechartering of the Russian-American Company, extending Russia's claims down to the 51st Parallel and put all that part of the North Pacific Ocean off limits within a hundred nautical miles of that point.

Even as Anglo-American tensions rose in the Pacific Northwest, they shared a common interest in preventing Russian expansion and both separately negotiated treaties in 1824-25 establishing a northern boundary of Russian colonization at 54-40. Nicholas did not enforce the Ukase. At the same time a wave of revolutions raging through what remained of the Spanish empire in the Americas, creating the potential for other European mischief, prompted Adams to issue one of the most famous documents in American foreign relations...the Monroe Doctrine, placing the hemisphere off limits…except to the United States, Tim noted as he reflected on the fraught history of America's hemispheric relations since. Manifest Destiny unleashed with a vengeance.

The Civil War brought another test of Imperial Russian-American relations. Again technically neutral Russia signaled in word and deed its tacit support of the Lincoln administration, sending war fleets to New York and San Francisco, interpreted as confirmation. There was much talk of the Czar's and Lincoln's shared humanitarian impulses, each abolishing un-free labor: serfdom in Russia-peacefully; slavery in the United States in a bloody civil war.

In the ensuing years following the sale of Alaska to the United States in 1869, the two nations interests and foreign policies remained distant but generally cordial and mutually beneficial punctuated by occasional points of cooperation and friction. While the two nations recognized their respective interests in exploiting China and militarily defeating the Boxer Rebellion in 1901, anti-Jewish pogroms created a backlash among some Americans resulting in the termination of the 100-year old commercial treaty in 1913.

The final diplomatic interaction between the two nations was Theodore Roosevelt's mediation and peace treaty negotiations at Portsmouth, New Hampshire, ending the Russo-Japanese War in 1904, a catastrophic defeat for Czar Nicholas II that had equally tumultuous consequences for Russia and tragic outcomes for him and his family, Tim reflected, as he put pen and yellow legal pad down at last. It had been a long day. His hand was cramped and his head buzzed from too much coffee. But he now had what he needed…a refresher on the tangled history of relations between two nations so different in their interests, history, culture, religion and governance.

Later he sat in their living room with a cold beer, Tweeks the cat and Ralph the dog curled-up nearby. Abby was at the market. In front of him on the coffee table near his pile of books and articles were the objects he and Abby had found in the cabin. Looking at the gold coins with Czar Nicholas IIs likeness and the Smith and Wesson 'Russian', he felt a connection or correspondence between these inanimate objects and the history attached to them in some fashion. Only a historian, he chuckled.

And then he picked-up the disc collar insignia. What about it? How did these pieces fit together if at all? But he was certain they must. Like archaeologists on a dig evaluating an artifact or fossil…it wasn't merely the object itself but the association among objects and the soil or rock they were found in that could be dated and contextualized that mattered.

Taking a long last pull on his Pabst Blue Ribbon, he rose and walked into his study…once his deceased wife Karen's office that Abby refused to use, where he kept a small library of reference and other scholarly and rare books. He kept twice as many in his office at the College but these had personal meaning, brought-up memories of grad-school and studying for orals.

A few years back on a lark he'd bought coffee-table sized book in a used book store titled: International Encyclopedia of Military Insignia on a day he was haunted by flashbacks of his tour in Nam…something that happened every so often without warning. Pulling it off the shelf he barefooted back to the sofa, checked the index and began flipping through pages until he found what he was looking for…WWI.

Abruptly he realized he had no clue what country or branch of service the disc represented. This would be work. It required another beer. He studied his way through the British, French and Russian sections when it struck him to think about 'association' as in where they found the disk…Show Low, Arizona…not London, Paris or St. Petersburg. It only took a few seconds into the American section when he was staring at a photo of exactly what he was holding in his hand.

He dropped his eyes to the descriptive entry below the photo and there it was 'I.P.'...Intelligence Police. Intelligence Police? He'd never heard of it. Quickly he turned to the short essay on this section and read: 'United States Army, American Expeditionary Force G-2, Corps of Military Police, formed in August 1917 with units deployed in the US in counterintelligence and to Europe, redesignated the Military Intelligence Division from June 1918 to March 1942.'

There it was. He knew the service branch, dates, and designation. Armed with that, he could now investigate more deeply and in what likely archives and collections and journals. His curiosity surged. What did the IP do, where exactly was it deployed, what did it accomplish? And most importantly did it have any presence in St. Petersburg in 1917-1919? These and other questions began to chew on him and he knew he was hooked.

"Hi," Abby called out happily as she entered through the kitchen, setting her bags on the counter. Ralph leapt up to greet her. Tweeker barely moved. "Market was jammed," she said as she began the choreography from fridge to cabinets to drawers, paper bags rustling. "Discover anything?"

"I did but I don't know what it means. It's like the tip of the iceberg. The collar disc is WWI era, something called the Intelligence Police. I'd never heard of them before."

"So how does that fit with the rubles and a Russian revolver?" She was almost afraid to ask, knowing Tim.

"That sweet girl is what we're going to find out."

It was the tone of his voice she didn't like. "What do you mean...we?"

"I've always wanted to see St. Petersburg. It's six weeks until the new semester begins," he offered with a sheepish smile. How about it?"

"How about what? Oh, you can't be serious, Tim," she protested.

"Abby, where's you sense of adventure? Ok, ok," he held his hands up in defense reading her 'are you fucking kidding me' expression. "A week that's all. St. Petersburg and nowhere else, I promise. Prescott's only going to get hotter. And you don't start back at the non-profit until September anyway," he tried his best to sell her.

"Isn't this…research something you could do here or at least in the states?

"Some of it yes, of course. But actually being in Russia will be important and a critical opportunity. Not only is the Czar's Winter Palace now one of the world's mind-blowing museums-the Hermitage, but the Russian State Historical Archive is there- the 'RGIA'…everything from Peter the Great to the Bolsheviks. There may be nowhere else to get the clues we need."

"Do you think it's safe...I mean the Berlin Wall just came down last November and the Soviet Union looks like it could come apart anytime from what I read and you've told me. I don't know much about what would you call it…the 'political dynamics', she air-quoted, "but the whole thing seems 'ify' to me. I mean couldn't there be another revolution… or worse?"

"Yes, you have a point. God knows we experienced some of that political chaos in Armenia. But St. Petersburg isn't Yerevan…earthquake or not. Regardless of what happens…if it happens, it won't be anything like 1917…revolution, riots, full-scale warfare. If nothing else, whatever the Kremlin decides to do it will want to prevent the worst for economic reasons alone. Remember these guys are experts at squashing dissent. Then too there are dozens of major American and European corporations based in the city doing serious business, from what I read. Even if things in Moscow get dicey, I think St. Petersburg will be insulated from any immediate political fallout in Moscow. It's nearly a thousand miles and a seven hour plane flight away from the Kremlin."

'But there are phones and secure communications and military installations around St. Petersburg right?"

"True," Tim conceded. But there is also one of the biggest airports in Russia and all of Eastern Europe-Pulkova. They're not going to shut down the only way to fly in or out of the city. If there's trouble, we book a quick flight. Air France, Swiss Air, KLM…they all fly in and out of Pulkova. Worse case… we spend a few nights in Paris, Geneva, or Amsterdam."

Still, we wouldn't be going as tourists. I'd be going as an accredited academic and you'd be accompanying me on a diplomatic mission of sorts."

"Oh please. Since when are you in the diplomatic corps or whatever it's called?"

"Since about," he checked his watch for effect, "a half-hour ago."

"What do you mean?"

"I mean as in reaching out to an old acquaintance and professor of mine. He gave a series of lectures on diplomacy and foreign policy at the Naval War College in Monterey when I was studying there. I wrote a paper he took me aside to compliment me on. Guess I made an impression. We've kept in touch and we've bumped into each other at a couple of conferences over the years. So, I called him because I read about something the other day in the NY Times that I remembered. He confirmed what I'd read and offered to appointment me a special academic liaison with this mission he's taking to Russia…leaves in a week….plenty of time to make arrangements."

"You've got to be kidding." She stood in the kitchen still holding the shopping list she'd begun to check. "So, who is this old professor?"

"Someone you know…or I should say know about," Tim corrected. Nixon's Secretary of State, Henry Kissinger."

"You can't be serious! It was pretty clear from your lectures that you totally disagreed with his foreign policy and especially in Vietnam and Cambodia. How can you say that after what those two did to Southeast Asia? And you told us he and Nixon sold-out the South Vietnamese in '75 for Christ's sake!" she bristled

"I know, I was there remember. No question I was and still am critical of his views in terms of policy decisions, Abby. But that doesn't make him any less brilliant a scholar or practitioner of the art of diplomacy. Being attached to his mission will give me, and us, much greater access and credibility than if we were merely curious tourists."

"What is his mission exactly…and what do you mean us?"

"Henry told me that the American Consul General, a guy named John Evans, and the CEO of Proctor and Gamble, created a US-Soviet bilateral commission or something, with the involvement of the Center for Strategic and International Studies, to promote trade and foreign investment. Sessions are planned for Moscow and St. Petersburg. I will be an unofficial advisor to Henry and given my former rank and military service, I can actually offer some advice that might be worth something. But he made it clear this is a personal courtesy not formally a working gig. We'd be there three days. In and out."

Abby joined him in the living room, sat next to him on the sofa. "What would I do?"

"You could explore one of the great cities of the world, capital and cultural heart of Imperial Russia home town of the Czars. People who I know who've been to the Hermitage say it's easily the equal of the Louvre. The city's a mecca for international designers and artists with galleries and boutiques galore, palaces, and majestic Russian Orthodox cathedrals. The night life rocks…so I hear. Think of it as a fun get-away…a vacation. I'll be attending a meeting or two and doing the drudge-work in the archives during the day and then our time is ours." He could easily read her expression. It wasn't encouraging. She starred out the large glass window offering a view of the high desert vista of the expansive Prescott Valley.

"Remember what happened to me last time, Tim. I still have nightmares. I'm terrified of things I can't see. The dark unnerves me. I'm now claustrophobic. I see than man's face who attacked me and I shot…the bobcat that stalked me in the catacombs under Ani."

"I know. You wake me up some nights."

"Sorry."

"Don't be. Honey, believe me I do not want to experience anything like that again or put you in any jeopardy. Armenia affected me too and not just the earthquake although that was bad enough. There were moments when I thought neither your or I would ever get out of there alive and that I would be responsible…that I am responsible." It's a lot to carry around and I don't carry it easily…not for a moment. So, I get it."

"I know that. I can see it in your eyes sometimes. That experience still haunts both of us. We swore-off any more misadventures like that one…or Montana for that matter. All we wanted was 'normal'. That's what we promised each other. How is this normal?"

He took her hands in his. She was right. What was he thinking?

"Abby, You're right. This whole thing is so sudden…definitely not what we meant by 'normal'. I'm being unrealistic and insensitive. Of course this is something you wouldn't want any part of. I'm being presumptuous…and…" he focused on his hands clasped between his knees. He had to start thinking more about her he berated himself.

"Tim, I'm sorry. You make it sound like so much fun, exciting and all and it's probably a chance in a lifetime but too much as happened too fast for me in the past two years, I'm overwhelmed emotionally and, I guess, just plain exhausted physically too. You go. No, I want you to," she said as Tim began to protest. "I think it's something you need to do and besides I am seriously interested in what you might discover about what we found. I hope you're not too disappointed in me?"

He kissed her gently on the lips. "You could never disappoint me. I'll miss you but I'll know you're here safe with Ralph and Tweeks. I'll be back before you know it no worse for wear and missing you terribly. I'll bring you back a babushka nesting doll."

"A what?"

Kissing her on the forehead, he left her on the sofa and went out on the back veranda lost in his thoughts. The sun was setting behind Granite Mountain and already the lights of downtown Prescott were winking to life.

Joining him, she handed Tim a beer. There was nothing more to say so they sat in silence as gold turned to purple and shadows deepened. Ralph trotted out to join them. For another moment they were all together, happy, secure…at home. All seemed copasetic and balanced. And then the moment was gone…

CHAPTER FIVE

Tim pushed through the heavy glass doors and into the lobby of 350 Park Ave. and 52d Street walking past corporate signage for major banks and other assorted world class entities. It was one of New York City's more exclusive addresses. He didn't bother with the marble computerized address kiosk because for security reasons Kissinger Associates floor and office number were not listed. Access was by prearranged clearance and appointment only. Tim had it…number 26.

With a soft whir the elevator floated up a few seconds, its door opening into a different world but also a space Tim had not anticipated. He stepped into a windowless, unpretentious recessed-lighting illuminated waiting room with the usual assortment of chairs, small sofa, table with magazines…Foreign Affairs, Forbes, American Heritage. In the background an announcer from the BBC spoke in barely audible commentary. He was alone.

An attractive administrative assistant sat behind a desk adorned with the objects one would expect to find in any office. Lamps glowed a warm yellow, framed but unremarkable artwork looked down from the walls. The carpet was industrial, Tim registered as he introduced himself to the admin and was told to take a seat. He could hear muffled voices down a hallway. There was no identifying letters or plaque to distinguish this from any other office. Everything was decidedly understated.

Tim had done his research. Kissinger Associates raison d'etre was to 'offer expertise to corporations in economic, diplomatic and geopolitical matters and offer international planning', the firm becoming in essence a corporation's own in-house national security advisory body. The top 'Associates' included Lt. General Bret Scowcroft, Ford's National Security Advisor and former Under Secretary of State Lawrence Eagleburger. In short, KAs letterhead reeked of 'gravitas' and provided its 25-30 who's-who of clients with world-class analyses and strategic advice in strictly oral presentations. Tim found it hard to pin down but a heavy dose of secrecy hung in the air like a cloak.

With Nixon's demise after Watergate and three years with Ford as his Secretary of State, Kissinger had established himself as a later day 'wise man,' doing consulting, public speaking, academic writing and becoming what some called uncharitably a 'statesman for hire,' although God knew that was becoming a growth industry and highly lucrative revolving door for former government heavyweights. It was insidious and reeked of conflict of interest but no one seemed to care.

Unannounced Kissinger emerged from what Tim assumed was his private office, displaying his crooked smile, hand outthrust like a lance. "Professor, great to see you again," Tim offered his hand in return gesture. He hadn't seen the man, except occasionally on the news, for several years. The former Secretary of State wore his 5'9", 170-pound frame well…same square chin, hint of cheek and jowl, pronounced nose, heavy brows, forehead creased in 'thought furrows' as Tim described them, still chestnut brown curly hair, dark blue eyes lurking behind thick black square-framed glasses. And same arrogant grim-faced smirk but this one bearing a hint of smile.

It was a perfunctory but stern handshake accompanied by a curt nod…followed by a quick, uncharacteristic man-hug. "Professor Strange good to see you again," he effusively greeted in the distinctive, burrbally-throated, heavy German accent, Tim remembered. A master of faux-flattery, Kissinger was a ruthless, blunt, take no prisoners negotiator, Tim reminded himself, while incongruously also an Alfalfa Club comedian and even something of a ladies man of late, if the tabloids were to be believed. The man was nothing if not enigmatic.

Kissinger invited him into a more extensive yet intimate L-shaped office decorated with much more impressive paintings, indoor plants, and numerous framed-photos of family and notables, and closed the door. "Thank you for allowing me to join the Commission, Henry. It's an honor," Tim volunteered as he took the offered chair.

"Think nothing of it. I'm pleased you reached out and happy to have you along. You're looking hale, clearly Arizona suits you, and it seems your career is going well," he launched into small talk. Tim reciprocated sitting across from the former Secretary of State feeling Kissinger's appraising gaze fixed on him.

Abruptly Kissinger rose. "These are momentous times for the world…Communism collapsing at least in Europe," he qualified, "the Wall coming down, German unification underway, the Soviet Union on its way into the ash heap of history. Hardly what Trotsky, Lenin, Marx had in mind, eh," his shoulders shook with a derisive chuckle.

"Never in my lifetime did I think I'd see what we've witnessed these past months," Tim agreed… "and without the kind of bloody upheaval so many predicted."

"Not yet," Kissinger cautioned. "There is always a chance of miscalculation, the unexpected, the accidental. We are not yet out of those woods. The superpowers often behave like two heavily armed blind men feeling their way around a room, each believing himself in mortal peril from the other, whom he assumes to have perfect vision…when uncertainty, compromise, incoherence, are frequently the essence of policy making, rather than consistency, foresight, or coherence. Of course, over time, even two armed blind men can do enormous damage to each other, not to mention the room!"

"I remember the lecture," Tim offered as a compliment.

"Ah, well I think my observation is as valid today as it was back…when was it?"

"The Naval War College 1977."

"Of course, I remember that paper of yours on Native American diplomacy and conflict resolution. I've kept a copy in my files. Tim was about to reply when Kissinger cut him off. "We'll need all our diplomatic skills to manage events as they unfold in real time these next few months. "Let's hope Gorbachev has opened a Pandora's box of clarity and sanity. We can never relax our vigilance when two nations possess upwards of 10,000 nuclear weapons pointed at each other. I've counseled Bush to tread easily. This is a dangerous period…but also one of especially ripe opportunities," he abruptly brightened. "But we'll get to that in a moment.

"So last time we met you were about to be married, as I recall?" he probed.

"I was and I am. She's a lovely, smart woman I'm lucky to have her as a partner."

"A younger woman I believe?" Tim swore he winked.

"She's a woman experienced beyond her years," he deflected not wanting to go down that particular road. Kissinger let it go.

"I gather from our brief conversation she's not accompanying you?"

"No, unfortunately Abby has some commitments in Prescott," he fudged. That was definitely a subject he didn't want to get into as conflicted as he was about pressuring her to go and missing her already. This would be the first time they'd been apart for longer than a few days in three years and it was already an adjustment he wasn't enjoying.

He changed the subject. "Can you give me a briefing on the mission?"

"Of course, Tim. As you no doubt know the United States has had an economic relationship with Czarist Russia going back to before the Revolution. Through the early 1900s American corporations remained of considerable economic importance to the various czarist regimes. After the Bolsheviks took power Wilson broke off diplomatic relations in December 1917, and within a year intervened militarily in hopes of preventing the communists from seizing power. That accomplished nothing except gaining the enduring animosity of the Soviet Union."

"Yes, I know the broad strokes," Tim confirmed.

"The United States did lead humanitarian efforts to relieve the great famine in Russia, Ukraine and the Volga River Valley in the early 1920s, with Hoover's American Relief Administration efforts which prevented the starvation of millions. Through the 1920's

American business pursued financial opportunism and Lenin's NEP policy facilitated commercial and diplomatic relations. Henry Ford, Armand Hammer, Averill Harriman…many others were in the game. Tim knew that Ford tractors became a symbol of American friendship and that Ford even contracted to open an automobile factory on the Volga River in 1929 in the Dearborn agreement. Republican administrations believed that the best antidote to communism was capitalism. All that began to change when Stalin came to power and relations withered".

"Still, FDR reversed US policy," Kissinger continued, "and officially recognized the USSR in November of 1933 for two reasons: he hoped to thwart Japanese expansionism in the Far East and he hoped it would help fight the Depression with increased trade and commerce." Business and Corporate profits prevailed over ideology. One must sometime compromise principles to achieve other purposes."

"I believe that was your point about 'legitimacy'…distinguishing it from justice…a pragmatic realism, I believe?"

"Very good…Precisely. So Roosevelt takes a necessitarian position and sends William C. Bullitt and Henry Morganthau to bait the hook with American trade and investment. They approach a Russian diplomat in Washington and he passes word on to the Chairman of the Central Executive Committee with an unsigned 'invitation' from FDR…very cleaver, plausible deniability!" Kissinger approved.

He paced his office now animated and in his full professorial persona, Tim appreciated.

"A favorable response comes quickly with the arrival of the Soviet Commissioner for Foreign Affairs Maxim Litvinov and following extensive negotiation a deal is truck. Unfortunately violence in Russia and the first wave of purges by Stalin cause this first initiative to collapse. But three years later a disillusioned Bullitt, who'd gone to Russia as our first ambassador since David Francis in 1916, was recalled and replaced by the prominent business executive Joseph Davies and talks restarted."

Tim nearly asked if he should be taking notes then thought better of it.

"Suddenly it's 1939 and Hitler and Stalin reach their infamous non-aggression pact which sours relations again as Britain and France align against Nazi Germany and the Roosevelt-Churchill relationship deepens. Only after Hitler breaks the pact and invades Russia in June 1941do the US and the Soviets overcome their animosity and, however unlikely, join forces to defeat the common enemy," he concluded his seminar. "Being Jewish in Germany was no place to be and we were able to escape the year before the war began..." he seemed to lose himself in the memory. Tim knew the family's history. He also knew the fraught history of what came next.

"While the Cold War began at Yalta even before Germany surrendered with Stalin and Churchill agreeing to separate 'spheres of influence' in Europe, the 'big chill' deepened precipitously into a deep freeze until the late 60s. Nixon, I, and Brezhnev, worked to thaw things out as part of Détente and it resulted in the reopening of our embassy in Moscow, a consulate in St. Petersburg in July 1973...and a Soviet consulate in San Francisco. Direct air routes opened, cultural exchanges flowered, American's studied at Leningrad University. Some called it the 'Babushka summer' although Kennedy and Johnson hammered out a preliminary consular agreement in '64. 'It's been a long strange trip indeed,' he quoted the Dead.

"Now we are at another watershed and this International Action Commission of ours will endeavor to grease the wheels of commerce and mutually beneficial financial opportunities. An old acquaintance of mine is in Saint Petersburg and is a well-connected heavy-weight in Soviet politics. He's currently on their city council and is positioned to become mayor in the upcoming elections. Some even say he could be president. He's also a Ph.D., law and economics...Anatoly Sobchak. He and I put this thing together with the help of my firm and a foreign policy think tank in D.C. "

"So you'll be meeting with companies, financiers, bankers, investors who see opportunities should the Soviet regime open-up to the West?"

"Nothing serves like seizing the moment." We've set-up a first round of meetings in Saint Petersburg with Sobchak and two of his deputies, a guy named Yakolev and another deputy- Vladimir Putin. Putin's in charge of foreign investment and six months ago became an advisor to Sobchak. He's KGB and was stationed in East Germany until the Wall came down. An ambitious, ruthless character and extremely clever, I'm told. From what I hear he and I should get along well, both of us getting our start in security and all."

Tim had never heard of him and had no reason to but the word KGB gave him pause. Its reputation earned in the Siberian Gulags and Stalin's mass murder of millions defined the darkest side of the Cold War in Europe and beyond. It agents and espionage networks were everywhere…even penetrating into the US confirmed by some sensational spy scandals

"I hear from Anatoly that Putin's in line to become Deputy Mayor in charge of the Committee for Foreign Economic Relations. So he's the guy who issues licenses and contracts and a man we need to have onboard. There's whispered rumors of corruption of course with so much money sloshing around…money laundering, off-shore accounts being set-up by the rats fleeing the sinking ship so-to-speak. But saying there's corruption in the USSR is like saying there's no candy eggs at Easter," he chuckled. "Apparently he doesn't speak English or ever met an American before so it should be interesting. For all that they say he's a 'law and order' guy so we'll see."

"Sounds like a man with an ambitious agenda."

"That's what Sobchak tells me. Now, while I'm negotiating…or 'triangulating' with Putin and Gorbachev, I'm tasking you with a small research project in the Saint Petersburg archives…shouldn't take you more than a couple of hours. We'll be in the city for three days. The delegation will be staying at the Belmond Grand Hotel….five stars of course and right in the center of town…"

His desk phone rang, "You'll have to excuse me Tim. Lawrence Rawl, head of Exxon Mobile, needs a consult. Seems they want to enter into a joint venture with Rosneft and wants to know what the lay of the land is…metaphorically where the land mines are. I'll see you at JFK in the morning," he closed the door. Meting over.

Three minutes later Tim sat in back of a Yellow Cab headed for the Radisson on W. 52d, affordable and convenient. Back in his room after a quick bite and draft at the hotel bar he called Abby….

CHAPTER SIX

She watched her husband drive off that morning headed for Prescott Regional airport…'Love Field' they called it ironically enough she thought with a twinge. The man she loved would soon be 5,565miles away in St. Petersburg, Russia of all places. She'd looked it up. The house was quiet. Mid-afternoon brought the usual thunder storm but it was already rumbling off to the east in flashes of lightening. Unlike most dogs Ralph actually sat in the big picture window seemingly enjoying the show. Nothing seemed to bother that dog, Abby marveled. Tweeks lie curled-up in a ball on the top of their sofa. She'd cracked an eye at the first clap of thunder but then simply curled-up tighter in a ball.

The reality of her decision to stay was screaming at her. She was alone in their big ranch house. Of course she had the animals for company but it wasn't the same has having Tim with her. Four-legged companionship went only so far.

Technically and in far more pleasant ways they were still newlyweds and they had indulged that status with abandon. But it wasn't just the sex as great as that was. It was everything else. They'd married in heat and adrenalin rush of shared danger. What happens when passion cools, when lovers stop being lovers and become partners and companions…roommates? He had needs, so did she…physical, emotional and no doubt others she couldn't even name. Were those needs compatible? How could they even know? God, she needed to stop reading Cosmo," she laughed in spite of her introspection. Besides it was way too early in any relationship to be asking such questions much less a marriage. Mellow out, girl!

They'd shared so many harrowing moments together, almost like soldiers in combat was how she imagined it. Love might be a 'battlefield' but it was one she wanted to fight on with him by her side. So, yes, it was all still new and giddy and…she confessed she didn't quite have the word for it. But she knew damn well she missed it and him…his scent, the feel of his skin, the sound of his voice, seeing him, sharing their day's little routines. All of it suddenly seemed so important.

But on the other side of that coin she had to admit she missed the thrill of the adventure and even the danger that had been their lives for the past three years as twisted as she knew that had to be, right? Was she simply an adrenalin-junky or was it something else? Tim was strength and security…'safety' was a stretch, but he had other qualities she'd come to respect and admire. Honestly she'd wrapped herself in all of it, in all of him and snuggled into it, she glanced over at Tweeks.

Anyway she figured marriage was a package deal. There was a lot to unwrap. She was coming to terms with the ways they were different and with how some of those differences were more than minor annoyances. Relationships were about adjustments and adaption and compromise, right? Still, there were some things she would not sellout on. She was who she was and had no obligation to change or intention of doing so for anyone much less apologizing for not doing so. That included Tim…as it had with every man she'd ever had a relationship with. 'Abeline's rules' she called them.

Some of those men, boys really, had been abusive verbally and emotionally…a couple physically. It had been that abuse, coupled with her father's lechery that she'd tapped into on the road to Leninikan, Armenia, when she'd killed the man who tried to rape her. He became the focus of her pent-up rage and 'issues'. Bad day for him. Good day for her. Some lines you didn't cross and not expect to pay the price. She didn't berate herself for that either however much the act of killing tore at her. Like everything else in her life she rationalized it.

She tried to look at this St. Petersburg thing from Tim's perspective and part of her understood how he could have misjudged her reaction. It probably made perfect sense to him logically. There was a mystery to solve. Some of the answers could be in St. Petersburg. There was definitely a Russian connection somehow and where better to start looking? He made a plan. It was all tidy and straight forward. But he failed to factor her into the equation. She couldn't help that she screwed-up the math. She was the 'unknown' factor he couldn't so easily solve for. She was an incongruence that he hadn't anticipated when, in her mind, he should have.

Still, to put it politely she'd brought a boat load of trouble into his life…turned it upside down and inside out. Yet for all that he hadn't walked away, had he. He'd chosen her despite it all eyes wide open. He must know what he was getting into with her…didn't he? But that begged another question…what did he see in her? And no she didn't mean the obvious.

Had he really looked more deeply, considered that her crappy life's experiences and the violence of her family's murder had probably damaged her and in ways she didn't fully understand herself? That hers was a fragile strength…that there were limits to what she could give? Obviously one of those limits had been St. Petersburg and their mysterious discovery and the unknowns it represented. She needed the predictability of routine, the simplicity of a normal existence, a merciful deliverance from drama. It was exhausting!

Now as she sat alone, contemplating all this, lost in her own head, her thoughts turned to Karen. She had come to understand and admire who Karen was and how much Tim loved her. Her death had devastated him as the loss of her mother and little brother tore her apart…and still did. Empathy did not equal equivalence however. These were different emotional journeys, she was certain of that. She'd taken a couple of classes from Karen Strange and had gotten a sense of the kind of person she was. 'Genuine' was the word she'd come-up with…a genuinely nice woman, an inspiring teacher, a woman of moral conviction and principles and someone committed to her students. 'Empathy' was the other trait she ascribed to her.

And so what she knew for certain was that she and Karen were two very different women. She didn't feel genuine at all. No, her life had been one endless unspooling of deception, of never quite syncing self-image with reality. She had few strong convictions she recognized, a moral compass that gyrated all over the dial, a well-honed, self-absorbed defense mechanism out of a need for self-preservation, empathy for no one, except for her mom and little brother, and raging cynicism. God, wasn't she the complete package!

Lightening forked again in the distance like an incandescent exclamation point. She felt Ralph lick her hand and the surprise of it snapped her out of her brooding. She tussled his ears, got-up and decided she'd go for a walk...clear her head in the rain-cleansed air of late afternoon. "Come on Ralph let's go for a walk." He jumped a foot and barked. She found a jacket and her Diamondback's baseball cap, leashed him and closed the door behind them.

Three minutes later the phone rang. It rang nine times…and stopped.

CHAPTER SEVEN

Air France flight 1732 touched down at Pulkova at 5:40 A.M. after a nearly 15-hour flight via Paris and Amsterdam. St Petersburg twinkled like a crescent jewel as the approaching dawn lit the east with a purple hue. The broad, dark sweep of the Neva snaked past the city as it had since Peter the Great's engineers laid the first foundation stone.

Tim was hammered not by alcohol but sleep deprivation. His flight into Yerevan two summer before had been brutal too but much of that he could be attributed to off-the-charts anxiety about his predicament and Abby's abduction in London by Turkish agents. Miserable and hungry at the same time he grabbed his coat and carry-on from the bin and made his way towards the rear exit reserved for their exclusive deplaning, leg-cramped, butt-sore and red-eyed. Welcome to St. Petersburg, comrade, he derided.

On the tarmac they were met by Counsel General Evans, the attaché and, plain clothes security and whisked away in two black Lincoln limos.

Diplomatic delegations were exempt from foreign customs clearance so their drivers had the eight-member delegation at the restored four-story pre-Revolutionary era Consulate at 15 Petra Lavrova in less than a half-hour. Tim rode in the second car behind Kissinger and Evans as they sped down the broad boulevard nearly every structure seemingly out of a time capsule in its ornate Baroque and Neo-classical architecture.

Entering through the gated entry they were met by several others of the 24-member staff. Five US Marine security guards stood at attention in their khaki blouses, red-stripped blue pants, holstered .45s on their belts. A medium-sized American flag tugged overhead with a flap of fabric and clink of its lanyard against the breeze scudding off the Volga.

Secure in the confines of the embassy grounds and after shaking hands all around, the Marine guards resumed to their duties. Without a word Evans and Kissinger disappeared into the embassy. The attaché or Under Secretary, Tim presumed, escorted the group to a comfortable conference room where they were instructed to wait. Twenty minutes later Evans and the Secretary walked-in. Both were smiling which Tim interpreted as a promising sign.

Kissinger sat knees crossed, Evans stood to address them. Of medium height with dark hair and a perfectly trimmed mustache, meticulously dressed in a dark suit, Evans personified the image of 'diplomat.' It was a not the perfunctory welcome they received at Pulkova but a thorough recitation of the political situation in the city and in Moscow, their next stop. It was not what Tim or anyone else expected to hear.

"Gentleman- they were all men, we live in perilous times," he said without preamble. "How perilous remains to be seen," he said with attention-demanding gravity. "As you know there has been growing unrest in the Baltic Republics, Armenia, Georgia, Ukraine, the Caucasus, and Moldovia, since Gorbachev pushed his Perestroika and Glasnost initiatives in 1987. He opened not merely a Pandora's Box but triggered a Pandora earthquake, I dare say- not unlike the one you survived in Armenia, Professor Strange." Everyone turned eyes on Tim. He was about to reply when Evans held up a hand. "It's my business to know the backgrounds of anyone who passes through this embassy and especially this commission," he nodded to Kissinger who dipped his chin over tented fingers, shot Tim a what-did-you-expect confirmation.

"Moscow has tried to hold things together with heavy doses of censorship and some violence," Tim could personally confirm that, "but this new cable news service, CNN, has made that impossible. Everything is coming unglued. Once Gorbachev abandoned the

Brezhnev Doctrine making any move to leave the Soviet Union illegal, the six once hard-core Warsaw Pact allies of Eastern Europe bolted and joined the others in February of last year, followed by the Central Asia republics… eleven of sixteen."

"I have been informed by our people in Moscow that a military coup is underway to force General Secretary Gorbachev from office. The resistance is being led by President Yeltsin. The parliament building is being shelled. It is utter chaos and extremely fluid. The Soviet Union itself may well cease to exist in the next few days, weeks, or months. No one can predict the timing. Under what specific circumstances and with what amount of violence, if any, is anyone's guess." The room went deathly silent.

"It is hard for me or Secretary Kissinger," he turned to Henry, "difficult for us to believe that hard-liners in the Politburo, perhaps elements of the Red Army, KGB, perhaps the Orthodox Church hierarchy and others will allow this liberalization to continue unchallenged. We are witnessing truly historic, world-changing events we haven't seen since 1917…and you just flew into the middle of it! We are all in a very real sense now hostage to an uncertain future that is unfolding as we speak."

"Jesus Christ," Tim muttered to himself.

"Henry?" Kissinger rose as if weighted by some heavy burden.

"I thought I would see the collapse of the satellite empire but I did not think I would see the collapse of the Soviet Union or the Soviet empire," he said gravely. "Regardless I thought it would take much longer. I know one certainty. Whatever may happen now in Russia, a post Tito type Yugoslavia, wracked by conflict from St. Petersburg to Vladivostok, from Europe, across the Middle East to Asia, is not in America's interest. We must do all we can to help President Bush navigate safely through these dangerous waters. I further suggest," he offered a note of optimism, "that our little commission and our meetings with Sobchak and Putin over the next couple of days can contribute importantly to that end and perhaps offer some stability. Now if you will excuse us we need to make a call on the secure line to Washington."

As the two men left the attaché requested their attention amidst the chattering of voices that erupted following Evans' potentially alarming announcement. "If you will please follow me to the courtyard, a car will take you to your hotel. Unless otherwise informed you are to be in the hotel lobby at 8:00 sharp. Enjoy your evening," he invited as he led them out.

The Grand Belmond had been an aristocrat's residence dating from the mid-19th-century located on Nevsky Prospetk in the Tsentrainy District downtown near the Russian Museum. The location suited Tim perfectly. It was a short drive from the embassy to the Belmond through the heart of the city. The old school opulence and charm were dazzling if understated as he was directed to the elevators after registering. They all shared adjoining rooms on the same floor. In less than five minutes Tim was unpacking his suitcase and ready to collapse into bed after a long, hot shower.

Three hours later although unable to really sleep he still felt together enough to call Abby. He'd called her from Amsterdam in their brief layover but she hadn't answered. He'd left a message. He checked his watch and calculated it was mid-morning in Prescott. Where the hell was she?

CHAPTER EIGHT

"Father…is that what I should call you? He nodded. "My name is Abeline Strange. Thank you for seeing me." She was way out of her comfort zone here.

"At your service miss Strange. To what do I owe this pleasure?" Aleksey Bakakov, Russian Orthodox vicar of the Southwest Region of the Metropolis of San Francisco, born in Kalingrad, smiled benevolently but was clearly puzzled by the young woman's presence. He was a caricature of an Orthodox priest with longish gray-streaked hair and rather scraggly beard…at least the prelate in a photo she'd looked-up looked exactly like him.

"Mrs. Actually. You probably realize that I am not part of your…she fought for the word…flock…congregants?"

"Parishioners," he clarified benignly.

"And to be completely honest I confess I'm not the least bit religious."

"No confession necessary and besides that's for our Western Catholic brethren. But that makes me even more curious Mrs. Strange."

"Please call me Abby. May I?" Father Bakakov indicated she should take one of the plush leather chairs in his office smelling slightly of incense. Brilliantly colored icons of all descriptions adorned spaces while a cross like none she'd never seen before occupied an illuminated alcove. She settled into the comfortable beige leather chair setting her purse and light sweater on the floor next to her…fidgeted nervously.

"Happily I have a few unstructured minutes this morning, hence my jeans and turtleneck, so please…how can I help?"

"This is major off-the-wall and I don't really know anything about the Orthodox Church except that it's Russian…"

"My dear, our church's origins date from the time of Jesus and the Apostles and it is formally known as the Eastern or Orthodox Church. We are that part of Christianity that was centered in the Middle East, Mediterranean, and Southern and Eastern Europe…and yes including Russia. As you can tell from my accent I am Russian. Strictly speaking we are the Greek Orthodox Church and in what historians call call the 'Great Schism' in the 11th-century we and the Latin Church centered in Rome parted company. In ancient times our spiritual and cultural center was Byzantium or Constantinople…today it is called Istanbul, as you may know."

"I do remember that from my Western Civ class," Abby recited. "And actually my husband and I were in Armenia during the earthquake, not far from the Turkish border near Ani," she disclosed without going into any detail. Who would believe it? And she had no intention of resurrecting memories of the Ottomans or her Turkish abductors.

Bakakov regarded her with greater curiosity. "I am relieved you and your husband survived that terrible ordeal. The Armenian Apostolic Church is closely related…we share the same lineage, you might say. But I don't believe you came to me for a history lesson? What are you seeking here at Saint George?"

"My husband, Professor Tim Strange...he teaches at the college is away on a trip to St. Petersburg…business," she offered keeping it simple, "and well, I thought you might know something about the situation there."

"Are you worried for some reason?"

"Not really. But I read the paper, watch TV."

"Of course, of course. The Orthodox Church in Russia, one of the most historic and influential institutions has regained much of its legitimacy and power since the bad old Stalinist days. I have friends in both Moscow and St. Petersburg and they keep me informed. Not all reliable information makes it into the Soviet or the Western press," he smiled.

"The Church is…has always been a powerful force for tradition and Russian nationalism. Given recent events and the political turmoil unleashed by ill-advised policies the USSR-the communist experiment really, as the world has known it for 75, years appears to have run its historic course. We, that is the Church, will do all in our power to assure that whatever comes next will adhere to Mother Russia's cultural heritage. Regimes come and go. The Church and all it stands for remains. It will be the rock, the spiritual center of the new Russia…whatever that looks like."

"My husband says democracy and liberalism won in the battle of ideas and systems."

Bakakov shrugged. "I would not be too quick to celebrate. There are elements…interests in Russia that will shape the transition and they must be served: apparatchiks, the bureaucracy, the military, security services…and, yes, even the Church. All is in a state of flux with swirling political and economic currents. Instability breeds uncertainty and fear…perhaps even paranoia, conspiracy theories...all manner of nonsense. Russians prize order and stability, strong leadership even at the expense of personal liberties. The Church is expected to help provide that leadership. For Russians democracy is chaotic, inefficient and notoriously individualistic. This is not what Russians or Russia needs or wants," he offered authoritatively.

"What does that mean for Americans like my husband? The USSR and the US haven't exactly been friends since 1945."

"My dear, America and the USSR have never been friends not even during WWII," he corrected. "That was an alliance of necessity…of convenience. They are antithetical systems. What is your husband doing in St. Petersburg…exactly if I may ask?" Bakakov pressed.

"He's part of a commission invited to explore economic cooperation…as I understand it. It's headed by Henry Kissinger." At that the vicar's eyes widened slightly.

"Your husband, he is an economist...political scientist...in the government?"

"Historian."

"Ah...a scholar...an intellectual. I shouldn't think he'd be in any danger so long as his activities are related to this official commission's work. Last I checked they are not shooting historians or 'disappearing' them to Siberia...not unless they cross the line."

"That's comforting...what line?"

"Well," he shrugged, "that can be a problem. The lines are always changing. One never knows for sure. Your husband and the others will be closely monitored of course by the security service...the KGB although I hear it too could be a casualty of the present troubles. State security will never go away it will merely change names," he offered a 'what can one say' gesture. "Normal tourist activities should not raise any eyebrows."

"I'm relieved to hear it," Abby's insides stopped churning quite as aggressively as they had been.

"But my friends tell me there are new alignments forming. What is being called the siloviki network consisting of Kremlin-friendly liberals, criminal syndicates, a new class of oligarchs, the bureaucracy, security services, old line Communists, state-controlled media, pro-Kremlin intellectuals...and yes even the Church are the main elements fighting a new Patriotic War against the 'enemies of Russia that are emerging and organizing as we speak The siloviki are dedicated to crushing liberal values, democracy, and westernization generally. For them...for us liberty and human rights are secondary to the greater interests of society...the collective state." Abby visibly winced.

"The rift in the Orthodox Church provoked by the Revolution of 1917 is being finally healed with the Russian branch welcomed back into the world community led by the Metropolitan. The goal in Russia is nothing less than restoration of a thousand years of monarchist tradition and authoritarianism. As is often heard in Russia, 'hell is a democracy. Heaven is a kingdom.'"

"I can see that these conservative perspectives and values trouble you. You are not alone. Some of our parishioners here in Prescott have concerns, and there are those in the West generally who have difficulty reconciling their history and national experience with ours…speaking from the Russian perspective." He laughed in a deep baritone disarmingly. "I am thoroughly westernized and left the USSR years ago emigrating to Nikolaevsk, Alaska in the mid-70s, then to Woodburn, Oregon-large Russian communities, before accepting this appointment," he explained.

"Who knows what the future will bring in these times of upheaval and transition. But have faith, my dear, I believe that Professor Strange-your husband, will be perfectly safe in St. Petersburg," he offered encouragingly.

Having little faith in anything anymore, Abby still found his assurances comforting. "Again thank you for seeing me like this. I know you must be busy with church business. Oh, one thing Tim hoped to do was to visit the Hermitage, I think it is, and the State Archives. He's trying to solve a family mystery we just became aware of that has a definite Russian connection…czarist Russia to be precise. Have you ever been to the Hermitage?"

Bakakov had begun to rise from behind his desk and stopped. "Yes, many times but not recently. Czarist Russia? How do you know? Ah, your husband the historian," he queried.

"Yeah. Tim teaches primarily US history, he's really into Native Americans, but he knows about all kinds of stuff. He was in Vietnam…all sorts of secret military stuff," she volunteered.

Bakakov took that in showing little interest but making some assumptions he thought that information warranted.

"This is wild," she effused. "We found an old bag hidden in the wall of a cabin Tim inherited that contained a bunch of old Russian items…an old, fancy revolver, Tim said was a Smith and Wesson, some gold ruble coins and banknotes, an American military insignia we think… and a large silver coin. The gold coins Tim said had the likeness of Czar Nicholas…first-second, I can't remember exactly. We don't know anything about the other coin but it had one of the other czars on its face. Tim was hoping to do some research to learn more about how it is that it ended-up in this cabin of all places. He can't help himself…kind'a goes with the 'historian territory,'" she laughed easily.

"Well, indeed that is a mystery isn't it Mrs…ah Abeline," Bakakov offered his hand. "I wish your husband luck." It was clear to Abby that their interview was over. "Forgive me but duty calls. I have enjoyed our conversation and I do hope I have put your mind at ease." Abby assured him that he had.

In minutes she was cruising down Gurely in Tim's Ford pickup, feeling better thanks to the priest's assurances and his solicitous manner. Now for the gym, a killer workout, and lunch with her friends at the Lone Spur.

Father Bakakov closed the door behind him…and locked it. The church was deserted except for a gardener doing his bi-weekly blow-and-go on the grounds. Sitting behind his desk he dialed an overseas number. "Andre-privetstviye," he greeted, "it's Aleksey…yes from Prescott. You'd better hold on to your ushanka comrade….

CHAPTER NINE

"Henry, my friend," they gripped in a quick man-hug.

"And it is good to see you Anatoly," Kissinger said looking up at the much taller Russian. "You are looking well," Kissinger offered, although not convinced of that as the normally ebullient Sobchak seemed off somehow. It was a few minutes past nine and cool with morning fog lifting off the Neva, the sound of traffic constant white noise.

Massive Mariinsky Palace, built in the mid-1800s for "Maria' the daughter of Czar Nicholas I, sitting across Isaakievskaya Square from St. Isaac's Cathedral, had been the seat of the city's government for decades. It's dove grey stone facade and green metal roof glowed with a pinkish hue in the cold sun.

Standing slightly behind Sobchak another man waited and watched appraisingly. At 5'6" Vladimir Putin nevertheless had a presence about him that conveyed power, ambition and intensity that Kissinger easily recognized. His CIA file confirmed he was in his early 40s, although he looked ten years younger, thought Kissinger as he sized him up. Well-groomed, sharply dressed, and ramrod straight, Putin impressed with an aura of extreme confidence.

Henry, I'd like you meet Lt. Colonel Putin of the KGB, although I think I've persuaded him to become Dean for International Affairs here at Lenningrad State University." Sobchak introduced the two men. Vladimir was one of my better students in his law studies. If I win the contest for Mayor, I'm planning to name him my deputy and chairman of a committee of international relations, I hope to promote. This conference and our little commission will be an ice-breaker and step towards implementing that vision."

"Priyatno vstretit' tebya…chest," Putin strode forward extending his hand with a curt nod, followed by a stilted 'hello,' his hawk-like eyes an intense, penetrating blue. There was a hint of smile but it struggled to break through. Kissinger liked him immediately.

"I have heard impressive things about you Colonel Putin. By the way I, too, was in the secret service many years ago so we have that and no doubt much more in common. All decent people get their start in intelligence. I hope our talks on improving our economic relations prove fruitful." Sobchak translated. Putin, clearly studying the famous American intently, now smiling broadly, replied quickly in Russian.

Kissinger turned to his friend. "Valdimir says, "Everything will probably never be ok, but we have to try for it, yes?"

"Spoken like a true realist. Unblinkered vision has always been dear to my heart," Kissinger beamed. Introductions were exchanged all round among the other assembled commission members. Tim found Putin's handshake vice-like which fit for a man known for mastering the tools of manipulation and intimidation. Tim squeezed back as forcefully as he dared. Pleasantries behind them, commission members broke into their designated working groups each with a translator for talks, while the three principals disappeared into the cavernous building….

That night he finally reached Abby. He was ten hours ahead of her so it was just before noon her time. She picked-up on the third ring.

"I've been trying to reach you for two days," she heard him say with some exasperation.

"I'm sorry. One message recorded…maybe I missed the others if you left them. I've been running errands, this and that, and I had no way of getting back to you anyway so I've just been waiting until we could connect. How's it going over there?"

"About as you'd expect. Lots of pleasantries on the surface, everyone trying to get along but under that there's a palpable undercurrent of distrust and skepticism compounded by tedious translations, definitions, clarifications and on and on. Not my idea of fun," Tim recited.

"How's things in Prescott?

"Hot, upper 90s with a breeze and scuddy clouds…typical August weather. Tweeks and Ralph are fine. No issues with the house," she scrolled through a mental list. "All good, except I miss you like crazy."

"Miss you too, babe. So good to hear your voice. What are you wearing?"

"Stop," she protested but smiled in spite of herself.

"Look, I need to apologize again for dropping all that on you like I did. You were absolutely right to react the way you did. And actually I'm happy you're safe at home although it's damn lonely without you."

"It better be, Tim Strange."

"Not to worry. I'm still trying to adjust to the time change. I don't have the energy."

"That's the only reason?" she teased.

They bantered-on for a few more minutes.

"Sure as hell a lot cooler here but nice enough and the city is spectacular, although I haven't gotten out much. It's just nine here but I'm so jet-lagged I'll crash pretty soon. Henry says he'll need me for our morning session then I'm free, so I'll be heading first to the Hermitage…do the tourist thing, and then tackle the State Archives for fun."

"Lucky you."

"The hotel we're staying at, the Mariinsky, is this massive 19-century place. It is no Motel 6 that's for sure! Rooms are first rate. It's very Old World beautiful. You'd call it charming."

"I don't do charming."

"I need to tell you that when we landed the Counsel General informed us that earlier today Gorbachev resigned as Secretary General so we're entering a period of extremely serious tensions. The USSR's imploding. He could be arrested or worse. That's another reason I'm happy your home. Henry thinks the Kremlin will keep it all locked-down but it's potentially volatile."

"That's what I heard today too," she said without thinking.

"What? What do you mean?"

She thought furiously. She didn't want to tell him she'd grilled a Russian Orthodox priest. That screamed insecurity. In retrospect it seemed silly and she was embarrassed. "I just meant that's what I've been reading and hearing on the news, that's all. But I'm happy that's what Kissinger thinks too." He seemed satisfied with her explanation.

"I met a couple of St. Petersburg heavy-weights today, Sobchak, I told you about, and this guy Putin, who Henry seemed to make fast friends with. Putin's KGB…like our CIA and FBI combined- and a hard-case little guy who I have the impression punches above his weight. Sobchak is very tall, good-looking, speaks fluent English unlike Putin. Henry said he's even overheard talk that he might be a serious candidate for leadership and the analysts with our commission agree. Oh, and I've been watching a bit of that new news channel CNN. It's quite a concept that Turner has come-up with. It might just take off. The networks better watch out."

"Honey, I've been missing you and can't wait for you to be home with me, Tweeks and Ralph. They know you're gone, you know... at least Ralph does. Hey, cats are cats," she laughed.

"OK, well I'm going to climb into a very empty bed and I don't need to tell you how much I miss your warmth next to me."

"Well then hold that thought. It sucks for me too. Night...love you."

"Sweet dreams from St. Petersburg honey...."

It was just after 3:30 in the morning when she woke with a start. Ralph was growling.

CHAPTER TEN

Throwing off the covers she hurried into her slippers and robe while calling to Ralph, standing alert at the foot of the bed. It took her a second to pull herself out of a deep sleep. Disorientation let go grudgingly. The few nightlights glowed in little amber halos of light but otherwise the house was dark. "shit," she breathed. She'd forgotten to switch-on the exterior security lights. Outside it was pitch black. It was a waning gibbous moon she reminded herself so it wouldn't be much help either.

Ralph kept at her side as she made her way into the living room. His tail was not wagging but arched over his back like a rapier. "What is it big guy?" Ralph weighing all of 25 –pounds but he'd proven his courage and tenacity on more than one occasion.

He stood head down, ears perked, looking straight at the front door. There was definitely something...or someone out there. Did she toggle the lights or remain concealed in the dark? A dilemma.

It was probably an animal…raccoons, skunks and an occasional Coyote were nocturnal visitors to the neighborhood rummaging for garbage. But, she abruptly froze in terror, they didn't usually turn door knobs! It was dark but there was enough light to see the glint of the brass knob quietly, slowly turn first left then right…didn't it? Maybe the light was playing tricks on her…was she imagining it…just paranoid? Ralph growled again then erupted in a bark that made Abby jump and scream.

She couldn't be sure but she thought she heard footsteps in the driveway. She ran to the light switch and abruptly the outside floods sparked on. If there had been someone at the door, there was now no sign of them. But in her state of anxiety there was no 'if' about it.

She was seriously freaking. What should she do!? Call the neighbor…call the cops? No, she didn't want to raise a ruckus and alarm anyone unnecessarily. Since the scandal of her dead father's corruption in the department and his complicity in the murder of her family, her relationship with law enforcement was conflicted to put it mildly. So, no to that too.

Besides she knew she could protect herself…she'd proved that on more than one occasion over the past couple of years. Tim's .45 was in a gun safe in his office. She hadn't even thought of it until now but that gave her a sense of security. She had no trouble with self-defense if it came to it but the moment seemed to have past. Her heart-rate and breathing were back under control. Even Ralph resumed his spot on the sofa no longer on alert mode.

But all of this rumination begged the question: who was at the front door at 3:00 A.M. and why? Did some creep know she was alone…was it someone trying to rob the place…a home invasion? Those were the only explanations. No one borrowed sugar at 0-dark-thirty. Tim's place was far enough from downtown it was unlikely that it could be some homeless person.

One thing was for sure: she wasn't even going to try to go back to sleep…not after this. Good luck with that. Instead she made sure all the doors and windows were shut and locked, fed the animals, made herself some hot chocolate, and switched-on the TV and CNN.

She'd gotten hooked by its streaming, real-time coverage of the Gulf War back in January and now it was her go-to station for reporting events she felt she could trust. She'd always been an engaged student…curious, disciplined, 'desperate' for knowledge was the truth of it. History class more than others had become a refuge from her dysfunctional family and her father's abuse. If nothing else history, at least the way Tim taught it, allowed her to see how screwed-up and contradictory the nation's past was, while at the same time offering inspirational human stories of triumph over adversity…the searing nobility of struggle. Now she wanted to be able to have informed conversations with Tim on politics, the economy, international affairs, and know her sources of information could be trusted. Hot and heavy 'chemistry' went only so far after all, and she always believed smart could be sexy too or damn well should be…

Abby rocketed out of her chair and turned up the volume. Jill Daugherty, CNN's Moscow Bureau Chief, was just then reporting that an on-going coup by die-hard elements of the Communist Party and the Red Army against Gorbachev was escalating and being opposed by President Boris Yeltsin's rallying of the pro-democracy opposition in strikes, mass demonstration and a show of force by loyal elements of the military.

She watched transfixed as a large building burned, tanks rumbled down streets, masses of people churned shouting slogans. It was like something out of a movie. But this was all too real…and terrifying to her with Tim way to near to the unfolding chaos.

It had been mesmerizing to watch tanks and armored vehicles race across the desert towards Baghdad in CNNs coverage of Desert Storm, and now here she was virtually carried into the protesting chaos and violence of an unfolding revolution.

Abruptly Paris in 1789, the barricades of 1848…even America's own 1776 moment or 1968 took on a new, visceral meaning. In its own unique way the 60s seemed less like a weed-fueled abstraction than a real moment of cultural revolt against a corrupt system…the 'Establishment.' Her 'forgettable' history and political science classes abruptly took on a coherence she'd never fully appreciated before. And for the first time she glimpsed the love Tim had for his field. It wasn't a job or even a profession…it was truly his passion. It was like a door opened not only into his world but also one opening new vistas for her as well…or so she hoped.

She woke with a start with sun lighting the big picture window. In spite of herself, she'd fallen asleep on the sofa an afghan tucked around her. Both animals were down as well. Ralph snored slightly. The kitchen clock said ten-after-seven. The timer had clearly worked as the aroma of coffee filled the room. It was probably what woke her, she registered as she folded herself off the sofa and headed for the bathroom. It was as she looked back in the direction of the front door, remembering her fright that she saw it. Something- an envelope, had been dropped through the old mail slot of the vintage mahogany door Tim bought because it was…historic. It lie there inert, non-threatening. It was what mail slots were for. She stood staring at it. Maybe it was the electric bill…a credit card statement…junk mail. Kid's pranks? But it wasn't…

CHAPTER ELEVEN

Tim stood in awe taking it in. The famous Winter Palace now the Hermitage Museum loomed before him across the huge square, its pale green, gold, and white –columned facade, it had once been a deep ocher, beckoning invitingly but intimidating in its scale. He couldn't help but see in his mind the grainy black and white photos of Russian troops firing into demonstrators where he was now standing. It was an eerie feeling but he also admitted he hadn't felt this kind of excitement and anticipation in years.

He'd inquired about booking a guide but decided he wanted the freedom to roam at will. Besides he had an appointment. Entering through one of its three massive wrought-iron gates, each adorned with the Russian Imperial crest, he found the court yard's ticket office, purchased a guide book on the first floor and, with a throng of other visitors, ascended the red-carpeted, white marble grand staircase-one of over 170, to the exhibition floors above. Snow white walls, vaulted ceiling, set off by blue columns and rococo giltwork, dazzled the eye. Overhead a massive gilt-framed artwork hinted at what the museum's 20-kilometers of some 350 exhibitions among the palace's 1000 rooms, offered. It was said that spending just one minute in front of each painting or exhibit would require eight years to see everything the Hermitage contained.

But Tim wasn't there to admire the art work and other priceless artifacts as he would otherwise have enjoyed. His time was limited. Consulting his guide he finally arrived at the ornately wood-paneled grand library of Czar Nicholas II. There was no public access, of course, but as chance had it a member of the commission had a contact who arranged for Tim to meet with the curator of a temporary exhibit of the czarist Ministry of Finance in a non-public office.

After pleasantries, fortunately for Tim the man, spoke very good English, Tim got to the point. "Thank you for taking time to meet with me. I am doing research on the events surrounding the succession of Nicholas I following Czar Paul's death. My understanding is that there was some controversy? Tim knew the broad strokes but wanted to test the local waters.

"Yes, well," the curator, Andre, replied diffidently, "Czar Paul had three sons in line of succession: Alexander, Constantine, and Nicholas in that order. When Paul did Alexander became czar as Alexander I. In November 1825 he contracts Typhus and dies in early December."

"Because he has no legitimate male heir and both his sisters died as children, the succession devolves to the two surviving brothers Grand Duke Constantine Pavlovich and Nicholas. Problem was that neither of them wanted the throne, but before Alexander's death they had informally agreed between them that Constantine would be czar. Unknown to either, Alexander learned of the arrangement and had a secret document executed which made this arrangement formal.

"Unaware of this document all, including the brothers, expected that Constantine would become czar. So when Alexander's dies but before the secret document is produced and presented to the State Council it was assumed that Constantine was in. But Nicholas changed his mind and there was an impasse for twenty-five days. No one was in charge. And in Russia that was unthinkable…as it is today," he offered with clear meaning."

"That is a problem," Tim agreed, but left current events unaddressed.

"This uncertainty is then complicated by the Decembrist Revolt fomented by some liberal factions in the army who had opposed Alexander's increasingly autocratic rule. In part because Nicholas was never intended to be czar, the army pledged allegiance to Constantine. Nicholas crushed the revolt and seizing the opportunity simply proclaimed himself czar, stating publicly that 'the morning after tomorrow I am either czar or dead.' It was a naked power grab.

If Constantine had decided to press his claim, there would have been a grave crisis," he finished.

"And I thought our politics was messy," Tim said "What happened to Constantine?"

"He exercised power as Emperor Konstantin I in Poland until his death from Cholera in 1831, surviving an earlier assassination attempt by his brother. They did not play nice together," Andre added with a thin smile. "Nicholas II turned out to be a reviled tyrant and roundly hated even more than his father. And he sold to you Americans our colony in Alaska," he added as if the affront happened yesterday. Tim ignored the Alaska dig.

"That is quite a story. What tangled webs we weave, eh?"

"There was one curious aspect to the story not many are aware of you might find interesting?"

"I'd love to hear it, if you have the time," Tim indulged.

"Dah…for sure yes."

"The Minister of Finance was a man named Georg Von Cancrin. He was in office in 1825…right here in the palace when all this drama transpired. Actually there are plans to refurbish the offices and have a permanent exhibit one day," he interjected. "It will be the centerpiece of Imperial Numismatics." Tim offered his enthusiastic approval, wondering where this was going..

"So, now during the succession crisis," Andre continued, "and assuming Constantine's elevation, Cancrin is commissioned to issue two coins…a very special commemorative birth medal and a silver rouble…since known as the 'Constantine Ruble'. Two well-known artists, Jacob Reichel and Vladimir Alekseyev, were tasked with the artwork, each designing one side of the coin-obverse and reverse, which were then given to three engravers at the St. Petersburg mint which pressed a few proof coins from the dies and tin presses whose edges and obverse sides differed slightly." Tim was following with mounting interest.

"When it was certain that Nicholas not Constantine would be czar, Cancrin ordered the proof coins, dies, and Reichel's drawings to be locked away in the Ministry vault. The coins virtually disappeared and were never circulated. Only the brothers, Cancrin, Reichel, and the engravers, sworn to secrecy, knew of their existence." This was indeed becoming a gripping story, Tim conceded.

"But somehow Alexander II learned of the coins in 1879 and ordered the Ministry of Finance to produce them. They did and he took possession of them. He kept one coin which is now on display at the State Historical Museum in Moscow." Tim registered that and took a mental note. "He gave three others to relatives which have now disappeared into the hands of foreign collectors." Now Tim really took note. "Reputedly three other originals were struck, two have also been traced to collectors. The third, once owned by Grand Duke Georgy Mikhailovich, is actually in your National Museum of American History at the Smithsonian. Thus there were actually seven Constantine Rubles…or perhaps eight. No one knows for sure," he added with a shrug.

"I'll be damned Tim thought. Next time he was in DC…

Tim did a quick calculation. "I believe you've accounted for seven rubles unless I miscounted."

"You didn't. The last remaining proof coin we know of is right here along with the original drawings, presses and dies," Andre grinned at his theatrical disclosure. It was compared to the original dies and found to be exact in every detail.

"One of the proof coins is here?!"

"Yes, I can show you momentarily if you have time?"

"Of course!" Time nearly shouted "I mean that would be exciting…marvelous to see given the history."

"As you might imagine over the years many fake coins have surfaced and all have been debunked as forgeries, some very, very good facsimiles, the so-called Trubetskoy ruble allegedly eight of them-five in silver, three in copper- were minted in Paris in the 1860s. One is here and your Smithsonian coin is another one. But…"

"But?"

"We know that one genuine proof ruble was sold by the Tolstoy estate…yes that Tolstoy, to a Russian émigré collector living in the US in 1913," Andre confirmed. "It was examined for authenticity in

1961 and then sold to another American in 1974." Tim was sitting on the edge of his chair.

"There is more. It has long been rumored that Reichel secretly kept a coin for himself. The story, never fully confirmed, is that it was bought by a Soviet collector Josef Richter around WWI. The coin was examined by a Russian expert in 1962 and authenticated. After that the coin was seen in Germany, owned by a coin expert who tried to auction it off at Sotheby's but had no takers. It then disappeared never to be seen again. No one knows where it is but rumors say the United States."

Tim worked furiously to collect his thoughts and calm his exuberance. "That is an amazing story, Andre. Thank you for sharing that with me."

"Would you like to see the Constantine ruble?"

"If it's not too much trouble," Tim made light.

"Certainly, follow me Professor Strange. It is on display four rooms down.

Tim followed the curator with a mix of anticipation and hesitancy, torn between his wild imaginings and reluctance to hope for too much. What were the odds?

They entered a small but ornately appointed room filled with glass display cases. Andre led them to one prominently positioned under a brilliant light. And there it was or 'they' were. There were two coins that appeared identical! Tim bent closer and stared. The silver coins were displayed so that both sides were visible. A chrome rod extending from the top of the case attached to a surrounding metal band encircled the coin around its circumference. A card underneath explained the provenance and history.

Tim took a sharp inhale he tried to disguise his excitement with a discrete cough and throat-clearing. It was the same coin he and Abby had found in the hidden bag! But as he examined it more closely and compared the coin to his mental image he tried to visualize it clearly but couldn't be sure.

"You said that the coins were not all identical?"

"According to records at least six rubles were produced with Cyrillic edge script of which five can be accounted for. The one on the right is one of the Trubetskoy fake rubles. The one on the left is a genuine proof ruble. Note the Cyrillic lettering on the edge. The sixth has disappeared.

"Disappeared?"

"Vanished without a trace or even rumor as to what happened to it or where it might be."

"You seem inordinately interested in the Constantine ruble Professor Strange?" Andre eyed him curiously, Tim noted.

If he only knew! "I collect historic coins mostly American, like silver dollars," he explained as in fact he did. I love the artwork and engraving of old coins and I've always admired the Russian double eagle…like I admire the Saint Gaudens walking liberty on our old silver dollars and gold coins," he explained.

"Yes, coins of this mintage are works of art and of great historic and cultural significance," Andre agreed. If there is nothing else, I do have another appointment," Andre announced with neutral bureaucratese. "It has been a pleasure." They shook hands and Tim cast one last glance at the Constantine Rubles suspended in their glass case. His heart raced even as he forced himself to dial it down.

He spent another hour taking-in, if barely scratching the surface of the breathtaking grandeur of the former Winter Palace. When he finally retraced his steps out the massive gates it was late afternoon. The weather had turned brisk as it did towards evening even in summer. He couldn't wait to share what he'd learned with Abby but with the time difference he'd have to wait a few hours. He was hungry and a drink or two sounded perfect.

With over 7,000 restaurants in the City and several near the museum, his guidebook indicated, he certainly had choices. He settled on Little Sicily, characterized in reviews as 'very cozy and friendly' and the menu offered Pizza! Just what the doctor ordered…or was about to, he relished the prospect. It was a short walk along the Neva. He just missed the highpoint of the fabled 'white nights' season of high northern latitude 20-hours of sunlight, but it was still bright and pleasant enough for a city along the same latitude as Oslo, Norway and Anchorage, Alaska.

After checking with Henry tomorrow morning, he intended to visit the State Historical Archive to see what local primary sources he might find on the events of February 1917 that might shed light on their other discoveries. What were the connections that inexplicably linked his cabin with its hidden artifacts to St. Petersburg?

Savoring a Baltika and waiting for his wood-fired pizza he thought too of the significance of what he'd learned in the Hermitage about the Constantine Ruble and actually being able to confirm that the coin he and Abby found appeared identical to the museum's coin. He wasn't able to take a photo, they weren't allowed, but there had to be something in the archives he could photocopy. His fallback of course would be the Smithsonian if necessary, but he'd cross that bridge when he came to it.

What was that coin worth? He didn't dare ask Andre for obvious reasons but that too should be something he could find out by exploring the rare coin market and checking with dealers back home. In fact he knew the owner of Ancient and US Coins on Cortez St. and had purchased coins for his own collection of Morgans. It would be one of his first calls.

Pleasantly full and with three Baltika under his belt Tim walked to the nearest metro underground marked by a large letter M he'd studied in his guidebook. It was a straight shot to the hotel…a five ten minute ride. He bought a card for his personal use when not on commission business. The metro was surprisingly cheap, modern and clean.

It was nearly 6:30 so his train was fairly crowded. He consulted the 'scheme' in the station to be sure he was headed in the right direction. Thankfully it was in English as well as Russian. He entered as the door snicked open followed by a bustling crowd of locals and foreign tourists. Among them were two men of medium build, short hair, in jeans and dark hoodies. Tim stood holding a loop as the train silently whisked them away, swaying with the acceleration.

CHAPTER TWELVE

Abby slid into a booth at the Lone Spur under the giant black bear hide mounted on the wall. As its name suggested the place screamed 'cowboy.' She'd arranged to meet two longtime girlfriends for lunch. She was early or they were late. She couldn't think strait. The place was half-full…a decent lunch crowd for a Tuesday, she guessed. She was all about supporting local businesses and minimum-wage workers. Having been a waitress and 'hostess'…even working shifts at McDonalds not too long ago, she knew all too well what it was like. She always left generous tips.

But what was gnawing at her was not labor inequities but the note slid through their door in the dark of night. Not only was that creepy enough it was what it said. She pulled the note from her purse, sliding it out of its envelope to read it again…for the umpteenth time:

> 'Thumb Butte. 1:30 tomorrow afternoon. Tell no one.'

The note was typed. Clearly 'tomorrow' meant today. She checked her watch again…nearly noon. It was only a ten-minute drive from the Spur but she didn't want to be late. Fuck it. What she really wanted was not to go at all…meeting who knows who with who knew what motive was not her idea of smart. Even in a well-used public place like the Butte there were many secluded areas and circuitous trails. She thought of the insane shoot-out there of three going-on-four summers ago between the cartels and police and her own brush with death compliments of her psychopath father. No, Thumb Butte held no fond memories for her. "Hey you!" the chorus of female voices called out…

If nothing else she could walk-off her lunch. In fact she was beginning to wonder if this wasn't all just some sort of prank…all the drama and theatrics. It was just like some guys she knew. She'd even dated one of them so she knew he might try to punk her like this. But after Tim and her rather dubious profile in town most of her so-called 'friends' had distanced themselves. Abby was toxic…someone to steer clear of. Danger and bad shit seem to attach to her. It was one reason her lunch with Hailey and Marissa had been such fun.

"Miss Davis." She whirled around caught off-guard. Who would be calling her by her maiden name?

"Oh my God! Mr. Clarke…John, what are you doing here?"

The old Arizona Ranger, using a silver and turquoise-headed cane she noted immediately, stepped forward, removing his Stetson, reached out to take her hand. She nearly knocked him over with her embrace.

"Easy there girl you give an old man a heart attack," he smiled affectionately, his weathered face deeply tanned, eyes crinkled.

"What…what are you doing here?"

"You mean in Prescott… or here at the Butte?" he feigned ignorance.

"Well both. "I obviously got your note.

"It's been a cool summer in Montana especially up along the Hi-line in Glasgow. Thought I'd come down for a little sun and warmth…see some old friends while I can still get around," he patted his leg. "…See you and that professor friend of yours…guess you're more than friends now," he took her hand in his big paw. Right pretty ring. Congratulations."

"Thanks John. We got married last year in Sedona."

"Handsome country. I knew it when all you'd see were Indians, outlaws, a few ranchers and coyotes…before the tourists ruined it. I had a hunch you'd rope him in," he chuckled. "Here let's sit," he indicated the bench just off the trail.

"Why all the secrecy, John?" Instead of answering her he looked-up to the summit of the Butte.

"This old hunk of rock has seen a lot going back to when I was a young Ranger and to the Spanish and the Indians long before me," he offered philosophically. She'd let him get to it in his own time. "In that shoot-out with your father, Buck, down in that hidden canyon, I was sure he had me. When you drove off that afternoon, I never thought I'd see you again. I would have regretted that…." the words hung there with undisguised emotion.

"How's the museum?" she deflected her own.

"Well now that's a ripe question. Doors are still open, locals drop-by to chat, tourists seem to like all the curios and memorabilia, amateur historians and an occasional academic from the college use the archives, teachers still bring their classes in for a tour and to satisfy some lesson plan-or-other, so it's business…or hobby as usual, I guess you'd say."

"Tim hung that old shotgun of yours over the fireplace," Clark wasn't convinced she approved.

"That MacNaughton is a fine old gun…maybe I should take her back," he winked.

"Don't you dare. Tim's attached to it for some reason. I swear: men and their guns," she rolled her eyes. "He's got those Colts of yours in wood and glass cases in his office. "Clarke nodded approval.

"Speaking of guns, you won't believe this but the other day we found a bag hidden in a wall in this cabin of Tim's in Show Low and in it was a large revolver of all things. Tim said it was Russian…a Smith and Wesson Russian."

"You don't say…has a little hook on the trigger guard? God, I haven't seen one of those in years. Wonder how in tarnation it got there?"

"That's what we're trying to figure out. It's a complete mystery. I wish Tim were here. You two could talk guns or history."

"That's the other part of why I'm here, Abby. Tim called last week, explained he'd be away for a few days…asked me to look-in on you if I had business in Prescott. So I made you my business. Figured I'd take a little Road trip. Nobody would miss me anyway.

Tim mentioned St. Petersburg…Russia not Florida, but didn't say what it was about."

"He finagled a spot on a trade commission with an old acquaintance-long story. They have business in St. Petersburg and Moscow for a few days. He hoped to be able do some research in their archives that might shed some light on the things we found, including some coins that could be worth a ton."

Clarke studied her for long moment. "Guess I'd better come clean. I left you that note the way I did because I did not want to put either of you in danger and did not want to be seen. I don't much trust phones. You never know who's listening."

"Danger…danger from what?"

"In my experience there are few authentic coincidences," he began. "You remember Colin Campbell?"

"The dirty cop in Glasgow…my distant relation? How could I not?."

"After all the fallout with the Seal narcotics enterprise and Colin's murder by your father in Red Lodge, Duncan spent the last eighteen months in Montana State Prison in Deer Lodge."

"Tim told me Duncan was apprehended up near Flagstaff but I didn't follow it after that. I'll never speak to him again…ever. The way he used me, my mother…even Tim's wife Karen pisses me off big time every time I think about it. Of course I read how Seal was assassinated down south somewhere," she added. "Good riddance. Whatever Duncan got he had it coming. Wait," she searched John's face, not liking what she saw… "what about him?"

"Seems there's a new operation that's moved into the vacuum Seal left and it's been recruiting aggressively in correctional facilities. Duncan was released a few weeks ago.

"And?"

"Apparently he violated parole and disappeared. Speculation is about three weeks ago at his last probation check. Further speculation is that he now works for the new kids on the block."

"And who is that exactly?"

"Well a report by former FBI chief William Webster identified it as the Russian Mafia which is aggressive, brutal and global in its reach…a real bad bunch."

"But what's that got to do with Tim and me? Wait…you don't mean…"

"An old friend of mine works in corrections and specifically at Deer Lodge. He hears things. He sees things. He said that a cellmate of Duncan's hoping for expedited parole turned CI, sorry- confidential informant, in exchange for information… conversations he'd overheard. According to my friend the cellmate swears Duncan told him he was being recruited inside by the Russian mafia and that he had 'business' to take care of in Prescott...that he and his cousin Colin had been betrayed and that payback was coming and overdue. State Law enforcement believes that Duncan has gone underground as a paid assassin or mule for one of these 'krysha'.

"How do you know all this?"

"Abeline, I sit in a museum all damn day. Some days not a single person comes through the door. I've been in law enforcement all my life. I have a scanner for entertainment. Friends in the department bring me copies of local bulletins and alerts-troopers, marshals, sheriffs…even the feds- BATF… FBI. It's a hobby or an illness I'm not sure which," he snorted.

"What if it's all just rumors and speculation, John? After the Seal business, it makes sense Montana would be on edge…a little overly suspicious, right?"

"By-golly you're right about that. But are you willing to take a chance? Anyway, that's why I slipped you that note and why I asked you to meet me. I needed to warn you in person. Thumb Butte was my last gunfight. Look at me, darlin'. Another month or two at this rate I'll be in a Goddamn wheelchair. Probably should shoot myself first," he proposed. "I'd better stopover in Denver to see my niece before I do something rash," he chuckled with a wink.

"You'll do no such thing!" Abby scolded knowing he wasn't serious…at least she didn't think so. "You are a good and dear friend, John, and I'll take what you just told me seriously…I promise. And as soon as Tim gets back we'll figure out how to deal with this. I'm praying your wrong but as you say neither of us can ignore it if there is any chance its true…so I promise."

"You do realize the penalty for lying to an Arizona Ranger…and the last one at that," he shook a finger at her but was smiling as he did it.

Abby kissed him on the cheek. "Now I insist you stay for dinner…our place or we can eat out?"

"Anytime I get asked out by a lady as pretty as you the answer is you bet!"

"Does that line always work?"

"Pretty much," he winked.

They chatted easily as they made their way down the trail towards the visitor's parking lot...the same one where she and Tim had said good-bys three years ago should they not make it off the Butte alive. Parked next to Tim's pick-up was a new black and silver Mustang GT 5.0. "This is yours?"

Clarke beamed. "Always love the ponies and this baby's got a whole herd of 'em!"

"You amaze me."

"I get that a lot now saddle-up. I'm driving this time."

CHAPTER THIRTEEN

'Senatskya Ploshchad' the modulated tone announced as the train ghosted to a stop at the underground platform at the Admiraltyskaya station. The car was half-full, the lunch crowd having dwindled in the early afternoon back-to-work routine. Tim, exited, headed for the escalator, backpack slung over his shoulder. Ten minutes later he was standing before his destination-the Russian State Historical Archive.

The archive was housed in one of the most immense, imposing structures in the city: the Russian Synod and Senate anchored right on the bank of the Neva, its high Neo-classical edifice and scores of Corinthian columns a testament to Imperial power and glory, and the intimate relationship between church and state that had characterized Imperial Russia. For how much longer, Tim wondered. Or might it enjoy a resurgence liberated from communist rule?

He had a brief conversation with Henry at their commission breakfast meeting in the hotel. The members would be in negotiations all day with their counterparts at Smolny Palace, where the Bolshevik leadership had governed and Lenin himself had kept a small study. Talk about coming a mind-blowing full circle, the thought struck him.

Word from the embassy and the newly arrived Ambassador Robert Strauss was that in the wake of Gorbachev's resignation as chairman of the Communist Party and the failed coup, it appeared that Yeltsin had at least momentarily stabilized the situation or was at best managing the chaos. There was talk of forming a successor state, replacing the now defunct USSR with the CIS- Commonwealth of

Independent States but that was a very tentative work in progress. Regardless the commission's work, Strauss indicated, should proceed and he'd been assured it would be warmly welcomed in Moscow.

Tim strode purposely towards the massive triumphal-arched entry that connected the two hundred yard-long wings, armed with a letter of introduction in Russian he had a colleague in the foreign language department draft before he left Prescott. To gain entrance one had to present their credentials and accreditation. He'd been altered that the Archive closed for a month in the summer but the July-August hiatus had ended two days before their arrival.

The state archives had been notoriously closed to Western scholars with a presumed animus towards Communism or fear of airing dirty laundry. But access had begun to open-up as the winds of change swept through the crumbling empire and a desire to distance the new from the old gained momentum, Tim had learned.

Still, it wasn't as if his research interests threatened Soviet security or state secrets. All he sought was greater clarity on the events of February-March 1917 as the Revolution unfolded in the city. Above all, of course, was the hope of making the connection between what he and Abby had discovered and how those objects got from St. Petersburg to Show Low, Arizona. It seemed inconceivable yet undeniable that there was a connection. Andre had confirmed as much.

Finding records or a document that might shed light on the mystery was going to be a monumental challenge, he'd been warned by a Russian specialist he knew and reached out to. In all the seventeen state archives held over 65 million files on 300 miles of shelving, not to mention regional and local depositories. It would all depend on the finding aids and staff, but on that score there were red flags. Still, the real enemy was deterioration, insufficient funding, and indifference that many scholars, even Russian academics, were warning posed an existential threat to preserving history.

Tim saw this moment of infatuation with all things western as the shackles of communism fell away- a moment of euphoria for some, dread for others, as a golden opportunity. It might not last long.

There could be a severe backlash all was so unpredictable. But he was a believer in 'timing is everything'...sometimes. Perhaps this was one of those times.

"Vam pomuch?" the young woman behind a large oak desk that could have been early 19th-century asked.

"Tim handed her the requisite letter and his passport. She turned to her Soviet-made Poisk-IBM compatible machine and entered some text, connecting first to the EUnet through the RELCOM network to the USEnet global network. Tim had been briefed and knew that one of the commission's goals was to secure license agreements for the import of Apple and Microsoft computer and software. That would be Mr. Putin, Tim surmised.

"Here you are Prof. Strange," she handed him a cardboard pass with his passport photo copied onto it. Please fill out this questionnaire, she instructed as she scanned his credentials. "Oh dear."

"That didn't sound good," Tim tried not to show his misgivings.

"I see you wish to research our collections on the 1917 Revolution. Unfortunately those files are closed temporarily," she said with terse finality while smiling. But there was no warmth to it.

"There is no access…to anything…since when?"

"That is not my decision. Is there anything else we may be able to assist you with?"

"No thanks but I've come a long way and only have a day or two in St. Petersburg and…"

"In that case please return your pass. We look forward to assisting you another time. Good day," she began…

"Tim Strange! What on earth are you doing in St. Petersburg?" Abruptly turning on his heels, Tim recognized the woman immediately.

"Judith, I'd ask you the same question. Gosh it's good to see you," they hugged briefly. Judith Forston was head of cataloguing in the Hoover Institution at Stanford and one of Karen's dear friends. "I haven't seen you since the service…gosh five years now." Five minutes of catching-up and explaining how she came to be in St. Petersburg she elaborated further.

"So we have a wonderful opportunity. We've been given permission to microfilm the Communist Party's archives here and in Moscow. Seems like everything's suddenly accessible! I'm here leading that effort…dotting the 'I's'-crossing the 'T's'. And you?"

Looks like I'm out of luck. I'm doing some research on the events of 1917 here in the city but apparently the entire archive is off limits."

"Ah, there is a newly formed Commission on State Secrets that has been muscle-flexing of late as all this political turmoil rages. Here, come with me," she said conspiratorially. The young woman had done her job and seemed uninterested. Down a long hallway they entered a well-appointed office. Sitting behind the same kind of desk was a large man who beamed at Judith.

"Tim, this is Rudolf Pikhoia. Dr. Pikhoia is head of the new Russian Archival Administration. They shook hands, exchanging introductions.. "Rudy, we have a problem I'm hoping you can help us with. It would be a great personal favor…" she cooed demurely.

"This is amazing," Tim took her hand in his a scant ten minutes later. "I can't thank you enough Judith for your intercession. I think Rudolf is sweet on you." She smiled indulgently, dismissed that with an airy wave.

"How long will you be in St Petersburg and where are you staying? We're all billeted at the Mariinsky except Kissinger who has a suite at the embassy. And sadly we leave tomorrow for Moscow on a charter at 11:00AM…or I should say Henry and the others are. I'm catching a Lufthansa flight to JFK and then back to Prescott. I'd love to have dinner, catch-up and hear details of your project but there's just not time…speaking of which mine here is ticking away," he glanced at his watch. "I'll call you at the Hoover, promise."

"I'll hold you to it to. These are exceptional times and I'd enjoy having your perspective. And I understand completely. You've always taken your research seriously."

"As one old professor once told me 'it's where the bodies are buried,' he laughed.

"Careful Tim, in Russia that's true…literally!"

Ten minutes later Tim was seated in an expansive reading room surrounded by boxes of documents brought to him on a dolly by a young archival assistant for his use. He had his work cut out for him but it all looked familiar except for the Russian labels with English translations below. Over his career he'd logged many hours in the National Archives, Smithsonian, Library of Congress and presidential libraries. He knew the drill. As always he felt a tinge of excitement, the thrill of the unknown and potential discovery. He was also glad he'd remembered to bring his Visine and a bottle of aspirin. 'If past experience was any guides, he'd make liberal of both!

He had a battle plan; one he always used. He'd written himself a set of key questions that would help focus his search. Who were the Americans in Petrograd at the time of the revolutions? Could he identify anyone who had served with the military and specifically the Intelligence Police? Was there anyone who had access to Russian rubles? Could he link the revolver to any particular individual…this last question being the real longshot. If he could narrow the scope, eliminate what he could, compile a short list of plausible individuals, check the boxes as it were, he'd consider this time well-spent.

But finding the answers to any of these critical questions much less all of them was the longest of long shots. Experience reminded him how elusive or ambiguous documents and sources could be…even back home where archives and collections were open with few if any restrictions. Here, it was a challenge altogether different and daunting and where every source could be tainted. Still, the task was before him and he dare not waste a minute. The clock was ticking literally and figuratively.

Six hours later he sat there stunned by what he had learned….

CHAPTER FOURTEEN

Petrograd endured nights of 30-40 below zero and days not much warmer that unusually frigid winter of 1917. Sunlight was in short supply in the sub-arctic latitude. Snow feet deep in drifts covered everything in its deep-freeze embrace. Smoke from thousands of coal and wood fires hung like ice-fog mingling with frost particles kicked-up by horses and sleighs sluicing across the frozen Neva and the city's canals.

It was a city beleaguered by shortages of food and every other commodity. Inflation and scarcity were symptoms of the same plague of deprivation. Women by the thousands stood in freezing temperatures for hours for bread. Children shivered in the streets. Feeding stations could not hope to meet the demand. Factory workers endured untold privations. Petrograd, certainly for the average Russian, was starving, dreary and on edge. Nightly blackouts and an Imperial decree banning vodka further darkened an already dismal mood.

But for others, the rich, the titled, and the entitled few, it was the best of times. The Russian aphorism, "I sit high and see far' betrayed delusional myopia of the impending doom.

Hundreds of foreigners were in the city of 2.3 million in the third year of the ghastly war that had begun three years earlier and which Russia was losing badly on the so-called Eastern Front. Casualties soared beyond imagination. The army was broken. Thousands of amputees crowded the city's inadequate hospitals or roamed its streets begging, trains disgorging the constant stream of wounded from boxcars pulling into Finland and Nicholas stations, also carrying with them endless misery, despair and anger.

Among those in the city that winter were scores of American and foreign journalists, as well as many more representatives of American corporations, banks and myriad companies profiteering off the war so that a flourishing expatriate community of writers, socialites and adventure-seeking war correspondents gave the city an even gayer illusionary flair. Russia's allies, Britain and France had embassies and consulates in Petrograd as did the formally still neutral United States, although there was little doubt about President Wilson's tacit if distant alliance, in all but name, with the Entente Powers.

All of this Tim knew but the visceral impact of reading through the accounts of those living in a city in the cross-hairs of what increasingly seemed like imminent German assault coupled with the unmistakable signs of military collapse and upheaval from within, affected him far more than he'd anticipated. The desperation was palpable especially as by February German submarine threats to shipping in the Baltic, the city's only real lifeline had become acute and hundreds of foreigners feared being trapped in the city.

A new American ambassador, wavy-haired, heavily-mustached David R. Francis arrived on board the Swedish ship Oscar II, then boarded the Stockholm Express through Tampere to Petrograd, presenting his credentials at the Winter Palace on April 15, 1916. Francis replaced George Marye whose sudden resignation some attributed to his overtly pro-Russian bias. Francis was not only America's chief diplomat, although speaking no Russian and knowing little about the country, Tim read with amusement, he was also a member of the robust diplomatic community and social circle. The embassy on 34 Furshtatakaya near the seat of the Russian Duma in Tauride Palace and the Smolny Institute was centrally located and not far from the Winter Palace.

The nine member embassy staff included Herbert Pierce, Minister Plenipotentiary and Special Agent of the State Department; First Secretary of Embassy; J. Butler Wright and Fred Sterling counsellors; John White, Second Secretary; John Ryan, Third Secretary; special attaché James Houghteling; First Naval Attache , Newton McCully; Military Attaches, Lt. Francis Riggs and Brigadier General William J.

Judson; Asst. Naval Attache, Capt. James Breckinridge, US Marine Corps. Ambassador Francis' personal valet was a man named Philip Jordan, one of the few Negroes in the city. By all accounts, Tim assessed, they were a solid bunch although unwittingly in the crosshairs of a world-changing event. He noted with particular interest that historians Samuel Harper and Frank Golder were among the many other 'unofficial' Americans in the beleaguered city.

They and others of the foreign embassies, expatriate community and those of social stature, some marrying into the Russian aristocracy, enjoyed the opulence of privilege completely divorced from the realities around them except as spectators and commentators. Glittering receptions and balls continued amidst a growing sense of foreboding. 'The air is thick with talk of catastrophe,' Tim read in one diary entry. Indeed, ominously even the more moderate Menchivicks had called for a nation-wide revolution only weeks before.

On the night of Friday 24 February, Tim noted the Old style date which by the Julian calendar was March 8, violence erupted in the working class and industrial neighborhoods as frustration and suffering and apparent indifference in the Winter Palace and by Czar Nicholas II, then absent in Stavka, combined in a convulsive reaction. Rumors flew as official censorship and seizure of telegraph and phone lines threatened to isolate Petrograd from the outside world. Fittingly given their stoic suffering it was International Women's Day.

Imperial troops and Cossacks confronted thousands of marchers pouring into the street and across bridges driven by rage and grievance. Sporadic gunfire became volleys as troops fired into crowds while the staccato of machine guns escalated. By that Saturday scores of thousands surged through the city. Draw bridges were raised and others heavily guarded to prevent protestors from accessing the city center. Sunday was even bloodier as hundreds were killed and wounded around the grand Nevsky Prospekt and in Znamensky Square. Outrage grew.

The following Monday, 'Red Monday', Nicholas ordered his commanders to crush the violence and restore order in the city.

Chaos reigned in the Duma with break–away members forming a people's soviet, the first mutinies among Imperial regiments signaled that events in the city were raging out of control of the government. Mobs were looting the city in search of food and seeking reprisals against anyone in authority. Government buildings and offices were being set afire. The Hotel Astoria was attacked and ransacked as were the private homes of the rich. A diary entry by Canadian nurse, Edith Hagan captured the moment and the 'ugly face' of stikhya… 'the elemental spontaneity of anarchy, the…primitive food of the oppressed classes…and now in Petrograd it was being unleashed…'

Ambassador Francis largely kept his staff within the locked-down embassy and was provided with a squad of troops for protection but was apprehensive about their loyalty to the government. He had reason to worry as throughout the city troops were killing their officers and defecting to the revolutionaries. Outside the embassy gates the streets had largely been left to the rioters. Nearly 70,000 troops had mutinied and the only parts of the city still in government control were the Winter Palace, Admiralty, General Staff and the telephone exchange and telegraph office, reports alleged. All over the city members of the Russian aristocracy and Imperial officers who had escaped the mobs appealed for sanctuary at foreign embassies under foreign flags.

Faced with the loss of Petrograd, unable to return to the Winter Palace, and on the advice of his remaining loyal advisors and generals Tsar Nicholas II abdicated at Pskov just before midnight March 2, rejoining his family thirty miles south of Petrograd gathered at the Alexander Palace in the city of Tsarskoye Selo.

A Provisional Government was formed from rival claimants jockeying for power at the Tauride Palace, consisting of members of the old Duma and the Soviet of Workers and Soldiers Deputies. In the following days crowds stripped Petrograd of all Imperial-Romanov symbols and coats of arms that had not already been destroyed, replaced by blood-red flags and socialist banners. Within days city services began to return, newspapers reappeared, and life seemed to return to a semblance of order…but it was a new order that foreigners and newly arriving correspondents struggled to come to terms with.

At the American embassy ambassador Francis saw opportunities for the United States and knew that the Provisional Government would be anxious for foreign recognition of its legitimacy. Francis drafted a cable urging American recognition of what he hoped would be a new democratic republic and had it wired to Secretary of State Robert Lansing. It was a bold move.

In his cable he stressed it was in America's interest to be the first foreign government to recognize the new Russian regime, positioning it as Russia's 'best friend', believing strategically it critical to keep Russia in the war that he was certain the United States would soon enter. He also wanted to get a jump on the British and the French and gain favor for American commerce and business opportunity. He received Lansing's approval two days later.
To commemorate the occasion Francis and the entire American staff took the ambassador's sleigh to the Mariinsky Palace where they were met by the entire Provisional government including its War Minister Alexander Kerensky, followed by a brief formal ceremony.

On April 3 Vladimir Ilyich Lenin arrived by train at Finland Station from Switzerland and the course of Russian and world history changed irrevocably. Ambassador Francis expressed concerns for the 'ultra-socialist' as an 'unknown quantity and what he might do confiding to his son, 'we are living somewhat in suspense.' He didn't have long to wait, Tim noted as he read deeper into the documents of these amazing events.

One question on everyone's mind was what all of this meant for Russia and the war? From the Kschessinska mansion Lenin, soon joined by Leon Trotsky from exile in New York, set in motion plans to overthrow the Kerensky government and withdraw Russia from the war. Three days later the embassy staff spent hours over code books deciphering an urgent message from Washington: the United States had declared war on Germany. Francis and the entire embassy were ebullient but wary.

The news as it spread electrified the city. It was popularly believed that American would save Russia. The embassy was besieged by scores of former Russian officers who came out of hiding, risking their lives by Bolshevik death squads, to volunteer, seeking American protection. At the same time hundreds of foreigners were returning to the city from their hurried exile to resume their activities. Much too soon as it soon became clear.

On the night of Sunday April 9 while entertaining guests Phil Jordan interrupted dinner with the urgent message from the police that a mob carrying 'black anarchist flags' and shouting 'death to American imperialists' was marching on the embassy. Ambassador Francis determined to defend it. Shouts of the angry crowd could be heard approaching the compound. Tim went rigid as he read the next entry.

> 'Preparing for the worst I instructed Jordan to load my revolver and bring it to me and I vowed to shoot anyone who tried to get inside the embassy…'

If he had fired into the crowd, Tim thought, the outcome could well have been catastrophic and a major international incident. The 'attack' which police dispersed before it reached the embassy, and the ambassador's 'last stand' was embellished out of all proportion, even President Wilson praising the 'gun-slinger form Missouri who'd faced-down the communist Bolshevik bear'…but it underscored the deteriorating situation in Petrograd. Anxiety and rumor raged in the absence of any sense of order, predictability or security. It was palpable. Could it be this incident was what he was looking for?

For Tim it was a revelation that hit him like an electric jolt. It was only one, isolated, piece of evidence but a tantalizing one. It was the first potential link, the piece of a puzzle that without question he would be following-up wherever it led, wherever it might fit… if anywhere. He could connect an individual, a weapon, a place and a date. All circumstantial but intriguing. He'd already filled one yellow legal pad with notes, took out another with anticipation because he knew enough of the history to know what came next. What more might these files reveal?

President Wilson dispatched two special missions to Russia after American intervention: the Stevens Railroad Commission, and a special diplomatic mission to the Provisional Government led by former Secretary of State and Secretary of War, Elihu Root, Tim read in the yellowed clipping from the NY Times dated April 27, 1917. The nine-man mission arrived in the city by train from Vladivostok and given an open-arms but feckless welcome as it had little impact on events or Russian policy. 'Cordial reserve' was how a San Francisco Bulletin reporter characterized the Russian reception by the Kerensky faction and indifference by the Bolsheviks..

In passing, Tim noted reference to an American who clerked for the National City Bank of New York and seemed to have easy access to the embassy and members of the Root Mission. His name was Leighton Rogers. This Leighton fellow bore further research. Tim scratched the name with a question mark.

In the end all the diplomatic formalities, speeches, and expressions of good will produced nothing and, Tim noted, encouraged an erroneous recommendation that an aggressive American propaganda effort would keep Russia in the war. As the situation in the city further deteriorated the Mission was advised to relocate to Finland for its own safety.

The Stevens Commission represented an effort by American experts to restructure Russia's collapsing railroads critical to its war effort. It arrived a month before Root and company. It, too, failed running afoul of chaos and political cross-currents, yet it had an important role in delaying American military intervention in 1918, Tim read with surprise...military intervention? This he underlined with a note to check thoroughly as he was not an expert on Wilson's foreign policy.

With the launching of the Kerensky-Brusilov offensive on July 15, St. Petersburg-Petrograd exploded in renewed violence and an alleged coup by General Kornilov, the so-called July Days, fueling growing opposition to the war. 500,000 thousand people mobbed the streets on July 17. Both Wright's and Roger's diaries referenced riotous protests, attacks on foreign embassies, and general violence.

Jordan witnessed a bloody battle near the American Embassy between Cossacks and mutinous troops and Ambassador Francis noted that the 'street was literally and actually running with blood' of dead men and horses.

Martial law was proclaimed in the city in early August even as the Bolsheviks gained support at the expense of the Provisional authorities who seemed to be losing all control. Foreign embassies began preparations to evacuate Petrograd both in fear of a Bolshevik uprising and a German assault on the city. Ambassador Francis arranged to have a ship anchored in the Neva that could evacuate all 266 Americans in the city on short notice. In his diary Francis wrote that 'the Bolsheviks had made a list of people whom they intended to kill' including the British ambassador and himself but dismissed it as rumor.

Soviets in Moscow, Petrograd and elsewhere continued to gain support as the Provisional Government continued to lose legitimacy and power to the Bolsheviks throughout the late summer and early fall. After a failed attempt by the government to close-down anti-government newspapers on November 6, the Military-Revolutionary Committee authorized military action against the Kerensky government. Naval ships taken over by their crews arrived to anchor off the city and Petrograd was soon engulfed in sharp fighting between Red Guards and government troops before most defected to the Bolsheviks. Jordan wrote in his diary that 'we are sitting on a bomb…if the ambassador gets out of this mess with our life we will be awfully lucky.'

Foreign embassies, including the American, had been cut off from the world. While they had not been attacked outright they suffered damage. Again food shortages and disease ravaged the city. All who could, especially women and children, were evacuated by the Trans-Siberian Railroad. Ambassador Francis, by then in frail health, and embassy staff were ordered out by the State Department before the order was rescinded in hopes he could somehow negotiate with the Bolsheviks.

A final assault on the Winter Palace met little resistance and the Kerensky government was easily overthrown and firmly in the hands of the Leninists by November 25th. In Moscow it was far bloodier. Rogers lamented that 'The Bolsheviks have stolen the Russian Revolution…the future is dreadful to contemplate…she is out of the world for a long time to come…'

Upon seizing power the Bolsheviks opened negotiations with Germany to end the war as German armies advanced to within a hundred miles of Petrograd. Fearing its capture the Bolsheviks moved the government to Moscow on March 11 prompting the evacuation of the foreign embassies. Ambassador Francis and staff finally abandoned the embassy on February 26 spending the next several months in Vologda, 350 miles to the south. He would eventually be evacuated to Arkhangelesk andMurmansk by an American cruiser. The Treaty of Brest Litovsk was signed on March 3, 1918. Russia surrendered and was out of the war.

Tim had one entry in the last file box still to be checked. His eyes stung and his butt ached from the unpadded chair, his fingers cramped. He needed a beer. With a resigned sigh he scrolled through the last entries and suddenly all his exhaustion vanished. It was a brief entry by Leighton Rogers. First an entry described the seizure of all foreign banks in the city around Christmas by Red Guards and their intent to confiscate all cash in the vaults and strong boxes, taking keys and placing the 'capitalist' clerks under virtual house arrest until the New Year. Thousands of rubles were carted off from American and British banks ending-up who knew where, he conjectured.

The last entry described how getting out of the city proved near impossible. 'Bolsheviks refuse to give me an exit visa,' Rogers wrote. And then…

'Thanks to the Brits able to secret myself on a freight to Murmansk. Fourteen days of misery and near starvation in freezing cold. Arrive London April 1, 1918. Enlisted in AEF, assigned to Military Intelligence Police, Britain and France until Armistice.'

After hours of mind-numbing research in a matter of seconds Tim found what he'd been looking for…maybe. It wasn't Jordan, the valet, who was the connection but Rogers! He had confirmation that a young American was in Petrograd at exactly the right time who then served in the Army's intelligence Police (the IP) in Britain and France! This lead he could now follow-up with deeper research back home. Chances were he left other papers in addition to his diary that could be found in archives somewhere. He found the 'smoking gun'!

All the way to the metro he imagined Leighton Rogers perhaps walking these same streets 70-years before dodging Bolsheviks! He was so lost in his thoughts that he didn't notice the two men-the same two men, who followed him to the metro station, boarding the same train he did, heading for the same destination…

CHAPTER FIFTEEN

She stopped waving only when she lost sight of the black Mustang. John Clarke was a gentleman of the old school she adored like the grandfather she'd never known. She insisted he stay the night and he'd obliged easily enough staying in the quest bedroom. After an initial protective bark Ralph remembered the scent and offered a vigorous tail-wagging welcome.

Abby hoped they could avoid talk of the Campbells or the Russian mafia but John insisted they had to before he left. Relaxing with drinks-Clarke was a straight bourbon man no surprise, he asked her what she know about the 'russkies', as he called them. She confessed the only mafia she'd ever heard about was Italian.

"These are very, very bad, scary people. Russian prisons are notorious incubators of these gangsters. I've read that there are as many as 5-6 thousand organized crime syndicates and separate groups organized around ethnic identity and various specializations. Dozens have a global reach. The collapse of the regime over there we read and hear about has been fertile ground and organized crime has lost no opportunity to infiltrate every aspect of Russian society. The corruption is like cancer."

"Now you're scaring me."

"I mean to."

"Inter-connected illicit enterprises operate through what are called 'krysha'…essentially giant protection rackets in every criminal activity that if to be believed, make Seal's operations seem like amateur-hour. They settle local scores, they send messages…they get even. But they can also manipulate state bureaucracies, institutions and even entire governments. They operate at all levels, infiltrate, corrupt and eviscerate. They eliminate competition and battle with the Mexican cartels, the Italian camorra, the Japanese yakuza, Korean gangs…you name it."

"OK, I get why Duncan would feel he has a personal score to settle with us. We did kinda' blow-up their shit." Clarke raised an eyebrow. "Sorry. Tim says I have a potty-mouth. What I don't get is how this is connected in any way with these Russian gangsters. What interest could they possibly have in Tim and me. We're just two people who got caught-up in a twisted situation three years ago we had nothing to do with…no responsibility for. Well, that's not entirely true," she corrected given their use of her mother's diary to unravel her dad's cartel connections. But we don't threaten anyone now or whatever they are into up there. So why us?"

"Abby, I honestly do not know." They sat in silent contemplation for a moment. "Could it possibly have anything to do with this discovery of yours?

"No, how could it? No one knows about it…we haven't told anyone else…." she stopped abruptly.

"What?" Clarke put his drink down.

"No, it can't be!"

"What?" he asked again this time more insistently.

"The other day I was missing Tim and watching the news about all the turmoil and upheaval in Moscow…you know how communism is collapsing…maybe the USSR itself with Gorbachev and all that. There was even some kind of fighting near the Kremlin. It looked really serious."

"And?"

"So I decided to speak to someone who I thought might know more about all of it…someone with personal knowledge or connections…had information no one else might have so I'd stop worrying about Tim."

"Abby who did you speak to...someone at the college?"

"No, I spoke to a Russian Orthodox priest here in town in his church office."

"What did you say exactly?" Clarke raised both think eyebrows.

"I just explained about Tim being in St. Petersburg and asked his opinion about the situation over there…if he thought I had any reason to worry. He was very nice and made me feel better. He was reassuring in a clam sort of way."

"And that's all?"

She shook her head. "I told him about what we had found…it just slipped out," she confessed. "We were talking about Russia and it just seemed I don't know…conversational. I didn't see any harm in it at the time and he didn't even seem particularly interested. John, he's a priest for God's sake!" Please don't tell Tim. It's between us, OK?

Clarke, squeezed her arm supportively. "Sure. I'm certain you're right. It all sounds perfectly reasonable and I'm glad he was able to put your mind at ease. I don't have much use for religion or men in robes waving the Bible around and sprinklin' Holy Water."

"My folks and late wife, rest her soul, were deep into the hallelujahs and the gospel word but I never took to it. All that righteous fire and brimstone like to set you ablaze!" he laughed. Hell, I hear there was a place in New York a way back they called the 'burned-over district' the preachin' got so combustible, you might say. Mercy, Lord knows I can use some moral and spiritual uplift now and again but I tend to look elsewhere for my inspiration. Good bourbon is a place to start. That will get me singing hallelujahs quick enough."

"So, no, I don't figure you meant any harm and sure enough it will be our secret," he patted her hand with his calloused paw.

But inside he was anything but convinced. Old instincts were kicking-in, warnings blared. What were the odds? He lived by rules or what passed for them. Rule first in line: there are no such things as coincidences. And that led him to this further insight. Abby was in real danger…again.

CHAPTER SIXTEEN

"I wanted to thank you for that report Tim," Kissinger said as they walked towards the embassy cars that would take them to the airport for their flight to Moscow.

"Happy I could earn my keep…make some small contribution to the effort. From what the others are saying it seems like we are on track to negotiate some encouraging commercial agreements with the emerging Commonwealth."

"I am sanguine but also realistic. There are many potential hurdles and unknowns-uncharted territory as they say. Gorbachev was briefly arrested but the attempted KGB coup failed. It seems that this Yeltsin has things in hand and ruling by decree. The one thing we must try to prevent is the re-imperialization of Russia. Sobchak agreed things went well and Putin assured me he would approve multiple contracts with many of our biggest corporations. Just as Kennan predicted: contain the bastards and allow capitalism to do its work, eh?"

"Revenge of the bourgeois!" Tim cracked.

"We'll miss having your counsel. I can always count on you for helpful perspective. Couldn't lure you away from academia could I? Kissinger Associates is always looking for top drawer analysts."

"Afraid not, Henry, but I am genuinely flattered. I need to get back to Prescott. Abby said it was important and I've done really all the research I can here. The other day was extremely productive….and certainly interesting. Lots of leads to follow-up."

"Nothing to worry about I trust?"

"At home? No, not that she said. She misses me…what can I say," he grinned.

"It is good to be missed, my friend. Nancy pretends to miss me," he laughed. Safe flight back and let's keep in touch Tim," Kissinger waved as he slipped into the back of the embassy car with the ambassador and security for the short drive to their waiting charter to Moscow.

Tim strode across this off-limits area of the tarmac reserved for diplomatic and other state delegations and their aircraft. His own commercial flight to JFK didn't leave until later that night. He had the day to kill. Showing his embassy credentials to the staff, he found a comfortable expansive window seat in the Priority Pass lounge an ordered a coffee. Given the hectic pace of the past three days he savored a moment of respite and reflection.

The Archive had indeed offered-up several intriguing revelations especially regarding Leighton Rogers but it was merely circumstantial at this point. Yet his service with the Intelligence Police and the collar insignia they'd found was a suggestive tangible link.

Tim knew virtually nothing about Rogers beyond what he'd read in the State Archive yesterday…that he'd been a clerk with the National City Bank in New York City when the war began and transferred to the bank's Petrograd branch, arriving from Kristiana, Norway on the Danish ship United States in early October. Rogers' descriptions, Tim noted approvingly, were vivid, objective but not sensationalized, admirable narrative qualities in such a young man. He was barely 24 in 1917.

He was shortly joined by seven recent college graduates recruited by the bank to join Rogers, as other staff was transferred to the bank's Moscow branch. It so happened that journalist, war correspondent and radical activist, John Reed and wife, were also onboard. His 'Ten Days that Shook the World' published two years later would become an international sensation, that Tim remembered reading as an undergraduate.

History was nothing if not fortuitous. There was no pattern of self-determined outcome to events but rather random improbability. He'd always thought the idea of 'fate' intriguing. If one meant by that chance or luck…being caught-up in events unspooling beyond one's control, he could buy into that. But fate as 'destiny' or inescapable design- no, that flew in the face of everything he knew about history and fickle human agency.

So, in his definition as fate would have it, Rogers, his fellow clerks, John Reed, Ambassador Francis, Philip Jordan, and scores of other Americans and foreign nationals were in the city for a rendezvous with uncertainty, observing firsthand the March and February revolutions that followed no script or preordination but simply happened. That wasn't to say that events do not have direction or that outcomes are not shaped by the actions of individuals and thus take on a kind of logic or calculus of their own. That was clearly true.

Kerensky, Lenin, Trotsky…starving, desperate Russian women…soldiers broken by betrayal and slaughter…actors instrumental and inconsequential…all had roles to play which interacted to produce the ever indeterminate 'present'. Tim thought of Nichoals II's ironic diary entry that while '1916 was cursed', 1917 will surely be better'! Delusional perhaps but no one ever knows what's coming next. Strange… strange indeed, he laughed…"Professor Strange?" Startled it took him a second to realize someone was actually calling his name.

"Yes?" It was the same young man who'd admitted him to the exclusive lounge.

"Sir, you have a phone call," the man indicated the receiver on the small desk in a private alcove.

Who would be calling him and how could anyone know he was here? Flummoxed, Tim made his way past scattered VIPs and cocktail servers. "Hello, this is Tim Strange."

"Tim, it's Judith. I'm so glad I caught you." She sounded serious, Tim thought.

"How did…?"

"A guess but knowing your plans and flight time, the Priority Pass seemed like a good bet."

"What's so urgent?"

"Shortly after you left the Archive two men questioned the front desk receptionist about you."

"Me? What about?"

"They said they were colleagues and needed to speak with you."

"I guess that's possible but…"

"No, listen to me. They were not colleagues unless you're hanging out with Russian security service agents."

"What?!"

"The State Archive has its own internal security. You probably noticed the cameras. They're everywhere." Tim confirmed that he had. Security and every department head has a monitor and direct feed. I was still with Rudolf in his office when the men entered. Rudolf has no doubt: they were KGB. Russians have cultivated a unique sixth sense in a security state like the USSR…or whatever comes next. I felt I should warn you, Tim. Be careful."

"Judith thank you but I can't imagine why I'd be on their radar? I haven't done anything."

"Tim, here there is no such thing as innocence: Suspicion is part of Soviet DNA. They don't need a reason. So, keep your head down and eyes open and for God's sake get on that plane as quickly as you can!" Tim assured her he would.

His one bag had been checked through from the hotel and his tickets confirmed and boarding pass by the airline through the Mariinsky concierge. Tim now more fully appreciated that convenience.

As he reentered the spacious if outdated terminal he saw two men standing by the main exit. Clearly they were looking for someone. They looked vaguely familiar but that made no sense…until suddenly it did. They were the same two men he'd seen on his train in the metro!

Shit, Judith was right: he was he being followed. He couldn't just stand there in the open. At that moment they were not looking in his direction and he took advantage of that by quickly reversing course and then ducking into a convenience court filled with people, pretending to consider reading material while keeping an eye on his shadows. What could they possibly want with him?

He answered his own question. Maybe Judith was right. He was American and this was the Soviet Union…or what had been the USSR a few days ago. He had a sobering thought: politics can change on a dime; institutional culture and bureaucracies do not. Had he attracted the attention of the KGB. The commission? No one else he was aware of had been surveilled by the security services, and why would a sanctioned mission which had been cleared at the highest levels of the government be targeted? Again it didn't track.

Maybe he'd been reading too many Ludlum and Le Carre' novels to be so paranoid. But no, he wasn't imagining this and Judith was right! These two guys were shadows for a reason. He had one advantage…maybe. How could they know which flight and airline he was on? Only if they'd gotten the information from the hotel could they have. Was he high enough of a priority for someone to have agents watching every gate? Obviously these guys had a description or a photo and knew who they were looking for, but he had no choice but to risk it.

Unbidden a memory flashed…a night mission in Nam when he and his team had gone full camouflage so as to be nearly invisible. He needed to do whatever he could to become invisible. Grabbing a nondescript woolie off the rack and a pair of reading glasses he paid the cashier, put them on and walked calmly out of the store hoping to blend-in, hoping it would be enough….

He only began to relax as the Lufthansa 747 banked right over St. Petersburg on a heading that would overfly Copenhagen on its 9-hour non-stop flight to JKF. Below the Neva glinted and the city spread along its arc in a mosaic of buildings, spires, bridges, and canals. He carried with him a briefcase full of notes he'd taken at the State Archive and that was it. No souvenirs, no duty-free vodka or caviar, no St. Petersburg tee-shirt. But he did have a slew of questions that begged to be answered.

He thought he might be incrementally closer to unraveling the mystery of the hidden stash of Imperial Russian objects but he wouldn't know until he got home and resumed his search for the truth…if it could be found at all. Perhaps there was no explanation of how they were secreted in a wall in Show Low. He'd often pursued research leads that in the end led nowhere. The art of historical detection was nothing if not aspirational. Still, he had the powerful sense that the answers were out there somewhere. He just had to find them....

CHAPTER SEVENTEEN

"You did what?!

On the way home from the airport she told him. She had to get it off her shoulders and it just spilled out. "I couldn't see how it would do any harm," she explained. "I was in a bad place…all the news…missing and afraid for you caught-up in the middle of it…lonely…needing some reassurance from someone I could actually talk to who I could trust. I mean if you can't trust a priest, who can you trust?" Tim let that lie, though he had his own views on that subject. But he didn't know anything about the Orthodox Church or this priest…not enough to judge.

"You're probably right, Abby. I've felt guilty for leaving you so I totally get that you felt abandoned. I apologize for putting you in a bad place," he reached over to squeeze the nape of her neck. She'd insisted on driving. "What did he say exactly?"

"He told me not to worry…gave me his take on the situation. He talked about the church and its historic role as a conservative, stabilizing force…the role it's trying to play now…that sort of thing."

"And about what we found?" Tim pressed.

"At first he didn't seem interested but when I said that you thought it all dated from the Revolution…the gun, rubles, insignia...and that silver coin., he…" She watched Tim visibly stiffen.

"You told him about that coin?

"About the gold ones with the guy you said was Czar Nicholas II on them, the paper rubles and, yes, the silver one you couldn't identify. Now that you mention it I did notice him react to that a little," she admitted.

"React how?"

"He…I don't know…his eyes narrowed…his body language changed."

"Do you know this priest's nationality by any chance?"

"Yeah, he said he was Russian but he's lived here in Prescott for a few years. Oh, and he's something higher than a regular priest. The word 'vicar' was a name plate on his desk." Tim considered that.

"Have you spoken to anyone else about what we found?"

She shook her head. "Only John." She read Tim's expression. "He asked…sort of."

"You know I called him...asked him to check-in on you if he was coming down this way."

"Yeah, he told me you did. That was very thoughtful…earned you points."

"Didn't know you were keeping score."

"Always," she laughed easily. He'd missed her playfulness. "You gotta' know he wasn't coming down this way until you asked."

"I know. I feel guilty about that too. I owe him."

"He asked me to meet him at Thumb Butte secret-like...in a note he slipped through the door in the middle of the night."

"A note…the Butte…why on earth…?"

For most of the rest of the drive she explained the other reason Clarke had come down from Glasgow. "Tim it was to warn us about this Russian mafia, about its activities in Montana and about…" she hesitated, "about Duncan."

"What about him?"

She told him the rest.

Tim sat silently staring straight ahead as he listened with growing unease. She could feel it from across the bench seat…see it in his body-language. "Is John certain about this?"

"He seems to be. It's sort of a hobby with him to keep an ear close to the ground since Seal and my dad and his crew's rampage through Montana.

"So he thinks they've been recruited in prison by this organized crime gang and have this vendetta against us…payback for their imprisonment?

"And do doubt a huge financial loss, don't forget," she added. "Christ Tim, he's dropped off the radar. Worse he knows where we live. You told me Duncan's even been to you house!"

"Twice, I'm afraid. Question is, is this a rogue, unsanctioned settling of scores or could it be something more?"

"What do you mean more...how could it be more?"

"If this is a Russian criminal operation as John believes it is, this could also be about business as in about what we discovered. Turns out they could be extraordinarily valuable and not just in monetary terms."

"How could this be…how could they know…how could Duncan know?

"There's only one explanation I can think of Abby: your priest. John sure as hell isn't the source. The only other person who knows is this priest you told. What's his name by the way?"

"Bakakov," she said dejectedly, "Father Aleksey Bakakov."

Tim let that sink-in, resisted the urge to berate her for her imprudence, her what…bad judgment? No.

"Honey, it's not your fault. Why would you or anyone have ever suspected? And we don't even know for sure," he tried to sound positive.

"But that's just it. We don't know what we don't know," she reminded him as they drove into the driveway and parked. "Except who else could it be? And why does any of this matter?

"That's what I'm getting to work on first thing as soon as I unpack, shower and get my head organized."

"Not the first thing. I'm badly in need of TLC. I'll meet you in the shower."

"What if I'm too jet-lagged?"

"Get over it."

CHAPTER EIGHTEEN

"Hey Thom it's Tim. How's the rare coin business these days? You too, huh. This global recession's is really kicking our ass isn't it." The oil price shock, that savings and loan scandal, interest rates and unemployment through the roof, construction and manufacturing way down…you name it. A perfect shit-storm all around. Even Bush's Gulf War cake-walk hasn't been enough to pull us out of the slump." He got no argument from Thom. "It doesn't look good for Republicans next year. President's get credit for a good economy and blame when it's in the toilet even though they have little to do with either." That elicited a grunt.

"Us? We've had to cut some classes, lay off junior faculty and part-timers but they're always the ones who take it in the shorts when the economy 's goes south," he offered colorfully. "Guess we're all looking for the light at the end of the tunnel…hoping it's not a locomotive on a one way track!" Another grunt. Thom was not a man of great elocution.

"Question for you: what do you know about old Russian coins? I know that's not my usual interest but I'm doing some research for a project and know you'd be the guy to ask," he said keeping it vague while baiting the hook with a little flattery.

"Shoot," but I may have to do some checking myself. I don't get a lot of interest in communist money," Thom snorted.

Tim ignored the expected comment. Thom was well-known for his right-wing politics as an old Goldwater Republican. "Actually the coin I'm interested in predates the Bolsheviks by about eighty years."

"So we're talking Imperial Russia…the czars and all that?"

"Yes, in fact I can narrow it down for you. It's a silver coin that was minted in limited proofs and never circulated. The date would be

1820s around the time of Nicholas II," again he was purposefully inexact.

"Hum, you don't say. That's the only description you have? Well, OK. I may have an idea but give me a half-hour and I'll get back to you."

"Appreciate it Thom, thanks. Say hi to Julie for me."

"Abby?"

"In here," she replied from the laundry room off the kitchen.

"I'll be in my study for a bit. Some pre-class prep. Fall semester's just around the corner," he kissed her cheek, squeezed her butt, poured himself another cup of coffee.

"OK," she replied brightly. "I'm going out later to do some shopping downtown," she reminded him. But she felt anything but 'bright.' Inside she was a jumble of warring thoughts. The revelations of the past couple of days, especially John's, had kicked her always simmering neuroses into high gear. She fought to keep it contained but knew she was losing the battle and probably the war too.

Tim sat behind his desk an hour later, class files put aside, with the revolver placed on a cloth under his mushroom table lamp. It was the first time he'd really examined it closely. Next to it Tim set a reference book 'History of Smith and Wesson' by Roy Jinks, reputedly the 'bible' on the subject. He glanced up to John Clarke's two Colts in their display cases. No offense, John, but this Smith has all my attention at the moment.

With a magnifying glass Tim examined the revolver closely. On the Flat barrel rib he found a string of Cyrillic writing and numbers that translated to: 'Smith and Wesson Weapons Factory C. (ity) America,' after which came the crown and double-headed eagle Imperial Acceptance stamp with the letter 'K0' below. According to Jinks the initials stood for inspector, Captain Kasavarii Ordinetz. Examining the cylinder chambers he noted the step machined for the .44 Russian cartridge not found in American models. The bore looked perfect with no rust and a light sheen of oil.

Then he checked the stamped serial numbers on the face of the cylinder, hinge strap, and, butt plate. They all matched. It appeared to be a factory un-molested original. The number was 0010. He found the relevant section in Jinks. "No, that's impossible," he breathed. To be sure he again examined the numbers. The revolver lying on his desk was a first model and among the first ten revolvers produced of over 130,000 sold to the Russian government beginning in May 1871. Colonel Alexander Gorloff, Alexander IIs arms expert and the Russian military attaché in Washington, facilitated the contracts for Gatling guns and Smith and Wesson revolvers. Tim sat back stunned. This alone was astounding!

But what about these grips Tim wondered. Service revolvers for sure weren't issued with pearl grips. Perhaps an officer's modification added later? There was one sure way to find out. Carefully using the small screwdriver he removed the right hand grip. There on the inside was a number…0010!

Suddenly something clicked…something he'd read about a Russian nobleman who toured America in the early 1870s. Quickly he found the article in a file. The nobleman was Czar Alexander IIs youngest son Grand Duke Alexi Alexandrovich who was a sort of good will ambassador during the Grant administration. General Sheridan, George Custer, and Bill Cody treated him to a buffalo hunt in Nebraska in January 1872. Weeks prior Alexi had toured the Smith and Wesson factory and was presented with a custom made engraved revolver with pearl grips!

Tim flipped a few pages back and forward…there was no photo of the revolver. The text indicated that no known photo or description of the gun existed and, more intriguingly, it had disappeared. No museum in Russia or any other in the world had it in their collections. "Damn!" he swore in frustration. Until five pages later he was staring at the photo of an elaborately engraved revolver with pearl grips identical to the one on his desk. It was a presentation by Nicholas III to the retiring captain of the Royal Yacht Standart or Polar Star in 1895. Except for the different engraved dates, the revolvers were identical. So, unless there were others like it, Tim's was one of two extremely rare guns!

He was no firearms expert by any stretch but given everything he'd just confirmed this was one rare weapon! The guys at Bill's Trading Post would drool over this, Tim appreciated.

For the moment he set aside the Smith and the notes he'd taken and once again examined the paper and gold rubles. Nothing notable stood out except that the bills were new or had been when secreted in the bag. The gold rubles stamped with the date '1906' and the denomination '15', looked like they'd seen some circulation but had been gently used. Tomorrow he'd take them downtown to Thom and let him have a look and get a tentative appraisal.

He'd already ordered a new IBM PS/2 Model 25 computer that promised to revolutionize education, communication, information, and research, with the rumored introduction of an operating system called 'mosaic' that could access what was being called the 'world wide web' linking computers in a global community of users. Aldus Huxley's Brave New World literally sitting on people's desk tops, he marveled. But for now it was reference books, journal articles and experts like Thom, he had to rely on.

Next he examined the military collar insignia of the Army Intelligence Police. For that he pulled another book from his bookcase a reference guide to US Military Uniforms and Insignia. He found the exact photo of the collar disk on page 218 and more importantly an authoritative article on the history of the Corps of Intelligence Police. Although predated by creation of Naval Intelligence, the CIP contributed importantly to wartime security, Tim read.

Shortly after American intervention a Major Dennis Nolan alerted the General Staff of his concerns about enemy agents, spies, and saboteurs present in the country among Americans of German ethnicity. While fueled by anti-German propaganda and wartime paranoia, those security concerns encouraged Colonel Ralph van Deman to authorize the enlistment of fifty 'secret service men' with police training and fluent in French for service as sergeants in the infantry specifically to do intelligence work in France.

In addition, fifty company grade officers were authorized to augment British and French counter-espionage efforts in the major ports supporting the war effort and on the front lines. All of this resulted in official formation of the CIP in August 1917 and arrival of the first agents in November serving with the AEF G-2 units. Another 700 agents were authorized but a little more than 400 actually deployed before the war ended. Now Time had a timeframe.

A third of these men- and all agents were men, served in the 'Front Zone' staffing over a hundred miles of checkpoints providing border security. The others were deployed in 'Rear Zone' areas protecting supply depots, leave centers and major ports in Britain, Scotland, and France, with still others serving in Spain and Italy. Agents also served along the US-Mexico border, and in Hawaii, Panama, and the Philippines. They complied files on 160,000 potentially disloyal people and tracked suspected agents. A few provided security for important civilian leaders and even for General Pershing.

There were few incidents of sabotage in the US during the war but dozens of suspected German spies were surveilled or apprehended. The porous US-Mexican border was especially vulnerable. IP agents in Nogales, Arizona, recruited an Austrian physician and former Colonel in the Mexican Army named Altendorf to infiltrate German spy rings operating south if the border. In January 1918 Altendorf altered agents that he was bringing across a former German naval officer named Witzke, who was ordered to subvert the American war effort through incitement, sabotage, and assassination.

Witzke was apprehended after crossing the border at Nogales, incarcerated at Ft. San Houston, tried for espionage by military commission, and sentenced to be executed. The war ended and Witzke subsequently had his sentence commuted by President Wilson to life in prison at Ft. Leavenworth. It was not uncovered until later that he and two other German agents had blown-up the Black Tom Munitions depot in New York harbor in July 1916, killing several and injuring many more. He was pardoned in 1923 and repatriated to Germany.

So what did Tim know so far? He knew that Leighton Rogers served with the IP in Britain and France from his own diary excerpts. In the citations accompanying the partial diary entries he found in St. Petersburg was reference to a book he'd written published in 1924: 'Wine of Fury'. Tomorrow he'd order it from Peregrine Books on Cortez. He'd already made a point of alerting the reference librarian at the college about tracking down where his papers and correspondence, if any, were curated. There was only an ambiguous reference in the Russian materials Tim had examined at the State Historical Archive.

But that triggered another thought: what about Judith Forston and her archival project for the Hoover Institution? Twenty minutes later as he put the phone down his mind churned with what the people at the Hoover had told him. Judith was still in St. Petersburg but was Tim aware that the Library of Congress had purchased over 2,500 volumes of Russian Imperial archives and books dating from Nicholas I in 1931? A special Slavic Division had been created just after the Revolution of 1917. The Bolsheviks were desperate for cash and all the Imperial treasures they nationalized-precious jewels, masterpieces, chalices and church icons, including records, they put on the auction block, selling to the highest bidder. At first reluctant, the Librarian of Congress, Herbert Putnam, had engineered the purchase for $10,000, although how the trove was actually acquired remained a mystery. Would Tim be interested in exploring them?

A preliminary search through the finding aids didn't yield anything specific but he knew from experience that it required hands-on digging. Perhaps he could hire a grad student from Georgetown to help? He filed that away.

With hard to contain anticipation he opened the small pouch and slid the Constantine ruble onto the piece of black felt he'd found in a drawer. He'd been prohibited from photographing the coins at the Hermitage but he'd purchased a color brochure highlighting the museum's most significant displays and artifacts for two dollars. He opened it to the page he'd marked.

The dull silver coin stared back at him he imagined with 'what-are-you-going-to-do-now' mockery. He pulled on a pair of white cotton gloves and examined the coin under his magnifying glass. There wasn't a mark or blemish on it that he could detect. It was like it had been struck earlier that morning.

Setting the brochure next to his coin his eyes shifting from one to the other, it only took seconds for him to feel the buzz of excitement building.. His coin's edge had Cyrillic letters around its circumference. What he had sitting on his desk was not a fake Trubetskov ruble like the one Andre had shown him. That left only the one that was known about…Cancrin's. But if this was the coin that Cancrin was rumored to have secretly kept for himself-the sixth proof, it was not supposed to have edge lettering! So what was this coin on his desk? Where had it come from? Was this the coin rumored to exist but shrouded in mystery?!

Beside himself, Tim leapt-up then sat back down again, got back up and began pacing around the office giddy with the thrill of discovery. The full weight of history asserted itself in the recognition of what this coin represented as well as the secrets and unknowns surrounding it…its provenance key among them because here was a mystery in a mystery! Had it been stolen by someone or lost somehow through misfortune…gambled away? And of course the most critical question of all: how did this coin come into the hands of the person who hid it in Show Low? It seemed inconceivable how it could have happened but somehow it had. First of course, he had to authenticate that the coin he had was real and not a fake. That would be Thom's task, even as his gut told him it was authentic.

He knew from past research surprises and serendipitous moments that often the least expected connections materialized and sometimes when other more plausible explanations proved unsubstantiated. Where to start was always his first question.

In this case he, Thom certainly, could approach it from two angles: trying to follow the coin along the Russian path of possession, and simultaneously attempting to trace coins from the path backwards from collector acquisition. But he could already anticipate the probably insurmountable problems with either approach. Collectors were notoriously secretive and largely anonymous, while following chain of custody through numerous revolutions, assassinations and two world wars was daunting in the extreme.

But there was a third angle and path and perhaps one no one else knew about or had explored and with good reason. There was no apparent connection…not even a hint of one. Except, there was one at least tentatively suggestive. And that was St. Petersburg in 1917 and the Americans in the city and specifically one American who met several criteria and linked all these disparate pieces together: Leighton Rogers! "Damn, if you could only talk Leigh!" Tim heard himself mutter as he stared first at the silent coin and then at the equally mute Intelligence Police insignia.

The he smiled. Perhaps you can….

CHAPTER NINETEEN

Abby's shopping took her all of two hours of aimless wandering up and down Montezuma, Gurley, and East Sheldon. She had nothing to get and no place in mind. She just felt like walking and letting her mind wander as she did without any particular direction. It was a beautiful day still in the mid-8os with a slight rustle of breeze in the stately American elms of Courthouse Plaza as she headed into Whiskey Row.

Aimlessly she strolled past the galleries, saloons, and boutiques that made the block famous. Once the home of 80 saloons Whisky Row was user friendly as establishments were within easy 'stumbling distance,' as locals enjoyed telling it. Preoccupied and almost without thinking she found herself in the Birdcage and ordered a draft. She and Tim enjoyed their alcohol but neither, save on rare occasions, over-indulged. She felt like it today.

Finding herself an elevated table in a dark corner, she sipped her cold pint, enjoying being alone in the mostly quiet pub, only Walter Egan's 'Magnet and Steel' leaking out of the corner jukebox as background noise. It was just past 2:00 and the day had now heated-up but in here the air conditioning offered welcome respite. People came and went, tourists gawking at the dozens of stuffed birds mounted or hanging from the ceiling as if in flight…hence the name.

What had her on such an edge today as opposed to yesterday? Nothing had happened to distinguish one day form the other but her mood sure had gone south. She guessed it was simply the stress of knowing that once again here they were in a shit-storm of trouble. Were she and Tim cursed somehow? Had one of them inadvertently violated some Native American taboo or burial ground? Released bad mojo into their lives? Tim assured her they hadn't and he was the expert, but it sure as hell was something because trouble seemed to find them without invitation or excuse. It was like a stalker waiting in the shadows.

But of course her unease was more focused than that. She was simply scared to death of Colin and Duncan and this Russian mafia connection. That sounded scary as hell. And why shouldn't it. Our lives are such menus of the normal and mundane, of habit and routine, until they are literally shocked into a different amperage. It's a jolt to the system. Well she was damn tired of being pummeled, of being emotionally mugged every few months. It wasn't that she was insecure. No, just the opposite. She was 'attuned' in ways that other people weren't. She likened it to having receptors that others didn't and that made her acutely aware…and wary. The jury was still out on whether that was a curse or a blessing.

No one was to blame. Neither she nor Tim went out of their way looking for grief. They weren't 'bad' people putting themselves in sketchy situations…deserving the consequences. No, it wasn't like that. Sometimes when she was really depressed she allowed herself to feel victimized and powerless. Shit happens and some people just get dumped-on more than others. Simple as that.

But it wasn't that simple at all and the thought of playing the victim sparked a visceral defiance in her, so those moments of despair never lasted long. She just hoped that well never ran dry. Maybe it was about optimism…believing that things would somehow always work out for the best…the 'glass half full' approach to life. In her deepest emotional crisis, she'd found Tim and he'd ben her lifeline while she recovered her strength and courage. So yes, she'd cling to that and hope the glass never shattered.

And then it did…

CHAPTER TWENTY

"Are you sure? Thom phoned later that afternoon.

"Yeah, pretty much. You'd better come down to the shop."

Abby was still out…somewhere downtown, she'd said when she'd called earlier to let him know she'd be a while. Tim could tell she was struggling with something. Better to give her space to work through it.

He left her a note and ten minutes later was standing in front of the counter at Ancient and US Coins. Thom, bearded and balding, with glasses and a pudgy frame, stood opposite with an expression Tim couldn't read exactly.

"I've checked all my references. Max Mehl-we call him M&M-his Star Book although published in 1914 remains the gold go-to…so- to-speak, but the Standard Catalog is pretty authoritative. Is this what you have…or think you have?" Thom opened the Star Book to the page he wanted and pushed it across the glass case. Tim looked, nodded.

Thom slid the coin from the pouch Tim gave him onto an examination pad. With a 30x jeweler's loupe he examined the coin in gloved hand for a full five minutes. "Come with me, he said finally. "Chuck I'll be in back for a bit," he alerted his partner and motioned Tim into what turned out to be a lab of sorts next to an office. "I'm going to conduct some tests to confirm or rule out authenticity. Noting I'll do will in any way damage the coin," he assured Tim.

I'm going to weigh your coin with this electronic jewelry scale that's accurate to 0.01 of a gram, check the circumference, diameter and thickness with this mechanical braille caliper, inspect

microscopically its markings, and put it under the x-ray florescence spectrometer to see if it's silver and its exact composition.
We call it XRF analysis. Then there is the magnet test that's pretty straight forward. Real silver is non-magnetic. I'd never use nitric acid on a potentially rare coin like this one but believe it or not you can also use an ice cube to test for silver. That will come in our drinks if this thing is the real deal.

Ten minutes later Thom was shaking his head. I've compared all the metrics indicated for the Constantine Ruble by the Hermitage Museum and Spassky. And you're in luck. A Russian named A. S. Melnikova just published a book on this very coin. The coin you have…is a true Constantine, Tim. I thought for sure it had to be a fake. I mean you can count on your fingers the known number of these in the world and four are in museums! How in the hell…?"

"You wouldn't believe me if I told you, my friend. But I'm as stunned by all this as you are…more.

"Does Abby know?"

"About the coin, yes; that's it's real, no…not yet.

"What are you going to do?"

"I don't know yet."

"You haven't asked me the question most people would ask right away: what's it worth?"

It's complicated, Tim thought of Clarke's warning. I don't want this to become public knowledge, Thom. Promise me you will not tell anyone…not even Chuck. He and Thom were among the very few gay couples in the city who'd 'come out' in a region where being homosexual brought out the worst in people. Tim admired their courage.

"Thom nodded. OK…I understand how you'd want to keep this quiet. So would I but I'd be jumping around the room. You look like you just got scheduled for the rectal exam."

Tim laughed. That would be bad, he agreed. "It's just that I got a lot on my mind. Let's just say we found some other items that are equally sensitive. Here, could you examine these? Tim gave him the gold and paper rubles.

Thom eyed him appraisingly with a 'what next' look.

In another five minutes Thom finished checking some sources and doing similar weighing and analysis. The banknotes are pristine but not especially valuable except to a collector. You're right that s Catherine the Great and these were circulated first in 1910. In this condition they're probably worth $200 each. There 50 of them in this sheath so if sold separately, well you can do the math."

These gold rubles are a different story. 1897 is what we call 'key date' meaning they're scarce. 12.9 grams pure gold. These 15 ruble wide rim coins are in all but uncirculated condition and would earn a top NGC certification. With the price of gold today at $350 an once and the collector's value we're looking at about $900-1,000 each. You've got ten of 'em so it doesn't take a calculator. You've got a pretty good day going for you so far, Tim."

"It's been interesting," Tim agreed. Out of curiosity do you know what the engraving says in Russian?

"Only because I have it here, he consulted Spassky: 'By God's Grace Nikolai II Emperor and Autocrat of All Russia'

"It actually translates 'autocrat?'

"That's what it says."

"Well they didn't mince words, did they? He lived up to his reputation from what I know."

"And then some. Say, is this some kind of inheritance or something? Don't mean to be nosy but you've never had any interest in foreign money or ever bought any that I can recall."

"Something like that," was all Tim volunteered. "Thom, thank you can I pay you for your service?"

Thom waved that off. "Enjoyed doing it and I don't often see rare stuff like this in such condition. Put this away in a safe place…like your safe deposit box if you have one. I swear it's like osmosis or something. Someone acquires rarities like this and before you know it the word leaks out. Can't tell you how many times it's happened. So be careful. This market can be cutthroat in more ways than one. Why I keep this under the counter," he revealed a sawed-off 12-guage 'hammer gun'. Bought it over at Bill's last year. Belonged to an old timer… Wells Fargo guard.

"I'm heading over to Bill's next, actually."

"Got something else, don't you?" Thom eyed him expectantly.

"Maybe, but I'm swearing Bill to secrecy just like you."

Thom drew his thumb and forefinger across his lips like a zipper.

As soon as Tim closed the door behind him with a jingle, Thom walked straight back to the office. "Chuck you won't believe it what just happened…"

CHAPTER TWENTY-ONE

"Would you like another, Abby?" the young woman about Abby's age asked. Would she? The debate lasted only a few seconds.

"Thanks Brenda. I'm good." It was her second and only half gone. She and Brenda had actually taken classes together at Yavapai a few years back. Not tight girlfriends but acquaintances. "Pretty quiet."

"Still early but it's been a bit slow; tips have been crappy. Folks are still tight with their cash," she observed. Can't blame them but it's the shits when you're working for minimum wage and tips."

"Tell me about it. I remember," Abby commiserated.

"How you doing?" Brenda asked casually enough, although Abby knew how quickly gossip, even innocent gossip, spread. She'd lost touch with many of her former classmates since graduation but Prescott was still a fairly small city and the social networks still thrived on whatever nuggets of information or rumor that could be ferreted out innocently or not.

"Doing well. Tim's gearing-up for a new semester and the non-profit got funded for another year so it's all good," she kept it to the basics. She sure as hell wasn't going to divulge the really juicy stuff, although part of her, perversely enough she thought, was dying to tell someone about the Russian mystery and Show Low.

"And you?" she reciprocated although having little interest in hearing about Brenda's drama.

Same old, same old," she shrugged, glancing around to see if any others among the five customers needed her. They didn't. "People still talk about your dad and all the fireworks on the Butte. Scary stuff." If Brenda only knew the whole story or about London and Armenia, she'd be in gossip-heaven," Abby thought.

"Here's some news," she's leaned-in conspiratorially. Word is on the Row that some organized crime types have been hanging around…asking questions. The Mexican cartels pretty much split after Thumb Butte but now some other guys are sniffing around…maybe looking to muscle-in. Foreign-types. Some say Russian. There was a guy in here the other day on my shift. Ordered a beer and just sat over there," she pointed to a now empty table top. He just sat there for an hour nursing his beer, looking around. It was almost like he was waiting for someone to walk-in. Kind'a creepy."

Brenda had Abby's attention but she asked casually, "so did he look or sound Russian?"

"Not unless Russians have red hair. No, he sounded more like a Brit or something."

"Scotland maybe?"

"Yeah, that's it. I can't keep them straight…Brits, Irish, Aussies. But yeah, I think he could have been Scottish."

Abby felt faint. Pushing back from the table, she threw some bills at Brenda and ran out the door, apologizing to the man she ran into. He grumbled something in return.

When she finally stopped in the far corner of the square she let her breathing steady and her heart rate slow. No use in denying the obvious: it had to be Duncan, Brenda was describing. God was he here in Prescott! She looked around frantically but saw no one so much as looking in her direction. "Get a grip, Abbs," she breathed.

But even that self-help advice ebbed away in the shadow of looming dread and at least one perplexing question: if the Russian mob was in Prescott, why hadn't they come to the house? She had to warn Tim!

One last look around the park revealed only an older couple feeding the birds, no gangsters lurking in the shadows, she admonished herself for panicking. Her car was parked on E. Gurley about three blocks away. In measured stride she set out towards her car unaware that Tim at that moment was only blocks away at Bill's Trading Post following his meeting with Thom.

She keyed the ignition and restraining her impulse to floor it, eased into traffic and headed for home. She was so preoccupied that she didn't notice the delivery van that pulled in back of her, seemingly just one more vehicle, its driver going about their business on a typical Tuesday afternoon in Prescott, Arizona.

CHAPTER TWENTY-TWO

"Got a minute Bill?

"HiTim. Haven't seen you in a while," the big man greeted him with firm handshake and broad smile as, by reputation, he did with all his customers. The Trading Post had a five-star rating for many reasons, Bill primary among them. "What's up?"

There were a half-dozen other customers perusing the glass cases, gun racks and other merchandise. "Would you mind if we went in back? I need to show you something I'd rather keep private."

"Well, that got my attention. Sure thing," he invited showing the way, as a young woman in casual business attire and name badge made her way towards the other customers to offer assistance.

Tim zipped open the foam-lined leather gun valise and carefully placed the revolver on a felt pad. Bill, in strict confidence I'd appreciate your opinion on this revolver. I've done some preliminary research but I need your opinion. You're one of if not the most knowledgeable guy around on historical firearms so I knew I had to bring this to you."

"I appreciate that, Tim. Of course I'd be happy to take a look but why all the secrecy?"

"That's what I can't tell you…not entirely. It's nothing illegal," he read Bill's fleeting expression and assured him. "You know me. It's just that how I acquired this is sensitive, shall we say."

"Good enough for me Besides I enjoyed working on those old Colts you allowed me to gunsmith on. You could have taken them to anyone. Here, let's have a look…"

Again Tim felt uncomfortable under the withering stare. "Now I am going to have to ask you how you came by this firearm. And I suspect you know why?

"I do."

"As soon as you removed the oiled gun cloth I knew…or believed I knew what I was looking at. Did you read the footnote credit for the photo and description of that presentation Russian Smith?"

"No, why"

"Cause I wrote it for Christ's sake!"

"You what?" Tim's jaw dropped.

"Years ago now the editors of The Great World of Guns, I think it was then in its 98th edition, asked me to write a short piece on the Smith presented to the Grand Duke and the other one. There were actually more than a dozen commissioned, and some of a different design were produced, but they were so enormously expensive only two identical presentation guns that anyone knows of were actually made: Grand Duke Alexi Alexandrovich's and Czar Alexander IIIs. But here's the kicker. They were identical except for one thing. The Grand Duke's pearl grips bore the Russian Imperial crest and the American coat of arms.

"What are you saying?" Tim could barely speak the question.

"What I'm saying is that before checking the serial number, I would have said it could be either. They are exact matches in every respect except when they were made and those grips. Tim the revolver on that pad belonged to the Grand Duke that he carried on the buffalo hunt with Cody and Custer. That gun disappeared over a hundred years ago and out of nowhere you walk-in and lay it on my damn counter!"

"I don't understand. You said the Grand Duke's grips bore the coat of arms of both countries. These are bare?"

"No, Tim, they're not. Look closely. Someone has very cleverly covered these grips with thin ivory veneer covers that match the originals exactly. It was done by someone for obvious reasons- to conceal and done a long time ago. I'm guessing it was to secret this gun out of Russia."

Tim was nodding, though unaware of it. "That makes sense to you…you know something."

"Can you remove them…safely remove them?"

"I can't be certain which kind of adhesive they used but yes, a heat gun should do the trick. Shall I."

Tim gulped…hesitated. 'Yes." It took all of two minutes. First Bill removed the right covering and then the left. "What is that?" Tim indicated the small bottle. "Goo Gone. Invented back in the '30s. Nothing better, I've found. Don't want to damage what's underneath." Using a wetted cloth he rubbed gently and gradually the adhesive lifted off the original grips. The left grip bore the Great seal coat of arms of the United States. The right grip bore the Imperial coat of arms, both beautifully inlaid and still in brilliant color.

"I need to sit down," Tim said.

"That makes two of us," Bill joined him.

"Well, don't this beat all," Bill finally managed. "This is by far the most famous, storied firearm I've ever held in my hand and probably ever will, he conceded readily. "I'm guessing you're not going to tell me anything more."

"Bill, I can't…not yet anyway. There's more than a little danger involved."

"Christ, you didn't steal it…or buy it hot, did you?"

"Tim shook his head vigorously. "I told you there's nothing illegal involved. That's the God's honest truth. Let's just say I have reason to believe there is someone else who knows…someone in town actually and now perhaps others. They will probably do anything to get their hands on it and some other things we…" Tim just caught himself.

"Wait," Bill finished his sentence for him … "you found this?! Where the hell you been…Russia?" he scoffed. Tim tried to keep his expression blank.

"Actually, I was just in St. Petersburg on a semi-official matter but no that's not it and quit asking. I suspected what this might be and have thought about what I'd do if it was authentic."

"And?"

"Haven't figured that out yet. Smithsonian probably.But until I do this has to be held in strict secrecy. Bill, I mean it. I'm right about the danger. Simply knowing that this Smith exists will put anyone smack in harm's way…and I mean serious harm."

"My God Tim do you have any idea what this gun is worth? I mean merely from a collector's perspective we're talking millions! I mean it's literally one-of-a-kind and given the history involved the damn thing's nearly priceless."

"As a historian just holding it in my hand gives me a rush. Who among the Romanovs handled and shot this same gun? So, I appreciate its intrinsic value…its provenance. Add to that how rare and irreplaceable it is and I totally understand what I have. It is amazing to me how human kind has always venerated even worshiped inanimate objects and symbols from the earliest times. Their value is subjective and assumes importance or meaning that can defy even rationality…assuming humans are ever truly rational! But think of Jesus on the cross, a nation's flag, the swastika, or the hammer and sickle…or sacred texts like the Bible, the Torah or Koran. Armies have marched, civilizations have risen and fallen, the arc of history has been given new direction," he lectured.

"Sure, on the one hand this is just a chunk of metal but then think of what it represents…the power of life and death in the hands of autocratic royalty over millions of people…the Romanovs of Imperial Russia…glory, power, prestige. Sure, weapons are merely tools but they represent power…the ultimate power to destroy, to defeat enemies, to alter the course of history in big and small ways, in ways both intimate and impersonal," he was warming to the subject.

"Well, that's a tad far down range for me professor," Bill grunted, "but I do know this chunk of metal as you so eloquently put it should be locked away in a vault somewhere with an armed guard just on general principles alone."

"I have a safe at home sunk in concrete in the garage. No one knows the combination…not even Abby. It would take C-4 to breach it."

“The way you make it sound for whoever might want to get their hands on this that would not be a problem.”

“You have a point.”

“Bill, there are only three people who know about this gun that I know I can trust: me, Abby and now you. The fourth was inadvertently told and perhaps that individual is nothing to worry about. But I cannot risk that. I have to assume that he has passed on this information and act accordingly.”

“Hope for the best, plan for the worst…always worked for me,” Bill confirmed. “Do you need security…some muscle? I mean I do own a gun store.”

“Bill, I appreciate the offer, I really do, but I won’t involve anyone else…risk their getting hurt.”

“Suit yourself but the offer stands,” he said as Tim left the store….

“Guys, may I help you?” Bill, not five minutes later, greeted the two men he’d never seen before and who did not at all look like Verde Valley residents.

“We understand that you are the guy to see for antique firearms?” the taller of the two asked with the slight hint of a Slavic accent that Bill failed to notice.

“Well, there are several guys in town equally knowledgeable but I appreciate the compliment, he offer affably. “How can I help?”

“What do you know about the 1873 Smith and Wesson Model 3 Russian?”

CHAPTER TWENTY-THREE

"And we know this how?"

"Last week I received a phone call from Father Bakakov in Prescott, Arizona. He's the Rector of that Diocese and one of our assets in the Orthodox hierarchy. It's a useful listening post like we have cultivated throughout western countries," Andre explained.

"Da ochen polezno-I agree," Vladamir Kumarin, head of the St. Petersburg-based Tambovskaya Bratva Gang, approved. Tambov had only recently emerged victorious from a bloody turf war with the Malyshev Gang and was consolidating its power. Tambov's portfolio included expertise in contract killings, money laundering, bootlegging, prostitution and human trafficking, and extortion, among other specialties.

Beginning in the late 1980s an increasingly close relationship was forged between Russian gangs and the KGB which 'exported' criminal elements to the US, Israel and numerous other countries, These 'emigres' then infiltrated into bureaucracies, home-grown gangs and other segments of society to facilitate their clandestine operations…and feed the KGB with all manner of intelligence. Father Bakakov ably fulfilled this function in his leadership office in the Orthodox Church, serving both God and the glory of Mother Russia.

Thus following Abby's surprise visit and revelations, Bakakov phoned his nephew Andre at the Hermitage. Andre was indeed an antiquities specialist but also KGB but with connections to Tambova. Bakakov's information immediately grabbed Andre's curatorial interest for obvious reasons, not least of which was his interactions with her husband and his interest in the Constantine Ruble. While fragmentary there was enough in Bakakov's characterization of what this young woman, Abeline Strange, had told him that Andre had immediately contacted his handler at the Bolshoy Dom on Liteyny Ave., headquarters of the KGB. It had once been the Imperial Armory until it was destroyed in 1917. Vladimir Putin still maintained an officer there.

Andre also passed on the information to a friend who did contract work for Tambova in case they had any interest in following-up on this intriguing bit of information. The Constantine Ruble alone, if that is what this could be, was such a high profile state icon that any possibility that the coin this woman claimed to possess could be true, however whimsical the notion, in his view demanded investigation. Finally after all these calls and receiving instructions he placed a call to Prescott.

And it so happened that other phone calls and connections were made and information shared, and decisions made. One such connection was to KGB Colonel Valdimir Khrenkov operating out of Billings and Butte, Montana. Based on the success the Krysha was having in prison recruitment, Billings had become critical criminal infrastructure. Inquiries then made their way down through the hierarchy and spread through the organization whose reach included the prison at Deer Lodge....

What do you think?" the man asked Duncan as they sat at a blistering hot rest stop table off US 160 near Kayenta, taking the long but sparsely-populated route down through Wyoming. Duncan had tried to dye his red hair a dark brown in an attempt to hide his most obvious physical feature but it wasn't a very good job. He and his companion had been given false IDs that matched the registration and license of the pickup they were driving legally obtained, provided by the Billings Krysha through a car dealership they conveniently owned.

"Prescott is 244 miles south...4-5 hours. We can be there by dusk if we push it," Duncan replied, sipping on a Coors from their ice chest. Eighteen months in Deer Lodge is worse than fookin' Barlinnie," he cursed Scotland's most notorious prison.

"Fignya!" the man spat. 'Bullshit. "Deer Lodge is nothing compared to Cheornly Del-fin-the Black Dolphin in Sol-Iletsk. My uncle was tortured to death there. They feed dead prisoners to the pigs," his Ukranian companion gestured obscenely. Duncan eyed his assigned partner, Vytali, with carefully disguised indifference. The guy scared the shit out of him and that said a lot for a guy who'd experienced the worst that Glasgow and Aberdeen had to offer…and that was ugly enough.

Soon after he'd made parole he disappeared…or tried to, seeking to escape law enforcement surveillance until he could slip back into to Scotland as his friends promised to help him do. But there was another even more compelling reason. Russian gang recruitment had been brutal and unrelenting. If you didn't embrace the 'invitation' you were blacklisted. Once you did, the other gangs targeted you. He had and they did. The last six months had been a living hell just trying to stay alive. There was no way out unless you got out and once he had, all he wanted was to do was vanish.

He had for two weeks under an assumed name staying in a dump of an apartment in 'malfunction junction'…otherwise known as Missoula, until Vytali knocked on his door one morning and everything instantly changed. How the guy had tracked him he never figured out.

Back in Billings Duncan received an assignment once the conversation he had with his cellmate had been confirmed. Khrenkov judged it to be a fortuitous conjunction and tasked Duncan and Vytali with the job: the retrieval of certain artifacts apparently in the possession of a couple living in Prescott. This was all Duncan knew until he learned the rest of it five minutes later.

"So what's in Prescott that's so important," he tried to ask casually.

"Vytali had been in the organization for three years even though younger than Duncan by several. He wore his hair in a thick crew cut and given the square shape of his head it made him look like a blonde erasure. At 5-10 and 190 he was a no nonsense guy to be reckoned with and Duncan had no illusions about what that would be like. Mixing it up with the Ukranian was a last resort.

"It has come to our attention that a couple have in their possession something they shouldn't and we are going to correct that. It will go easy or it will be something else," he shrugged indifferently. "Either way we retrieve the items and see them safely back here. They will then be flown out of the country from Logan International by Fed Ex to St. Petersburg. It has all been arranged."

Of course it has, Duncan thought. Seems our Russian friends have a hard-on for these artifacts or whatever the fuck they are. Ironic it was Prescott of all places. Last time he'd been in the Verde Valley was with Barry Seal escaping form that crazy shootout at Thumb Butte only to be apprehended on Hwy 17 headed for Flagstaff. He'd heard about Seal's assassination and wasn't surprised. The guy had made himself a target as big as his ego and prodigious belly.

"Who's the couple?"

"What is it to you?"

"Jesus, just curious."

"Need to know basis...you don't."

Duncan finished his beer, pissed on a tree in the otherwise deserted rest stop. Out on US 160 cars and semis crawled their way along the greenish-gray asphalt. Duncan and Vytali joined them...Duncan driving presumably so the Ukranian could keep an eye on him. He wasn't trusted and why should he be? So, let Vytali do his thing...Duncan would do his.

"Shit!"

"What?" Vytali roused himself from chicken-necking.

"State trooper behind us but he's hanging back not crowding us...probably reading our plate."

"Will he make stop?"

" Depends on how bored he is."

"What is speed?"

"75... right at the speed limit," Duncan checked his rearview again. Ahead a semi was doing more like 80 which in Arizona was almost always overlooked especially for big rigs. Behind the trooper was a long, long interval before a trailing vehicle appeared like a dark spec.

"What is in other lane?"

"Another semi maybe half mile off closing fast."

"Brake check the cop then accelerate around the semi in front when I say."

"That's fookin' crazy!"

"Do it, Vytali pulled the Glock from a belt holster.

"Duncan considered himself a pretty damn good driver but this was…Russian roulette, he choked off a laugh at the absurdity. The trooper was closing the distance…maybe getting seriously curious.

"Do it now!"

"Duncan tapped the brake and the trooper instantly braked in response. Duncan floored the pickup's 460 cubic inch supercharged Vortec engine and it leapt forward like a shot with a howl of its supercharger. In seconds they were around the startled driver of the semi. Right behind Duncan the trooper had erupted in pursuit his light bar flashing and siren wailing. In the opposite lane the oncoming semi was barely 100 yards off and closing at 80 miles an hour, its distinctive Kenworth grill filling Duncan's vision.

"Brake check!" Vytali bellowed.

Barely yards in front of the trailing semi, their truck's taillights flashed for an instant causing the semi driver to instinctively hit his airbrakes. The trooper's patrol car was now abreast the truck driver's door. Onrushing in his lane was the other semi the trooper had not seen until he pulled around the leading semi in pursuit of Duncan's pickup.

Two things happened: The trailing semi jackknifed in response to the emergency braking and the g-forces it generated, swung its trailer around into the opposite lane. The driver of the oncoming semi hit his brakes at the same time but his momentum and speed was such that he slammed head-on into the trooper's cruiser which had also braked but there was little the unfortunate officer could do.

Behind him the trailer now broadside across the highway filled the other driver's vision. It was the last thing he would ever see.

The combined impacts and carnage was horrific and truck tractor and trailer parts exploding and cartwheeling in all directions in an orgy of grinding metal. Fire erupted from fuel tanks. The patrol car simply disappeared. Both truck drivers and the Arizona trooper were killed almost instantly. Duncan nearly lost control of their pickup but managed to keep it in his lane, speeding-off leaving the smoking wreckage behind them.

"Nice driving," Vytali managed with a grin. "No witnesses."

Duncan glanced in his rearview which was filled with the receding conflagration and twisted steel. There was little chance the oncoming distant driver could have understood what happened to trigger the crash, except for seeing the cruiser's emergency lights pull around the semi. What had caused him to do so would remain a horrible, tragic mystery.

Duncan was still hyperventilating. "You crazy fucking son-of-a-bitch. You almost got us killed!" His head snapped back as Vytali's elbow brutally scythed into Duncan's forehead, blood immediately dripping into his eyes. The assault was sudden and paralyzing.

"Do not ever challenge my decisions!" he said in a chilling hiss, spittle drooling down his cheek, eyes glittering. "I had no choice of partner. You are no karahasho. You are no one to me. We've been given a task and we will complete it and complete it my way. You live because the syndicate believes you to be useful…your relationship to the professor and his woman. That is all…ponimat?

Duncan spoke no Russian but the message was loud and clear. He nodded.

To the southwest Prescott waited now 110-miles away.

CHAPTER TWENTY-FOUR

Abby eased her car into the driveway and was about to open her door when a small, black delivery van pulled-in behind her. She was slightly buzzed from the unusual early afternoon beers and still rattled by what Brenda had said to her in the Bird Cage, her apprehension-meter still pegged on full alert as she faced the unexpected vehicle

"Can I help you?" she asked as two men exited the van and approached her. They were in their early thirties, she guessed. Both lanky of build. One had reddish-brown hair. They were both wearing light khaki jackets. Abby's fight or flight instinct screamed at her but stood frozen in the driveway. It was only then from her new angle of vision that she could see behind the driver a logo of some kind on the van's door. It was the same odd-looking cross she'd seen in Father Bakakov's office.

"Sorry to bother you Mrs. Strange. The Vicar…Father Bakakov, asked that we return this to you. Apparently you left it in his office the other day," he explained with a heavy accent, holding out Abby's sweater.

Seeing it she realized she'd totally spaced that out only now recalling that she'd taken it with her and forgot it when she grabbed her purse, she'd been so preoccupied with her concerns for Tim and the prelate's soft intimidation.

The tension drained from her shoulders and neck as their words registered and she saw her familiar light blue sweater. "Oh gosh, I'm so sorry to have troubled you like this. Thank you for returning it to me. What an airhead," she apologized.

"No trouble at all," the red-haired guy approached handing her the sweater with a wan smile.

Abby could hear Ralph barking from inside the house. "Father Bakakov would like to speak with you again. He said to tell you he had received some information you would want to hear regarding your artifacts. The Vicar has many interesting, knowledgeable contacts as you might imagine," the man explained.

She thought of Tim' and Clarke's warning about being careful but certainly the priest was no threat? Still… "I…ah, I have some things to do around the house and you can hear our dog. But, sure, that would be great. Please tell father Bakakov that I'll come-by tomorrow in the morning if that's OK."

"Actually, he wants to see you now. Father Bakakov is a very busy man and he has managed to make some time this afternoon for you. He said it was rather important and the rest of his schedule is full."

Abby looked back towards her front door behind which Ralph was barking now more insistently. What it could be she couldn't imagine but…what the hell. 'OK, I'll follow you," she turned towards her car.

"We are instructed to take you to the Vicar ourselves. It is no trouble we assure you. We will bring you back, the other man now spoke for the first time, offering the same smile. But his eyes said something else. Abby began to refuse the offer that now really had her uncomfortable when the red-haired guy pulled back his jacket just enough to show Abby what could have been a shoulder holster but regardless she got the intended message. The other guy walked back to the van an opened the rear door. All nice and friendly. No one observing would think anything other than what it looked like.

With one last look back, with Ralph now behind the picture window barking furiously, Abby walked to the van and climbed-in. The door slid shut. The van backed out of the driveway and wound its way down the hill towards town. No one said anything further. Less than ten minutes later Abby was ushered into the office she remembered well from the other day. Nothing had changed. Father

Bakakov stood behind his desk and with a broad smile beckoned her in. The door closed behind her. "Please sit Mrs. Strange," Babakov invited.

As she did she noticed for the first time that the priest was not alone. In the corner another man sat cross-kneed regarding her with curiosity and something else she couldn't read.

"Ah, Mrs. Strange- Abeline, thank you for coming on short notice."

"I had a choice?"

"Of course," he offered solicitously. "As I believe my associates explained I am very pressed for time but I did want to see you briefly. After our most interesting meeting the other day I made some inquiries."

"Inquiries...about what?"

"Well, of course about the objects in your possession. Like your husband I too have a keen interest in history...Russian history as you might appreciate. So your description of them toyed with my curiosity. I would like you to bring them here to the church so that this gentleman and I might examine them if you wouldn't mind?"

""Who is he?"

"A representative of the Hermitage Museum in St. Petersburg: Andre Porsenkiya," he introduced the curator who'd arrived the day before and had driven-up from Phoenix. "He would like to offer his expertise to help you identify these objects you found." All still very nice. All still polite.

Andre rose, approached, bowed slightly and held out a well-manicured hand: "a pleasure."

Abby returned the gesture bur she wasn't buying it. This was all too convenient and suspect from the get-go, she decided. She was getting a bad vibe like she had when her dad and his cop friends had been anywhere near her. Think, think! Be cool.

"Father Bakakov...Andre, I'd love to but we don't have them any longer. Tim has a friend at the Smithsonian he told about what we found and sent them back to DC to be evaluated."

Bakakov and Andre exchanged glances and the exchange wasn't lost on Abby. These two were definitely up to something so her well-honed instincts were right on. Andre might well be who he said he was but that didn't mean he could also be something else.

"That is unfortunate," Bakakov said with studied composure. "We were looking forward to having the opportunity to view them."

"You understand Mrs. Strange," Andre interjected, "any authentic artifacts from the era of Imperial Russia legally belong to the state and…"

"Which state is that exactly?" Abby couldn't resist. I'm under the impression that your country is currently in the process of…ceasing to exist."

"I see you are a student of current affairs," Andre observed drolly. "Whatever the political outcome Russia, apart from the other republics and satellites, will retain possessory rights over Imperial Russian historical and cultural artifacts…just as your country does for example," he added.

"I'm aware of that. My husband is a professor of Native American antiquities. I know all about Cultural Property Law. That's why we turned the objects over to the proper national authority for evaluation and disposition," she hoped they'd buy the explanation she had to dig deep for.

"I am quite sure your husband had the items verified locally before sending them off to the Smithsonian?" Porsenkiya queried. "My information is that there are a couple of businesses in Prescott with that kind of expertise. Can you verify that?"

"I don't know where Tim is or has been today he's been gone since this morning. He said he had errands."

Again, an exchange of looks between the two men. "Indeed…of course you made the correct decision," Bakakov quickly assured her while Andre's expression was more quizzical but with a hint that he knew more than he was revealing. Had she said something she shouldn't?

"A missed opportunity then. I'm sure Andre will make the appropriate official inquiries of his counterparts at the Smithsonian, so all will be well in the end," the Vicar rose abruptly like the statement it was. "These gentlemen will drive you home he indicated the same two guys with the same van. Please give my regards to your husband. God be with you and keep you safe. Alas, it is a dangerous, unpredictable world.

To Abby the benediction sounded hollow and chilling. Ten minutes later she walked through her front door…and lost it.

Still sitting on the sofa where she'd buried herself in its soft refuge, arms wrapped around her shoulders, rocking gently back-and forth, head buried in a bolster, she hadn't moved since. It had been a soft kidnapping but a kidnapping and a warning all the same. There was no other way to interpret it. No uncertainty, none whatsoever.

Question was: what to do? Did she call Tim? No. Yes. He'd bought a Dynatac-8000 mobile phone for emergencies after Montana. This sure as hell was that! The 8000 was old technology now but still reliable. He was attached to it- an historical artifact, of course. Abby almost laughed in spite of her near panic. With trembling hand she dialed. Eight rings. No answer. Ten miles away downtown tucked into the door panel cubby, the Motorola rang in his empty truck.

Where did he say he was going? She couldn't remember ! Her mind refused to work like her thoughts were pulling themselves through cold molasses. Pouring herself a glass of wine, she paced their living room as if the walking would get her closer to an understanding of what was going on.

It didn't.

CHAPTER TWENTY-FIVE

"That's a highly sought-after collector revolver depending on its condition and other factors," Bill offered easily but thinking to himself after having that mind-blowing show-and-tell with Tim only a few hours earlier …what were the odds? "Sorry I don't have one, don't see them very often. Are you in the market for a S&W '73 Russian?"

"Well, as you say it would depend on the condition," Vytali stipulated "and price of course. But yes, I could be." Duncan had moved down the counter as if examining the glass-incased handguns.

"You must be new in town, welcome to Prescott…best little town in America," Bill enthused like the Chamber of Commerce member he was. They shook and as they did Bill took stock of the two guy's demeanor and body language. It's what you did constantly in a gun store. The loaded Sig Saur he wore on his hip wasn't for decoration. Something was off. These two sure as hell weren't locals and not tourist-types either. For that matter if they were collectors, he was Granny Goose. He had a sixth-sense he found invaluable in this business.

"Do you know anyone in the area, a collector perhaps, who we could contact? Bill never gave out personal contact information and anyone with half a clue should know the drill. He wanted to make this sound convincing. "You know around here guys are into first and second model Colts….44-40s and .45s- 'Peacemakers.' I do have a couple of fairly nice ones but I can't honestly think of anyone who's into those Russian models. Wait, I do have a Schofield Model 3 if you'd be interested? They're very similar in appearance for the most part."

The guy was about to say no, Bill was certain, until he glanced over to his partner and received a slight nod. "Sure, why not. We've come a long way from Tucson so might as well take a look."

"Sure thing. It's not on display so just give me a minute I'll be right back. When he returned the two men were gone…just as he expected they'd be. Tucson my ass," Bill laughed. The guy had pronounced it 'tuk-sun' with a hard 'k'. He had no idea what they'd been driving so he had nothing really to give the sheriff that could ID them except their physical description, but he'd toss him a head's-up anyway.

He'd better alert Tim as well. No telling who these clowns were but to say nothing would be irresponsible. Abby picked-up on the second ring. "No, not yet but I expect him any time now. Can I take a message?" Bill had never met the young woman Tim had described in an happy cross between Alicia Silverstone and Liv Tyler. Smart and easy to look at.

He didn't know how much about all this she knew. One never could be certain what couple's shared. And he didn't want to alarm her with a message that was bound to do just that however he phrased it. But what he was also sure about was that she'd been crying and was trying to cover it up. "No, just tell him that Bill from the Trading Post called and to get in touch as soon as he can. I don't mean to pry but is everything alright? You sound upset."

"No, no. It's nothing, thanks. I get allergies this time of year with a vengeance. I'll be sure to tell Tim as soon as he comes in," she promised. Bill noted her muffled sob, her voice breaking, as she ended the call.

Get it together, Abby, she slashed at the tears that welled-up from a reservoir of despair so deep she knew that if she let go entirely she'd drown. It wasn't Tim. It wasn't the present situation. Her angst tapped a deep well going back to a horrific childhood she'd wish on no one. But she'd be lying to deny that their discovery at the cabin in Show Low was a trigger or more accurately, it tapped through the thin patch she always managed to cover wounds that never seemed to heal. So once again it raged to the surface and she couldn't contain it…she'd learned not to even try. In time it always receded. Would there come a time when it didn't?

Where was he anyway? It was getting late. "See you in an hour," he'd said. That was two hours ago and the sun was already beginning to dip behind the Bradshaws. It would be dusk in another hour. Last she'd seen him was when she peeked into the office to say she was leaving. He had his face buried in a book…nothing unusual about that. But then she'd seen the artifacts they'd found together on his desk.

"How's the research…anything new? "she came-up behind him and laced her arms around his shoulders, kissed him on the cheek, staring down at the gun, the coin, the bills and the military insignia…and the pile of books askew next to them. He slipped off his reading glasses and kissed her back.

"Actually I've managed to verify some things, some even intriguing with my limited resources. But I'm going to run that by a couple of guys downtown whose expertise and resources are a lot deeper than mine. How long you think you'll be?"

Abby was adrift…she had no plan so she'd left it vague. "Not long. You?"

"Shouldn't take me more than a couple of hours. Let's BBQ…drinks on the deck?" he'd invited.

"Sounds perfect," she'd managed fighting against the unease that was gathering like storm clouds on a troubled horizon. That had been their last exchange. Had he come home already only to find her still gone? The Bakakov thing ate-up an hour so that was possible but there was no sign he'd been home and he would have let Ralph out in the now fenced backyard.

While Helen and Ralph had been best buddies, the new neighbor, following Helen's murder, made it clear he had no use for dogs…so up went the fence along their generous property line. What did they say about 'good fences? Maybe but this guy was just a plain, no frills asshole, she concluded.

She had to tell Tim about what had happened…she wanted to. There was no explanation other than Bakakov had passed-on what

Abby had told him she'd assumed had been in confidence. Wrong and naive in equal measure. He was part of something other than the Orthodox Church that was certain. Otherwise why would the Church be interested in a bunch of old czarist stuff?

But then she remembered what he had said about the Church promoting Russian nationalism. And this Andre guy? He was smooth and soft-looking like one might expect a museum curator to look, but he, too, was obviously connected to security of some kind...as were the guys with the van. Some operation, she reflected. This was getting seriously serious. It was all so messed-up.

Where the hell was he? One glass of wine led to another. The sun had set long ago and twilight had become full-on dark. The wine took the edge off. She began to relax into its sleepy embrace....

It was after 1:00 A.M. when Abby bolted from the sofa where she'd fallen into a troubled sleep, Ralph curled by her feet. Looking around frantically, trying to clear her head, the half-empty bottle of wine still sitting on the coffee table, she realized instantly she was alone. Tim had never come home.

CHAPTER TWENTY-SIX

Tim leaned against his truck, gas nozzle in the fill-tube at pump six in the first station he came to, a Chevron, pumping fuel into his near empty tank. With so much on his mind lately he'd nearly run out of gas on the way home…literally running on fumes, he'd guessed with the needle pegged below empty.

He'd thought about calling Abby but she was probably just getting home and he would be soon as well so he let it slide. After his meetings with Thom and Bill he decided he'd stop by his campus office to pick-up some files and check his faculty mail slot until he realized how close he was to being fuel-challenged. Now as he eased into his faculty space at the college he remembered their BBQ date. Shit. Checking his watch against the obvious signs of a not too distant sunset, he knew he'd better hustle. Tonight he'd share with Abby everything he'd confirmed and they would make a plan on how to deal with it all.

In a corner of the lot they were already setting-up stalls for tomorrow's farmer's market. Smells of the city mingled with the scent of pine and juniper eddying off the uplands on a gusty breeze. Lights were beginning to twinkle-on. A beautiful night. From where he parked it was only a minute to his office. Aside from the vendors there were few other people or vehicles in the large parking area. In another three weeks it would be filled as would the student lot and parking garage. Another semester.

It barely took him five minutes to retrieve the files he wanted and to walk down the hall to the faculty work area to check his mail. There wasn't much…the usual pre-semester forms and brochures from book reps trying to sell 'new' editions of textbooks…and a letter. The return address identified the sender as 'Kissinger Associates.'

The note was from Henry summing-up the Commission's efforts in Moscow. Together with St. Petersburg, Kissinger judged the mission a success as it resulted in a slew of contracts and 'memornanda of understanding' negotiated for the significant broadening of commerce and trade relations between the newly pronounced and stripped-down Russian Federation and the US.

> 'I do hope your research in St. Petersburg proved fruitful. I have always found in my own archival searches for materials for my books and articles inevitable surprises, oft times pleasant, sometimes not. Perhaps it was so for you in the Russian History State Archives? Again thanks for your help and good to see you again. Oh, and my offer still stands, Tim. My regards to your lovely, young, wife.'
>
> HK

Tim shook his head with a chuckle…Henry, ever the ladies man.' Speaking of ladies he missed his and needed to get home. He bundled-up his files and mail and headed back to his truck. Half-way there he noticed a vehicle parked next to his, odd he thought as there were perhaps a hundred empty spaces in the immediate area.

Approaching now with some caution Tim saw another pickup parked next to his with two men sitting in the front seat. He could only see the driver's profile clearly and it as no one he recognized. Chill out Tim. Dial down the paranoia he upbraided himself as he reached to open the unlocked driver's door. The movement caught the attention of the driver who swiveled his head to lock eyes with his. Tim could see his lips move. He said something to the other guy. Tim could hear and see the passenger door open and close…and footsteps. Quickly he put his bundle down on the bench seat with the intent of quickly following and locking the doors. Fears flashed.

What was this…a mugging…a car-jacking….somebody lost looking for directions?

He turned as the man came around the bed of the truck. Tim stopped. This man did look familiar…really familiar but there was something different about him that didn't fit a memory. And then suddenly it did. He was staring at Duncan, his hair badly dyed and wearing a mustache, fake no doubt, but it looked real enough to totally alter his appearance…except for the eyes and face pocked with acne scars.

It was just as John Clarke had warned could be possible and now here he was. Mind racing furiously, heart accelerating, he decided on the only thing he could think of. "Duncan, I hardly recognized you. I've lost track of time but obviously you must have been paroled. What are you doing here?"

"Hey, long time no see...eighteen long fucking months to be exact in that shit-hole Deer Lodge. But we'll have plenty of opportunity to talk about all that. Leave the truck and lock it. You're coming with us."

"The fuck I am," Tim bristled desperately trying to figure a way out of this. The farmer's market people were too far away for him to alert. Summer or not, where was campus security when you needed them?

"I said get in," Tim was abruptly staring down the barrel of a semi-automatic. He had no choice but to comply. He moved towards Duncan barely five feet away when in his peripheral vision he saw the distinctive markings of a campus police cruiser enter the lot. So did Duncan and so did the driver. Duncan hissed an expletive and the handgun disappeared but he walked up to Tim. Open the door and grab a file," he said just as the cruiser made a lazy turn heading for them. "Do it or our next stop is your house and it won't be pretty."

Tim did as he was told just as the campus cop pulled abreast of the two trucks on Tim's side. "Hello Professor Strange," the officer greeted as he looked over the scene. "Didn't expect to see you on campus for another few weeks."

Hey, Glen," Tim acknowledged the 45-year old retired Prescott City cop who'd hoped to pad his retirement with a little extra income a couple of years ago. His son had taken a couple of Tim's classes and managed to pass just barely with a lot of hand's-on mentoring. Clearly Duncan expected Tim to say something.

"Me neither but I needed to return Don's term paper. He's headed down to Tempe for a graduate program he's accepted into."

"Congratulations," Glen offered eying the guy who sure as hell wasn't the 'traditional' student. The guy was probably pushing 40 at least.

"Duncan nodded reading the cops expression. "Guess you'd say I'm a late bloomer…just stuck with it," he shrugged, smiled. Glen smiled back. "What was your paper on?"

Jesus Christ, Duncan fumed inside. He racked his brain to remember what Tim's specialty was. "It was on Native American kinship and reciprocity," he remember a long ago conversation at Tim's one night when he was staying with them when Karen, his step-sister was still alive.

Glen's expression, and Tim's, changed but for different reasons. "My son did a paper of Native American warfare…got an A from this guy. He's a notoriously hard grader, is the word. You guys have a nice evening," he said as he eased the cruiser down the lot toward the exit.

What Tim couldn't see was Glen watching in his rearview, especially looking long and hard at the driver of the pickup. He'd nearly reached the exit when it hit him. They'd just received a new set of wanted alerts from neighboring states as far north as Montana. He'd been flipping through them just the other day and he'd swear that guys face was on one of them!

Training said he should call it in and wait for backup but fuck it. Throwing the cruiser into reverse he accelerated into a violent turn, sawing the steering wheel and flooring it. Perhaps Vytali's radar was on alert or it was just instinct, but no sooner had the cop begun his maneuver than Vytali, automatic drawn, exited the truck and sighted over the hood even before Duncan could react. Tim stood frozen in place.

In seconds as the cruiser rocketed towards them, Vytali got off at least six shots that Tim registered and a tight group tore into the driver's-side front windshield spidering it into a million shards. At first confused once they realized it was gunfire, the few people setting-up the farmer's market scattered and dove for cover wherever they could find it…which in a parking lot wasn't much.

The cruiser lost momentum and glided past them the trooper clearly dead behind the wheel. Vytali yelled instructions to Duncan as he started their truck and drove slowly out of the parking lot. Following with Tim at the wheel, Duncan beside him gun drawn, the two trucks soon disappeared down the street unobtrusively intermingling with the five o'clock traffic.

Within minutes police cruisers, an ambulance and fire truck with lights and sirens tore past them in the opposite direction on Sheldon, heading for the college. Duncan followed Vytali onto Hwy 89A heading north towards Jerome and Flagstaff where it intersected with Interstate 40. Tim knew the route well. From Flagstaff it was 138 miles southeast to Show Low.

But he knew also that Abby was home alone, no doubt worried sick, and she had no idea where he was or who had him and he had no way to alert her. They'd found the phone and disabled it. Tim Strange was just going to disappear without a trace and that's all Abby would know….

CHAPTER TWENTY- SEVEN

She grabbed the phone on the first ring. It was just past two in the morning. "Tim! Thank God. Where the hell...?"

"A nooh, sorry. So, you'd be the new Mrs. Strange?" The man's heavy Scottish accent leapt from the handset. "I knew the old one...very well actually. Abby, right? Well, Abby, I...or I should say we have the professor and what happens to him now is all on you, lassie". Duncan, Vytali, Andre, and Father Bakakov were gathered in the prelate's office. Tim bound and gagged sat in a chain. At first he'd been stunned to see the museum curator but perhaps he had unwittingly aroused the man's curiosity with his questions and obvious interest in the Constantine Ruble? And it was clear Andre had other associations outside the Hermitage. And now this priest and thug Vytali...Christ was everyone KGB or Russian mob?!

Seeing Duncan again brought it all into focus and chillingly confirmed the possibility Clarke had alerted Abby to. Clarke's warning was now his and Abby's reality. The Scottish bastard had blackmailed and entrapped Karen in his drug conspiracies and then had done his best to silence him and Abby in Montana. There was only one reason he was here. Tim could see it in his eyes.

The reply froze in her throat but she'd known that only something like this, short of a heart attack or a fatal accident, could explain why Tim had failed to come home. What now? How did she play this? She'd learned a lot about Tim and about herself these past three years...about their strengths and resiliency...about what it took to outsmart and outlast...to survive. But ironically enough she turned to what she knew from her dead parents too: her father's unforgiving realism stripped of all emotion; her mother's cunning and fierce survival instinct. She'd learned through fraught experience she had ample reservoirs of both.

"Last time I saw your sorry ass, Duncan, you were kissing Seal's up in Montana. How'd that work out for you and your two dead brothers?" she taunted putting him on notice she wouldn't be intimidated.

"Shut your fooking mouth and listen to me. We persuaded the professor to tell us where he's got what we're after on behalf of the clients we work for. Someone is very keen and extremely motivated to have it returned to their safe-keeping. We're told it involves some czarist treasures of old Russia. They don't belong to you so you will give them back. Not complicated. Then we settle personal accounts. Business before pleasure. The bill always comes due, lassie."

Again a pang of guilt shot through her but one now amplified by Tim's abduction and the threat to his life this clearly implied. "I need to speak to Tim before I agree to anything." Indistinct voices.

"Abby, I'm OK. I need you to do what Duncan and Vytali ask." She heard a raised voice, the sound of a commotion and Tim grunt. He'd just given her the name of Duncan's partner and paid the price for it. She wrote the name down. "Tim, are you hurt?"

"Nothing that won't heal with a little TLC," he managed with a tinge of dark humor. "Abby, they've given me instructions so do precisely what I tell you OK?" She wanted to say more but didn't. "Listen carefully and hear what I'm saying…go into my office and you'll find the items in the glass display cases. Bring them with you to the cabin in Show Low. Oh, and bring that MacNaughton reference work. They're demanding proof that what we have is real. Finally, call the museum and tell than I can't keep our appointment tomorrow."

She couldn't believe what she was hearing. Was he drugged? He knew damn well that the artifacts weren't in the office because he had them! She didn't know anything about a reference work…and what museum appointment? What the hell was he talking about?

"Did you get all that?" Duncan was back.

"Yes, of course. Please don't hurt him. I'll do exactly as you ask…" and that's when what Tim asked her to do that made no sense suddenly did!

"Come alone. You tell anyone and he'd dead. I want you to…" he broke off. She heard muffled voices again. "OK, listen. There's a restaurant in Show Low on 9th in town called Aunt Nancy's. Be there at 6:00 PM sharp tomorrow. Sit at the counter and wait for a phone call. Don't be late. We'll be watching. We see anything we don't like he's dead and you're next." Abby had no illusions she would be next regardless and so would Tim no matter what they did. Whatever else was going on with this Vytali guy, Duncan was all about payback. Tim knew that for certain too and that's why he'd given her the instructions he had. Desperate situations called for desperate measures.

"I'll be there," she managed. "What then...you let us go? What guarantees do we have of that? We're supposed to trust you?" she scoffed.

"You can always trust a Scotsman," Duncan replied in a voice heavy with sarcasm. We need to get off the interstates for a while. Your cabin sounds ideal…private, secluded. Who knows, maybe there are more surprises stashed in your walls? We'll have us a scavenger hunt or better yet a game of hide-and-seek? Come prepared to play."

The phone went dead and then to dial tone. She looked at the kitchen clock. She had fourteen hours to make it work…not the scenario Duncan had just explained but what Tim had told her in code. They were coming to play all right. Duncan and Vytali had dealt the hand and what better place to shuffle the deck than in Show Low? She could only pray it would work.

Ralph stared at her like he knew exactly what she was planning…and didn't like it one bit.

CHAPTER TWENTY-EIGHT

There was no way she was going back to sleep not after that phone call. All her senses were on alert. And she was torn between incredible relief that Tim was alive and apparently all right and her other emotion which railed against what this was…another life-threatening, fucking mess. It was no one's fault. There was no one to blame for it. Christ, they innocently found an old bag hidden in a damn wall and then everything went to shit. So now the only thing she could do was to help get them out of a bad situation anyway she could. Tim's life depended on it. Everything else…recriminations, what ifs… and what comes after could wait.

The first thing she did was go to Tim's office. She'd listened very carefully. Clever guy! First she took the two presentation cases off the wall and removed the matched set of Colt .45s Clarke had given Tim. Next she went to the gun cabinet and lifted out the heavy MacNaughton 10-gauge hammer gun. Unlocking the ammunition chest she took out two boxes of .45 Long Colt cartridges and two boxes of 10-gauge double-ought shotgun shells. She also removed Tim's 9mm from his gun safe for good measure. The hand guns and ammo went into a duffle, the shotgun zipped into a soft case. She set them by the door.

It was barely 4:00 AM. Dawn crept into the desert vista like a wary animal from the east. The clock was ticking so she had to make the call. It rang twelve times before she hung up distraught. He's not there!

In a panic she paced the room until abruptly she remembered their last conversation. John had a niece in Denver and he'd given Abby the number in case they were ever up that way and needed a place to stay. She and her husband owned a big ranch in Cherry

Creek. She dialed. It rang and rang. She didn't realize she was holding her breath until finally…

"Hello?" She remembered he liked to get up to greet the new day with black coffee and a donut.

"Mr. Clark?"

"I'm here," the reassuring gravelly voice replied. "I told you to call me John," he scolded softly.

"It's Abby."

"I know, darlin'."

"They've got him," her voice broke.

"I'm on my way…

Glancing at her watch she did the simple math: three hours to go. But there was nothing 'simple' about any of this. Ralph sat beside her noticing everything with keen interest, nose out the window sniffing the air sluicing by them at 70mph. It was ten hours from Denver although in that 5.0 Mustang Clarke would probably make it in nine! Still, it would be close. They had to meet and figure out a plan. The miles seemed stuck in molasses even as her speedometer crept up to 90 in the clear straightaways.

It was twenty-to-five when Clarke's black 5.0 rumbled into the Circle K on the outskirts of Show Low, eleven hours after leaving Cherry Creek. He and Abby hugged. "Sorry, I would have been here sooner but I hit construction around Pueblo and had to get creative with a Trooper south of Albuquerque," he explained with a wink. "You OK?"

"I am now," she exhaled a deep sigh. "Thank you for coming all this way again. I don't know what I…"

"Not a'tall. Besides I wasn't doing anything 'cept watchin' the sun come-up."

"And having your donut and coffee."

"Well, that too but I was just finishing-up and besides my niece was getting sick of me so your call was perfect timin'! So, let's get at it."

For the next few minutes Abby explained the situation and a short version of her history with Duncan. "I can't tell you anything about the guy he's with but I think he's the Russian mob part of the equation; Duncan has the personal grudge part.

"Red hair like his brothers? I remember seein' 'em in Glasgow. Abby conformed it.

"Where is this cabin from here?

"It's a few miles out of town towards Fool Hollow Lake."

"Name has a nice ring to it," he approved. "First, you meet these guys as planned…that's in thirty minutes," he checked his watch. "I think our best move is for me to head out to that cabin and prepare a little welcome for our friends."

"But…"

"Abby trust me they'll never see me or know I'm there. I'm good at this, remember?"

She drew him a little map. He'd parked next to her in back of the station by the air and water kiosk. She opened her trunk handing over the duffle and soft case. "Feels like my old friend," Clarke approved.

"Tim made sure I brought it and your Colts are in the duffle with the ammo."

"I'm keen on not havin' to use the artillery but can't hurt to prepare…and it might hurt a lot not to."

"You OK? You've been in the saddle since the crack of dawn," Abby eyed him sympathetically.

"I'd be lyin' if I said I wasn't butt-sore and eye-weary but I bounce-back pretty well…or I used to. I think I got one more in me," he patted her hand. I'm going to get a couple of big-gulp coffees and a sandwich to-go and head out to the cabin. You'd better be on your way. Abeline, we can't anticipate how this will go-down but let me handle them. You watch out for Tim and for yourself…promise?"

She nodded but said nothing. Before she keyed her ignition she retrieved the model 1911 automatic from her glovebox and racked the slide, said a silent prayer. Good to go. These mother-fuckers were going to get more than they bargained for. And she had her own score to settle with Duncan. Ralph whimpered and curled into a ball next to her.

CHAPTER TWENTY-NINE

"Will she come alone?"

Vitali shrugged. "I wouldn't."

"Neither would I but who does she have to bring…the cops?"

"Net kopov," Vitali spat. "Not from what you've told me about her psycho-narco father. "Vozmozhno, kekotpryye druz'ya-perhaps some friends."

"Some burly college jock types maybe?"

"Da. "But whoever they are we will deal with them efficiently."

"This cabin is out in the middle of nowhere. There's big lake close-by but no big developments…just scattered rentals and a few homes. It was worth driving around out there today getting a lay of the land. It will be quiet and secluded. No streetlights to worry about," Duncan recited.

Vytali grunted. He wasn't much of a conversationalist, Duncan had learned on the drive down from Billings. That was good because he wasn't either and hated someone running his or her mouth in aimless chatter. He preferred talk radio although their truck had been outfitted with an after-market police scanner, radar and CB. It was how they knew the trooper following them on the way down hadn't yet run their plates. Even now as they sat in their truck the emotionless monotone of a female dispatcher provided white noise background to their conversation.

Tim, hands zip-tied and gagged sat alert but exhausted in the back seat. He'd hadn't slept or eaten since the day before. He felt utterly powerless to shape events and it wasn't a good feeling. But then he'd been in similar situations on more than one occasion over the past three years so uncomfortably this wasn't a novel experience. Not the sort of thing anyone wanted to get used to, he fumed.

The windows of the crewcab were dark tinted so he was virtually invisible from the outside. But he could hear and see and struggled to take-in every word. He hoped to hell Abby had deciphered his meaning in their brief phone conversation. Had she even been able to reach Clarke? It was all such a long shot…a very long one at that but he'd also learned that nothing was written in stone…until it was. Where there was hope there was possibility.

"So, this is what we do," Vytali outlined. "You will drive the other truck and meet her as planned at the restaurant. I will be watching from my truck with Strange in case anyone tries to intervene. They do you and she are just meeting for coffee. If not, you and the girl will drive in his pickup to this cabin. I will follow when I am certain all is clear. Once we are there and all is 'pervoklassnyy'…copacetic, we make the exchange there: the items for two dead Americans and then we are on our way back to Billings. The deal is done- sdelka shavershena!"

"Done deal," Duncan corrected the colloquialism.

"Bez raznitsy," Vytali shrugged. "Time to go," he tapped his faux Rolex.

"You are right on time," Duncan approved as Abby sat at the counter and was handed a portable hand-set by a waitress, confirming she was at the restaurant.

"Now what?"

"We wait."

"Where's your partner…where's Tim?"

"Close-by." Duncan ordered a beer. For the first time she realized they must have two vehicles. Scarcely noticed by anyone clouds had thickened and now it was beginning to drizzle and the temperature drop. A northwesterly breeze freshened. Raindrops pittered on the windows. Duncan downed his beer. "Leave your car in the lot and come with me. She hadn't expected that. The 1911 was in the glovebox where it would now be absolutely useless…and what about Ralph, she fumed. There was nothing she could do or was there?

"Wait just a sec. I brought our dog for company I want to make sure he has some water." It was only then that it registered: the truck Duncan was standing by was Tim's!

"Hurry-up," he waved impatiently leaning against the truck.

She opened the trunk grabbing a dish and water bottle and a duffle presumably containing the Russian artifacts. Ralph sat-up expectantly. Filling the dish and setting it on the vinyl floormat, at the same time she reached for the glovebox. Without warning a powerful hand gripped her wrist. Duncan stared at her with a bemused expression as he depressed the button. Ralph growled and lunged. Only Abby's quick reaction restrained him with her free hand. The door fell open and Duncan pulled out the .45. "Shame on you, lass. Is this your plan?" he asked sarcastically. "Always fancied one of these," he said as he shoved the gun into his belt.

Forcefully grabbing her by the arm he led her to Tim's truck. "Get in!" Sliding-in she sat as far away from Duncan as possible, hugging the duffle to her chest. He was one of the roughest looking guys she'd ever seen akin to a dockyard thug, she imagined. In truth Deer Lodge had aged him in unflattering ways, ways he preferred not to think about…and it was her doing he reminded himself now as they exited the parking lot. Across the street headlights flashed and soon they were being followed out of downtown by another truck. It must be Vytali and Tim.

At a stop light waiting for green they tensed as a Show Low patrol cruiser pulled alongside in the other lane. The deputy glanced over. Abby nearly squirming out of her seat stared straight ahead. She didn't dare make eye contact afraid of what she might betray. The light changed and the cruiser pulled ahead briskly, wipers sawing across the windshield, disappearing into traffic as they turned on to Fools Hollow Road. A mile back Ralph sat alone in Abby's car in the dark staring out the windshield.

The rain increased in volume and it became much darker as they left the city behind. Tall pines loomed. There were no other cars on the road except the other truck. It would not be long now whatever was going to happen. Where would John be?" Abby wondered. Her fingers were crossed in her lap. Her hands were sweating. And now she was really beginning to stress. What would happen when they opened the duffle and found… what they expected to find? And would they buy it?

As soon as he'd discovered in St. Petersburg that he likely had a real Constantine ruble Tim found the coin shop in the Hermitage full of replica rare coins and other artifacts for sale and bought a faux Constantine that looked identical to the original in nearly every respect. Only a closer examination could prove it wasn't legitimate.

The history of 'historical fakes' and forgeries was replete with examples going back thousands of years. It was big business. From 'Jefferson's wine bottle' to 'Paul revere's silver'; the 'Vineland Map' to the Piltdown Man'; 'period' furniture to 'rare' canvasses by the Masters. Even religious objects like the so-called 'Shroud of Turin' were not immune to fakery. And, of course, there was 'Princess Anastasia' who reputedly survived the Romanov massacre-one of the all-time hoaxes. All Tim needed was for the fake coin and other items to buy him time if that ever became necessary. He couldn't predict the circumstances but if history taught anything, it was better to be prepared than not.

Next he found a gun store, Zolotaya Pulya, on Konyushennaya Ploschad and bought one of several S&W model 3 Russians for sale as 'antiques'. He used his diplomatic status to have the gun mailed to Prescott. He substituted the Alexandrovich revolver for the one he bought in St. Petersburg, gambling that whoever the Russians sent after him wouldn't know the difference and hadn't done the research he had.

Finally, he left the gold rubles and banknotes in the pouch he and Abby found, keeping only the military insignia. What use would anyone else have for it? He knew Abby had generally described the pouch's contents with this Bakakov character so he needed it to be substantially as she'd represented it. Sometimes he thought he was too prudent, too risk-averse but now glad he hadn't second-guessed himself and taken the extra precaution.

However that left him with the other more deeply problematic reality. He'd been waylaid on the way home from the rare coin shop and Bill's Trading Post before he'd had a chance to secure and lock away the two authentic artifacts in his garage floor safe. They were now in a cloth-wrapped box under the bench seat of his truck…the one Duncan was driving!

He berated himself for being so careless but he couldn't have possibly known that Duncan and his partner would show-up that very day. Now as they bounced along Fools Hollow Road all he could do was hope that the box and its treasures wouldn't simply slide out from under the seat… or that Duncan wouldn't reach under it for some reason and discover it.

The cabin wasn't far now. He sat hands clenched trying to will the box to stay put. But that was the point. It was now out of his hands entirely, clenched or not.

CHAPTER THIRTY

Clarke had a powerful sixth-sense about these matters. Better to hold back than jump right in. See what developed, what the unknowns and unexpected were then act accordingly. And that's what he did. What he lacked now in speed, strength and mobility at 85 he made-up for as best he could in smarts, judgment and patience.

He had enough time to drive around and get a sense of the geography and roads even in the descending gloom. A camp ground near the lake and a mile from the cabin seemed an ideal place to park among the dozen or so campers and RVs already there. He put a twenty in the campsite box.

Locking-up the 5.0 he slung the soft case over a shoulder and carried the duffle into which he put some extra gear he always carried with him. He slipped into his black rain slicker. Good to go. Pulling the brim of the well-worn Stetson tighter on his forehead, he set out at a pace he calculated would put him at the cabin with a little time to spare...he hoped.

Twelve minutes later the cabin appeared in a stand of pine partially cleared along the gravel drive but denser around the back and sides. He approved. There was a single porch light illuminating a small elevated front deck and stairs leading to the front door. Approaching carefully and with little sound he stopped to listen. Night sounds and rain on the cedar-shake roof and dripping off trees was the only sounds he could hear.

As he was making his way around the near side of the cabin keeping twenty yards away and screened by trees, he heard it. The sound of tires crunching on gravel made by a slowly approaching vehicle...no, make that two vehicles. His hearing was still pretty damn good, he marveled. Hell most geezers his age were wearing hearing aids…or diapers.

The vehicles slowed further. Headlights swung into the driveway as Clarke disappeared silently into the concealing pines. He was now about fifty yards from the rear of the cabin's back deck revealed by another single light not visible from the front. Doors opened, doors closed…four doors, four people. Just right.

Indistinct voices except for one word… "inside." Foot falls on gravel then on creaks from the stairs, the sound of a key in the door lock. More squeaking but this time metal hinges. More voices. A door shutting…the click of a lock maybe? He couldn't be sure but it made sense. Lights flashed on inside in a couple of rooms. Old fashioned beige shades. He could see darker silhouettes behind them, moving, animated in conversation. But the rain washed out any words he might have heard.

Good thing the duffle and the soft-carry were waterproofed…not raining hard but a steady drizzle was enough to make things uncomfortable. It also meant that those inside were less likely to hear an errant twig snap or a creaky board. Question was how much time did he have? What were they using the cabin for…a rest stop…a sleep over? But then another possibility hit him: A kill house. Take the objects then use it as a kill house, leave the bodies there. Tim's and Abby's bodies could be there for weeks. If Duncan and Vytali were any good, it would be an unsolvable murder. Perhaps they'd make it look like a murder suicide…the tragic end to a lover's quarrel. So sad. But for the moment he would wait and watch s bit longer because his sixth-sense hadn't stopped nagging him.

"Kind of a dump," Vytali looked around at the sparse, rustic interior, setting down the duffel he brought from his truck.

"That's what I said," Abby couldn't help herself. The place still smelled faintly of paint from where they'd demoed the old wall and replaced it with new wallboard. It didn't help much.

Duncan sat heavily on the sofa and opened a beer from the twelve- pack he'd bought at the gas station. Vytali shook his head no at the offered beer. Tim went to the fridge and found two they left, handing one to Abby, taking one himself. Vytali shrugged indifference. "All right, hand me the bag," he ordered when they were settled around the table.

Abby handed it over, shooting Tim a look. Moment of truth. The Ukranian unzipped the bag, first removing the revolver and the coin, setting them on a towel, and then the other items. Watching him examining the gun, Tim could tell he was not a familiar with antiques at any rate. He set it aside. The coin he examined more closely, turning it over, feeling its weight, but he then set that side as well. He did the same with the ruble notes and coins, though he seemed to relish handing the gold rubles.

When he was through he pushed back from the table saying nothing. "So what now?" Tim finally asked. A wave of relief washed over him because for the first time he realized the guy had no clue what he was looking at. He was just a currier expediting a pick-up and delivery assignment. But the thing he said next was what none of them expected and it changed everything.

"Now we wait."

"What for what?" Abby demanded.

"Not what…who. We wait for Andre. He's late so we wait."

Andre?! This was a disaster! Tim recoiled. Abby looked stricken, before turning away so the two men couldn't see her expression. Andre was the expert. He'd be able to tell pretty quickly that the gun and ruble were not what Tim and Abby represented them to be. The walls weren't just closing-in they were about to come crashing down.

Over the past few minutes Clarke judged the time was about right. He made a slow approach to the cabin's back deck removing the MacNaughton from its soft-carry, checking his Colts which he wore in a brace of more modern shoulder-holsters under his slicker rather than his old ranger service belt he'd retired when he gave Tim the revolvers as gifts, thinking he'd never need them again.

Now here he was crouching through the rain and pine-needles in pitch dark carrying a humungous shotgun. His back and shoulders were already killing him…arthritis kicking-in, he rued. Why did he do it...put himself through this? He liked Tim and Abby well enough, had actually grown fond of her certainly, but he had no obligation to them that felt binding. He didn't go out of his way looking for trouble…at least not like he did when he was younger and full of piss 'n vinegar, and he wasn't necessarily a 'crusader for justice.' No, it was something inside of him, innate, he'd always felt.

He'd visited this question more than once over the years and pretty much came-up with the same answer. He figured the word was service as in the Good Book doing for your neighbor. Plain and simple he just liked to help folks with their problems if he could. Bad guys were just that and deserved what they got. But good people also deserved what they merited, sometimes with a little help…decent lives rid of that portion of predators, violence, and despair that one man might be able to provide. It wasn't too much to ask, he reckoned. It was just who John Clarke was. None of that that made the rain dripping down the back of his neck any less of a nuisance but it did his heart good. He was on the downhill side of things, he reckoned, so he'd better hedge his bets.

He was ruminating on that when he froze in place. The sound came from the covered back deck now barely thirty yards away. It sounded like the track-noise of a sliding door. Then there were voices carrying to him. It was Duncan and Vytali. "So why didn't you tell me about Andre?"

"There was no reason for you to know. My bosses insisted I have the artifacts authenticated before we leave for Montana. He's the only one who can do that. So I arranged with Bakakov to have him meet us here," he explained.

"Why not Prescott?"

We were fortunate to be tailing Strange when he left that gun store and then stopped for petrol. It was easy to follow him to the campus lot. Securing him there was the key to forcing his lady friend to bring us the items. I hadn't counted on that local cop but too bad for him. So what…you'd rather stage a home invasion in an upscale neighborhood in Prescott or take care of our business in a secluded cabin in the woods three hours away from the police activity back there? Someone in the group of people could have taken a license or gave a description. I don't leave things to chance. You live longer. And one more thing…"

Tires crunched as another car pulled alongside the two pickups. Headlights winked out. The car door opened and shut. Footsteps approached rapidly. A knock on the door. Hearing the car Duncan and Vytali were already back inside. Duncan opened the door expectantly. But it wasn't Andre. It was a community service patrolman, a guy in his 60s in a kind of uniform. He was armed…and looking from Duncan to Vytali immediately suspicious. "Christ Almighty," Duncan muttered under his breath.

"Ed," Tim walked briskly towards the front door as Vytali backed away as if to give himself a clear field of fire. "What brings you out on a night like this?" Water was puddling at Ed's feet.

"Hi professor Strange…Abby," he nodded towards her, smiled. "I was driving by and saw the vehicles and thought I'd better check. Few weeks ago when you were here you said you wouldn't be back until later in the fall? Surprised to see you. We've had a couple of break-ins since then so just doing my job. Everything all right?" he glanced again at the two men.

Tim was thinking furiously but Abby spoke first. "Duncan's my half-brother from Scotland, he glowered at her, "he's here for a visit. Thought we'd show him and his friend some Show Low western charm Obviously, we didn't check the weather," she offered a what-can-you-do gesture.

"Yeah, spur-of-the-moment trip...we're all good here, Ed. We won't be staying the night. Appreciate your checking things out for us. I'll put-in a good word with the Association."

"All right folks," he offered a wave. "I'm going to get on home to my supper and feed the dog," and they watched from the window as his tail lights disappeared around a bend.

"Sorry, I didn't even think of that. He's harmless... a widower…means well."

"Twenty-two minutes later by Tim's watch the sound of tires on gravel again and the scene repeated except this time it was Andre. Brief greetings, he refused the offered beer but brought his own vodka. Two shots in quick succession. "The roads here are terrible…worse than Siberia. There was a mudslide…some trees and boulders. Izvini ya opozdai…sorry I'm late. Pokazhi mne," he gestured towards the artifacts.

CHAPTER THIRTY-ONE

Carefully Andre examined first the revolver with the eye and movements of an expert. Tim and Abby prepared for the worst. There was no need for complex metallography of the weapon's microstructure to verify age, although Andre produced a small kit from which he produced a powerful jeweler's loupe and swept his eye seemingly over every inch from every perspective. He checked the serial number against the same reference Tim had used only a smaller paperback version...in Russian. At length he set aside the gun saying nothing.

Next he produced s small electronic scale and placed the coin on it, noting its weight and checking in a separate source that looked to Tim to be a 19-century binding. Andre used a micrometer to take measurements, then once again used the loups to examine the coin's reverse, obverse and edge. He took some notes, consulted his references. Finally he removed an instrument that Tim recognized as a portable XRF analyzer for testing alloys to ascertain positive material identification. It was all done very thoroughly and professionally and took all of ten minutes while the others watched and waited. Tim was as baffled as he was desperate.

While this had been transpiring Clarke had gained the back deck and had positioned himself next to the slider. This close he could now hear bits of conversation, enough to know that things were getting dicey. He had no idea that Tim had switched the real artifacts for fakes but assumed that once Duncan and Vytali had what they came for they'd kill Tim and Abby. Why keep them alive? He cocked the MacNaughton's hammers and positioned himself.

Andre looked-up at the expectant faces gathered around the table. "So?" Vytali demanded.

Andre cleared his throat. "The revolver is authentic, the serial number and other references confirm it. The coin is an authentic Constantine Ruble…all the tests confirm it's genuine," Andrea pronounced.

Tim struggled to keep his jaw fixed. Abby couldn't suppress her small gasp, her mind screaming. what?! 'You are sure?" Vytali pressed.

"Defintively."

"He's the Hermitage expert," Duncan reminded them.

"OK then." Vytali carefully retuned the artifacts in their protective coverings to a padded container he removed from his duffle. "We are done here."

"Not quite," Duncan corrected.

"I am done and I am leaving. You do what you need to do with them," the Ukrainian replied with little emotion. Finish your business and take their truck. We leave it here and that rent-a-cop will get suspicious. The professor said we weren't staying the night, remember?" Let's not give anyone an excuse to check until we're half-way back to Billings. We can dump the truck somewhere a couple hundred miles from here and that will confuse things even more for the authorities. Tell you what, we'll meet up in Cottonwood for gas and take care of that, agreed?"

"Suits me. I 'd rather drive alone with just me and the radio anyway, no offense." Vytali shrugged indifference. He didn't have much use for this dour Scot anyway. What was it with these people? They were almost as bad as Cossacks.

"Andre, you head back to Prescott and report this to Bakakov and give him this receipt," he handed Andre the sealed envelope. It case there is any question, this will prove that the artifacts were taken into possession of the Tambova. Securing these priceless icons of Imperial Russia will not only enhance our prestige- our reputation, but it will give us enormous political and competitive leverage to secure whatever advantages we seek in the new Russia…or we may simply sell them to the highest bidder and 'reinvest' the millions of dollars they command. Any way you slice it corruption always pays," he approved with a broad grin..

Tim tried to process all that had just happened. Clearly Andre was lying but why? He could see that Abby was thinking the same thing. Regardless, they were now in grave danger. With Vytali and Duncan splitting-up and Andre heading back to Prescott, they were left to Duncan's retribution and there was no doubt what that would be and it would happen in the next few minutes.

Andre packed his processing kit and left but as he did he mouthed to Tim…'maskirovka'. Vytali secured his large duffle and strode out into the rain without looking back. Duncan watched from a chair holding Tim's 1911 in his lap, an unreadable expression on his face but it could have been a smirk. The cabin door shut with finality to it.

First Andre's land Rover pulled away followed by Vytali's truck. The pittering rain abruptly became a maelstrom of hail and wind as a colder cell erupted over them. Minutes later lightening flashed followed by a thunderous boom. The lights flickered, dimmed and went out plunging the cabin into total black. "Don't ye fooking move!" Duncan hissed, as he grouped and found the flashlight he'd seen on the counter by the stove.

Thumbing it on, the Rayovac illuminated Tim and Abby standing right where they'd been when the lights went out. Oddly they were both smiling. The hail and wind were diminishing as quickly as the assault had begun. He thought he heard a noise and turned around with the flashlight. Three feet from his face illuminated in the beam were two enormous side-by-side black holes and behind them was the face of an old man in a droopy, soaking wet Stetson who looked vaguely familiar. "Hello there Duncan."

"Bluddy hell."

"And then some," Clarke chuckled. "Lower the sidearm and lay it on the table." Duncan did as he was told. "What shall we do with him?"

Tim retrieved his 1911 and handed it to Abby. He walked over to Duncan and staggered him with a vicious blow to the abdomen followed by an uppercut that lifted him off the floor, crumpling him in a heap. "That's for terrorizing my wife with a good measure added-in for Karen." Duncan wasn't listening because he was out cold but Abby and Clarks were. "Thank you…for both of us," she said in obvious solidarity with Tim's former wife.

"You throw a mean punch," Clarke complimented.

"I was motivated."

"We caught a break with them splittin'-up like that. Saved us a messy clean-up…maybe worse," Clarke observed.

"What I'm trying to figure out what the hell Andre's angle is," Tim confessed, explaining it all to Clarke as they sat around the table with beers after hog-tying and gagging Duncan.

"No honor among thieves," Clarke finally volunteered as Tim's story brought him up to date…except for the most important detail. "So… the Czar's gun and the Constantine Ruble, the real one, are under my front seat in a box wrapped in a towel. Vytali has the fakes!"

"You don't say," Clarke slapped his knee in approval. "You two are not half bad at this. Next time I'm stayin' home. He chuckled.

Abby threw her hand-up in alarm. She'd heard something out of place. Then something caught her eye. Sitting by the end of the sofa was a bag of some kind. It wasn't Tim's or Abby's. It wasn't Duncan's as he hadn't brought anything in with him. Clarke's duffle was near his feet. He shook his head now as he too noticed the other bag. That left only one possibility…Vytali. He'd somehow forgotten it and he'd come back for it! He'd been gone for barely fifteen minutes, probably had just reached the highway when he realized it was missing. Shit, shit, shit!

Duncan was groaning and he'd begun to struggle against his constraints. The rain and wind had let-up so the sound carried. "Kill the lights and get down!" Clarke hissed. Tim flipped the switch and dropped next top Abby…and then it was as if the world exploded around them.

Vytali stood on the front steps of the porch. He'd surmised that Duncan was now a hostage and that some unknown person had joined the girl and the professor in the minute he'd been standing there. But it was being duped by Andre that enraged him. The bag he'd forgotten had saved his ass. If he hadn't come back for it, the guys in Billings would have made sure this was his last assignment.

From his duffle he pulled an ugly-looking PSS H-41 sub-machine gun widely used during WWII through Vietnam and the Soviet-Afghanistan war. It was fitted with a 71-round drum magazine like the American Thompson gangsters used during Prohibition.

The front porch lit-up in a penumbra of brilliant yellow-white, the front of the cabin, door, and windows blowing apart in chunks of wood, glass and metal as he swept the weapon back and forth from right to left, ejected shell casings a shower of tinkling brass. At 900 rounds per minute it took all of ten seconds to empty the magazine, twenty more to change magazines and empty the second into the cabin that was now smoldering from severed wiring. The unmistakable, pungent odor of propane scented the air. No sound came from the cabin except things falling and breaking.

Vytali retreated off the porch as soon as he smelled gas. He'd have to leave the bag he came back for after all. It was a small price to pay for what he gained. Striding back to Tim's truck, he threw open the driver's side door, felt under the front seat and found…nothing but a wrench and an empty plastic water bottle?! When…how had Tim moved it? "Fek!" he screamed. But there was no time. He had to get out of there. He reached further back one last time…and there it was!

Throwing his gear, the bundle of artifacts and the still hot PPSH-41 into the back seat of the crewcab, Vytali drove away exhilarated, self-congratulatory and already anticipating his reception in Billings. Only a hundred yards from the cabin the sky turned a brilliant yellow followed by a heavy concussion. Tim and Abby's cabin blew-up showering the woods around with burning embers like fire from the heavens.

CHAPTER THIRTY-TWO

Thirty yards from the rear deck of the raging fire that a few minutes before had been the cabin they huddled dejectedly, fortunate to have escaped with their lives not feeling especially pleased about their situation.

As soon as they realized Vytali had returned they knew the reason and what would likely follow. Tim dragged Abby to the floor at the same time Clarke hunkered down next to Duncan in the kitchen behind the island and counter top. In seconds the refrigerator, microwave and cabinets behind them exploded in the maelstrom of 7.62 Tokarev rounds. The entire interior seemed to be coming apart in the deafening fusillade.

For Tim he was instantly back in Nam caught in a vicious firefight with the Viet Cong, incoming automatic weapons fire zipping through the foliage like wasps, the cacophony of battle all around him. It was not a pleasant flashback but a familiar one for those with PTSD.

He half-dragged Abby across the floor towards the back slider to the deck after he'd killed the lights and barely had time to drop before rounds tore through the cabin like a scythe, one nicking his shoulder. The glass patio door blew out seconds later in a shower of shattered glass. Her hair was full of small chunks. She realized she was screaming but Tim's strong, reassuring grip motivated her to keep moving towards the cool damp of outdoors the destroyed slider offered.

Clarke new what coming too. His sixth-sense was screaming at him. Before the first burst he dropped to a crouch and then to full prone as the kitchen island took two dozen rounds zipping over him like pissed-off wasps. "Outside," he yelled and crabbed across the glass-littered floor towards the back of the cabin. There was a short pause. "He's reloading come on!" It wasn't much of a respite but just enough to see them roll or scuttle out the opening on hands and knees now bloodied in the scramble to relative safety. Fortunately the drapes had fallen and now lay heavily on the shards of glass still in the track of the slider.

The rain had turned to a light misty-drizzle, Everything was wet and slippery and all each of them had was the light clothes each happened to have on. They were quickly soaked, cold and miserable but alive...so far. Tim and Abby huddled while Clarke said he'd watch their rear flanks for any sign of Vytali. But it was soon clear by the sound of his truck that he was clearing out. That's when they too smelled propane and wood smoke as the shifting breeze carried the rotten-egg odor to them.

"Away from the house!" Tim urged. They'd made it twenty yards into the woods when the cabin blew with a thunderous roar and fireball of debris. It could probably be seen and heard for miles. And even as that registered in the next couple of minutes as they watched what was left of the cabin burn they could hear distant sirens. In shock, it took Abby a moment to gather her wits and begin to think straight and the first question that tumbled into her head was… "where's Duncan?"

"I'm afraid one or more of Vytali's rounds ricocheted off the wrought iron work above the stove or something and clipped him within a few seconds. He was lying next to me with a head wound. If that didn't kill him the blast and fire did. It was all I could do to get myself out in one piece."

"No need to explain John," Abby assured him. "Duncan chose his path a long time ago. It was just a matter of time when he came to the end of it. What's more I think he knew that. I think guys like him with their backgrounds who have shit for childhoods…make wrong choices, have a deep streak of fatalism running through them. They draw the short end of the same stick they whittled away at all their lives."

"I wouldn't...couldn't have said it that way but damned if I don't agree with you Abeline," Clarke vouched. "Now look we'd better come-up with a story about all this and right quick," he alerted them. "Abby, head out front and see if there's any brass still lyin' around. Son-of-a-bitch had a machinegun for Christ sake. If so, get rid of it. That alone will ping the cops radar and give us real headaches."

"On it," she said as he ran for the front with a flashlight.

"Tim, you got the shitty part of this but we got to get that Scot's body outt'a there and hidden back in the woods."

Together they found Duncan's body which amazingly enough was not burned other that his shirt and hair. It was fairly easy even with Tim's bad leg and Clarke's bad back from years in the saddle to carry him a good sixty yards into the woods and underbrush. "We give the cops no excuse to start sniffin' around for anything and we'll be fine," he volunteered.

Retracing their track they met Abby carrying a plastic bag. Inside were 26 brass casings. "Couldn't see any others but I can't swear there aren't."

"Part of our story is that some ammo you keep cooked-off' during the fire."

"What about Ed? He's bound to show-up and he saw the others," Tim reminded them.

"They went into Show Low to do the town," Abby suggested. "They said that if they partied too hard they'd get a motel...see us in the morning for breakfasts. We were just getting ready to leave when the place blew." The sirens were close now.

"Well.... old Ed didn't see yours truly so I'd better get scarce. I'll be just out back and I'll be watchin'," Clarke assured them as he walked off carrying his gear and the MacNaughton.

Tim and Abby were sitting on a bench looking bedraggled and appropriately traumatized for good effect when the first police cruiser pulled into the drive, followed minutes later by two more...and by Ed.

CHAPTER THIRTY-THREE

The first thing they did flowing an hour of Q&A and a cursory examination by the police and firefighters on the scene was to get Abby's car back in Show Low she'd left in the Circle K parking lot. Instead of some terrible scene they feared, they found Ralph curled-up on back seat sound asleep seemingly without a care in the world. Once he realized who it was it was a different story with a lot of licks and tail-wagging and barking. By now it was nearly 3:00A.M. Hell of a way to start a new day!

Show Low police and State Troopers had walked round the destroyed cabin, snapped some pictures, took notes and taped a recording Tim had offered voluntarily to be cooperative. Parts of the floor had burned through and still glowed red in places so it wasn't safe to do much inside investigating so the cops didn't do a lot. A firefighter confirmed that it appeared that a fitting on the propane tank's regulator had cracked causing the leak. It had been Clarke's suggestion that they'd unknowingly hit it in the dark and rain parking to give the story greater plausibility. It seemed to have worked. The incident was preliminarily ruled accidental. Clarke had buried Duncan while Tim and Abby managed the first responders. The ground in a small clearing was wet and soft and the old army trenching tool proved equal to the task.

Bleary-eyed and on their third round of coffee the discussion turned to the obvious question: what now? Vytali had the Czar's revolver and the Constantine Ruble...it was the first thing Tim checked. They were gone along with the fakes. Why had Andre lied about his examination? He had to know Tim had substituted the authentic artifacts for fakes. It made no sense. Why would he lie?

What was the word he'd mouthed to Tim as he left…maserova…mosterosov? No… 'maskirovka', he came up with it. What did it mean? It would have to wait until they got back to Prescott and he could look it up.

And they were returning home. What else could they do? There was no way in hell they were pursuing Vytali much less going to Billings…into the heart of the beast. Abby wouldn't stand for it and Tim had no motivation to put himself, or her, through another such ordeal. The czarist revolver and Constantine Ruble and gold coins and bank notes were gone and that was that. They had serendipitously come into their lives and they had now disappeared just as fortuitously. Cosmic balance…stupid luck...whatever. But he still had the military insignia that had most intrigued him and his research had already confirmed tantalizing connections and possibilities suggested themselves. That mystery was still very much in play.

Later that morning they said good-bye to John Clarke. It was a bitter sweet parting as they all knew this was probably for the last time. "Here, this old thing is too heavy for me to lug around anymore," he said as he handed Tim the McNaughton. "I do miss firing it one last time though. Hell of a gopher gun! And the Colts too," he passed the duffle. It was good to feel them in my hand again…old friends.. You know where I'll be so look me up next you up on the Hi Line and in Glasgow," he kissed Abby on the cheek, gave Tim's hand a pump…looked away, coughed conspicuously. "It's been my pleasure knowing you folks. You're a hell of a lot of work but worth it. Now you two be happy and stay out of trouble!"

Climbing into the 5.0 he threw a wave and proceeded to burn rubber half-way to the stoplight. "Now that's a farewell with attitude," Tim approved with a slight hitch in his voice. Abby stood there tears streaming down her cheeks. There was nothing more to say….

CHAPTER THIRTY- FOUR

Home again, mentally and emotionally exhausted from their Show Low experience they collapsed into bed and were still there ten hours later. But sleep came grudgingly as it will when overtired minds careen among entangled thoughts and what Tim called 'mind worms' burrowed deeply into the subconscious, appearing and disappearing in a tedious pattern of M.C. Escher-like repetition. It was hard to shut-off the escalator.

Oblivious to Abby breathing softly next to him, Tim was ensnared in a dream he'd experienced variations of for years but this one more intense than usual. It was always about Nam, not so much the horrors of combat, though those were real and graphic enough, but the oppressive heat and dark of the jungle that turned the world a dark, malignant green.

All around you it clung seemingly with intent, 'wait-a-minute' vines eager to trip you, the sultry humidity sapping your strength, slippery mud banks plunging you into feted waters, land and water leeches, cobras, 'two steps' vipers, krates and giant constrictors lying in wait for a misstep, jungle centipedes, scorpions, stinging weaver ants, and spiders like small dinner plates, became intimate, often deadly companions in the murk. And the incessant buzz of insects- black horse flies, mosquitoes, wasps and hornets was a constant music of torment impervious to Army 'bug juice', requiring 'search and destroy' missions each morning to rid battle fatigues and helmets of unwelcome guests… and now constant companions in his dreams. The Nam- such a beautiful country of death from equal opportunity predators.

But this dream was different in a bizarre way. This battlefield was not jungle but deep, heavy pine forest nearly impenetrable to sun and sky. And it was not the hot, humid, sweat-dripping heat of Southeast Asia but the biting, unrelenting cold of snow-covered terrain with brutal gusts of arctic wind numbing his cheeks and ears. Shadows darted between trees in strange uniforms and headgear, gunfire came to him in mostly single shots and somewhere the thump of artillery rumbled the ground. Everywhere he looked were dead, dismembered horses their dead riders sprawled in the bloody snow their sabers beside them.

Suddenly someone was screaming in his ear. Someone was shaking him. He awoke with a start totally disoriented. Sitting beside him Abby stared down with a concerned expression. She knew his recurring dreams and torments. At first they really scared her but gradually she'd gotten used to his night terrors. Still, she knew this one differed from the others. He was not wet and clammy as he often was. This time he was curled in a ball, arms wrapped around himself as if he were freezing to death.

Slowly he came out of it but the images and lingering, visceral feel of his dream remained stark. "Wow that was really bizarre. Wonder where that came from," he shook himself awake. Hey babe. Sorry I woke you" he stumbled into coherence. 'What time is it?"

"You were having one of your 'time travels'," she'd decided that's what she'd call them rather than nightmares. I was awake anyway...sort of," she yawned. The sun poured through the curtained window.

"Crap we really slept-in, huh. Guess we needed it after...."

"I'm going to take a shower...another one to get the smell of burning wood out of my hair and skin," she alerted. She didn't ask him to join her like she often did. Not a good sign, he registered. But what did he expect. She'd hardly said a thing in the five hour drive back home and had actually slept most of the way. He could scarcely blame her after once again staring-down violent death, this time from a Russian mobster, Duncan dead, their cabin destroyed. And although hardly equivalent they'd lost what was potentially one of the great discoveries in recent memory…and one worth a fortune at that. No, not a good night.

Tim left the bedroom, let Ralph out, fed Tweeker, ground some fresh coffee and started the machine. It was Saturday August 23rd and by the look and feel of it promised to be a scorcher.
Coffee done he slipped into his office and found the translation Russian-English/English-Russian guide he'd be bought in St. Petersburg. He looked-up the word 'maskirovka' and set his coffee down, putting on his reading glasses to be sure .The word Andre used could be understood to mean 'disguise' or… 'deception'! Deception about what? Who was being deceived and why? And then the answer took his breath away.

Abby walked into the kitchen bare footed, in a robe with a towel wrapped around her wet hair. This wasn't going to be pleasant. She was already in a fragile mood and it was on him. He poured her a cup of coffee. "Breakfast?"

"No thanks, Coffee's good," she glanced at the Daily Courier front page Tim had set on the breakfast bar. The vibe was chilly. Even Ralph munching on kibble looked over warily.

"Abby, can I ask you something?"

"Sure."

"The day I was grabbed by Vytali and Duncan what did you do? I mean we haven't had a chance to talk about any of that crazy day and night."

"Why? It's over… right? You're not telling me you're going to still pursue this because if you are…"

"No, Abby, I'm not. They can have that damn coin and the rest of it. It's been a curse since we found it and it sure as hell isn't worth any more grief than it's already cost us," he reassured her. "But you should know that Andre whispered something to me at the cabin as he left."

She looked-up from her coffee. "Whispered what?"

"It was just one word-'maskirovka'. I looked it up…it's Russian obviously.

"What does it mean?"

"Deception."

"Deception…deception about what? Why would he say that to you?"

"That's exactly the question I'm asking myself. It's a confidence. We hardly know one another."

"Wait…you know Andre? Since when…?" Then it all fell into place. Of course: St. Petersburg! They'd never really discussed his trip except in generalities about the commission, Kissinger, his impressions of the historic city, and that he'd discovered some interesting history about St. Petersburg in 1917. But this made perfect sense…Tim's research at the Hermitage Museum. Andre worked there, Bakakov said in his office!

Tim confirmed it. "Yes, I met Andre briefly one morning when I was touring the museum. I asked him about the Constantine Ruble…they have one on display. He was very knowledgeable," and Tim explained his suspicion that the coin they'd found in the cabin was the missing Reichel Ruble and that he'd actually confirmed it, as well as the identity of the S&W the day he was abducted.

"Well that makes sense now," she volunteered.

Tim regarded her curiously. "What makes sense?"

"You asked me about that day. I haven't told you what happened."

"What haven't you told me?"

Then she told him. "My God you were abducted too the same day? You could have told me on the drive home."

"You could have told me all about St. Petersburg but you didn't. What else happened there you haven't told me about?"

"Abby, I was being followed and I think it was by the KGB…the state secret police. This guy Putin I met was a KGB officer in East Germany before being groomed by Sobchak for deputy mayor. A scary little weasel of a guy. He may well be somebody someday. I didn't want to worry you…everyone's followed and surveilled over there especially Americans. If I had any idea about this father Bakakov at the time, I might have connected the dots. And that's what I wanted to ask you about."

"What?"

"Bakakov…that day you were brought to him…was Andre there?"

"Yes. Tim, I had no idea who he was until Bakakov introduced him. It seemed like they knew each other. Why? Is that important?

"It could be huge if by 'maskirovka' Andre meant the deception was on Vytali…which makes sense if he and Bakakov are connected…if besides their day jobs they are both KGB or perhaps something else."

"Something else?"

"I became far more aware of how powerful and important the Russian Orthodox Church is going to be in the new Russia and above all as it was historically in Imperial czarist Russia. It was truly a dynastic, secular-clerical power-sharing relationship. No separation of church and state. Rather just the opposite much like the power and influence of the Roman Catholic church in Europe for hundreds of years. Remember Christendom was united for a thousand years before the Eastern and Western churches split. One major distinction is the Orthodox church's veneration of religious icons and relics. It is an institutional guardian, an illiberal bulwark against relativism and license. What more powerful symbol than the cross and nationalism?"

"So it could be that the Church and what… the Hermitage Museum engineered this deception…whatever it is?" Abby ventured, to seize these objects?"

"Not the museum per se but another historical-cultural group with deep roots in Russian history. I discovered it during my research in the State Historical Archives. I'd never heard of it before. It's called the Imperial Russian Military Historical Society chartered by Czar Alexander II in 1866 in St. Petersburg for the veneration of all things military and glorification of Mother Russia. It was widely respected and influential through the Revolution of 1917. The Bolsheviks disbanded it officially but it continued to exist unofficially…kind of like our veterans organizations or the old GAR- Grand Army of the Republic. I heard there's talk of returning it to a place of official prominence in the new Russia. My sense is that all kinds of patriotic groups once snubbed by the communists are coming out of the woodwork to reassert Russian nationalism, heritage, and past glories."

"I can see that but what I don't quite get is- what was the point of the deception Andre's involved in? Someone will figure it out eventually won't they? What then?"

"Good question. I can think of only one explanation: Andre pronounced my fakes as authentic…to fool Vytali and prevent the Russian criminal syndicate from getting their hands on the real ones."

"So this is a turf war for fucking bragging rights we got ourselves caught-up in and nearly got killed for?!" her eyes flashed.

Tim pondered reflectively for a second. "I guess you could put it that way, yes. But I think it's also far more significant. Abby, look at it in the context of national identity, of a proud country desperately seeking one when seventy years of its previous identity has been delegitimized…when the empire of a super power disintegrates literally before your eyes. For many the need for tangible iconic symbols around which to create that new identity becomes the existential necessity. It's human nature and humanity's history to venerate objects and symbols." She looked skeptical.

"Think of our founding documents -the Declaration or the Constitution… Lincoln's Gettysburg Address… the Liberty Bell and all they symbolically represent as talismans of democracy and liberty we venerate. What if all those were suddenly declared irrelevant, our system of government…our democracy and economy…our global stature…all that simply collapsed in a matter of weeks or months? Can you imagine? What would we do? How would we react?"

She nodded tentatively.

"I've been at this history thing for a longtime. Sometimes it does strike me as just one damn thing after another without rhyme or reason. And I still do believe it's a random universe…there's no preordination to anything--except death of course. But I've come to understand that a nation's identity is the sum of its historical memory, its stories and mythology, as those accrue and are passed down from generation-to-generation to create a landscape…a shadow land of memory and veneration where light and dark comingle to illuminate what we accept as reality, mythology or even…historical truth. And we seize on that moving forward, holding on to the comforting things we have known or accepted as guideposts to an unknown future. It's a corridor of time nations and peoples all subconsciously walk through even though along different paths of national experience."

Abby sat silently with her coffee warming her encircled hands. Unknown future precisely summed-up what she was thinking. Her past was so fucked-up she could hardly conceive living through it…her present was so conflicted it was nearly impossible to think clearly about a future that held any promise of a life she wanted. She was questioning everything, everything including life with Tim. These past few days had challenged her thinking and decisions…caused her to question her motivations like never before. Near-death experiences will do that.

She figured that kind of self-doubt and reassessment was probably a normal response but that didn't make the introspection any easier. It was nearly impossible to step outside oneself and judge objectively. Too much baggage…too much ego. And then there are the stories we tell ourselves to explain us to us. Could there be a more self-serving exercise?! But there were moments of clarity…like this one. This was not a life she would or could sustain. And she knew it was real when she admitted the reason: she enjoyed the endorphin rush too much.

It was addictive, seductive. Part of her fed on danger and uncertainty, the thrill of the chase, holding the power of life or death. Yeah…It was a side of her that attracted a kind of feral instinct at war with the other side of her nature she liked to believe made her a good person, a person of empathy and kindness. That part of her recoiled in horror at her twin. It scared the hell out of her. And what scared her more was that Tim seemed to somehow enable that darker side not through intent but a kind of coherence between them she couldn't explain. Did she even want to?

Watching Tim as he poured another cup of coffee, glancing over to see Ralph gnawing on a chew-toy, Tweeks stretched out in a ray of sunlight, she yearned for its warmth seeping into her forever in comforting, trouble-free embrace…sweet serenity.

CHAPTER THIRTY-FIVE

"Andre," Father Bakakov welcomed the curator expectantly into his office, seizing him in a brief man-hug. "Well?"

Rather than answering directly Andre placed a plain oak box on the Vicar's desk, smiled. "Success not easily done but success. Otkroy eto… open it," he invited. They'd met in St. Petersburg nearly twenty years before when Andre was a student at the Russian Pedagological State University and Bakakov a professor of religious studies. Theirs was a student-mentor relationship they sustained even as their paths in life parted…except that both had mutual overlapping allegiances to Church and State.

Bakakov lifted the clasp securing the lid and hesitating only a moment and hinged it back. In the center space bedded in red foam cradled the S&W 3rd model Russian with its gold engraving gleaming in dull patina against the perfect bluing of the revolver's frame and barrel. The grips bore the seal of Mother Russia and the United States. There was a sharp intake of breath. Bakakov crossed himself. "It is magnificent!" he proclaimed.

"Obviously this is not the original Romanov presentation case. We must assume that became another casualty of 1917 now lost to history but we have recovered what is most important."

The Vicar admired the gold rubles and crisp banknotes in their respective nooks but they were of interest but clearly incidental. In the last space sat the perfectly engraved silver Constantine Ruble bearing the likeness of the czar who never was. It spoke to him as a prelate and as a scholar of Russian history.

"This coin represents what might have been, Andre. Konstantin Pavlovich is our tangible link to Russian glory and patriotic sacrifice. His grandmother was Catherine the Great, he helped drive Napoleon out of Russia in 1812! Technically he was only czar for three weeks but still he was the ruler of all Russia in all its imperial grandeur." Andre demurred from reminding Bakakov that Constantine's rule in Poland was so harsh and incompetent that it sparked a revolt by the very army he commanded, and that he abdicated because the job was beyond him. History was as much about what, or who, is left out as about what is venerated…sometimes more, and who controls the narrative.

Still, he figured little harm could come of linking Russia's past glory with its future iteration whatever that might be. It was very much still a work in progress and a future in limbo. Without question the revolver would be a prize display for the Hermitage and even its historical links to the US might pay dividends of some kind. Who knew? What was certain was that keeping it out of the hands of the fartsovchik and shapana would further strengthen relations between the Church and Kremlin and that was essential. Neither institution was in the business of vorovkoe blago-criminal welfare…and neither was the KGB at least in this instance. But that was the conundrum of Russia…one never knew. 'Any law can be turned around to achieve the opposite result' was a popular proverb for a reason.

"What about Tambova? Tell me how you pulled it off?

They sent two men, Vytali was the hard-case; his souchastnik-Duncan, was along for the ride. I immediately determined that the artifacts the professor produced were fakes but assured the Tambova they were authentic. If they had been the real artifacts, I would have claimed they were fake and let the chips fall where they may. My assessment was that Tambova was going to kill them both regardless. There would be no blow-back on me. I don't think either suspected I am KGB…just a nerdy museum curator." Bakakov enjoyed the illusion.

"I left them to return to Prescott but something was eating at me. It struck me as I'm replaying all this in my head. Where were the real objects? Since arriving in Prescott the day before I acquainted myself the city, walking and driving my rental around. I saw a sign for a 'Bill's Trading Post' and I was about to go in just to kill time when I saw Tim arrive and enter carrying a box…this box. I put four-and-four together and guessed it had to be the items."

"Two-and-two," Bakakov corrected, shrugged.

"Bez raznitsy. Anyway, I wanted to make sure he wasn't going to sell or trade them so I watched very carefully until he left taking the objects with him. If he had sold them, I would have gone in and purchased them at any price obviously. I followed him until he eventually stopped for petrol and then went to his college. There he was met by Vytali and Duncan. A cop tried to stop or perekhvat-intercept them, it was very confusing, but they shot him and took off. I followed until I was sure they were headed for Show Low…what an odd name, where the girl said they had the cabin. That's when I called you."

"God was with us, Bakakov crossed himself again.

"It was clear the professor still had the authentic icons with him and they had to still be in his truck! And that's what struck me later as I was leaving the cabin. I backtracked quickly parked in some trees. Only minutes after I got there Vytali was back for some reason. It was quite a shock. I was hiding by the side of the cabin when I heard the professor reveal to those inside where the real objects were. I had to assume Vytali did too. Suddenly like a crazy man he machine-gunned the place. In all the mayhem, I raced to the professor's truck and removed the authentics. A duffle in Vytali's truck contained the fakes. I simply shoved them under the Professor's seat and ran off taking the real ones with me. I was at my truck hidden in the trees when Vytali came racing by. A minute later the cabin blew-up. Whew, that was slishkom blizko dlya comforta!" Bakakov agreed it was certainly that.

"What do you think they will do now?"

"Tambova? It may take them a while to realize they've been duped...twice," he laughed, "but I have a receipt!" he laughed. Then seriously…"what can they do? They're going to come after the

Church…after the Hermitage? No, even for them it would be too audacious and politically dangerous. Eventually they will get the word that this is how the Kremlin wants this particular matter settled. One palm greases the other as we know. There will be many other opportunities for mutually profitable ventures."

"I agree. But I also meant the professor and his wife. What about them?"

"That is less predictable. I think there may be conflicting dynamics at play between them. I only had a superficial impression of her the other day but she doesn't strike me as someone who is as zealous and certainly not as professionally vested in the artifacts as her husband. He, I got a pretty good read on in St. Petersburg. We may be able to exploit that if necessary."

"That's my observation as well," Bakakov agreed.

"All of this literally fell into their hands as she explained it to you. Hidden in a wall…seriously? Dr. Strange certainly-perhaps his wife knows their value. But we know they now understand the danger their possession brings to their lives. So I think they will be glad to be rid of them. I think they will accept the loss...easy come easy go…but it was anything but easy go. They almost got themselves killed."

"And you as well, my friend."

"What do the Americans like to say: 'ukhodit s territorii-goes with the territory,' Andre laughed.

"So, it is finished?"

"I believe so, yes. I will see to it that the Military Historical Society's first new exhibit will feature the Alexandrovich revolver. It will be on loan to them for five years before returning to the Hermitage for permanent display. The lost Constantine Ruble along with the other items will have a prominent position in our new exhibit space that will open in two years. The Church will have the satisfaction of assisting in the recovery of these objects of great historical significance and in forging the all-important ties between our Imperial past and the new Russia. It will give the people something to take their minds off the miserable lives they live. Undoubtedly someone will emerge after all the chaos settles seeking to be a new czar. He might even wear the pistol on his hip and ride around on a horse bare-chested like a Cossack!" They both enjoyed the image.

"Well," Bakakov chuckled, "It's not as grand as finding the lost library of Ivan the Terrible but it will do."

Bakakov veered off into another topic then stopped abruptly. Andre, I remember now the girl, Abby, she spoke of an American military insignia that was with the other items. I do not see it here? Andre paused, perplexed.

"I saw no such insignia."

"Could it have fallen out or something?"

"I did not do an inventory only glanced into the box to verify that the revolver and coin were there. Still I do not think so. I was very careful."

"Then…?"

"Then he must have removed it for some reason and still has it," Andre concluded.

"It cannot be of much value," Bakakov ventured. "So why keep it?"

Andre thought about that for a moment until finally. "To solve a mystery…or at least part of one"

"What mystery?"

"How did all these artifacts find their way into the hands of someone who brought them to America? I'm guessing Dr. Strange believes the military insignia is an important clue."

"That is the great unknown. I wouldn't mind knowing that myself," the Vicar admitted. "But how could he possibly unravel that conundrum after nearly a century?"

"He'll hope there are more clues out there somewhere hidden in the mists of time. If he finds them, he will follow them wherever they may lead. That's what these historians do, '"exquirentibus veritatem," Bakakov offered in Latin… "a seeker of truth."

"Ah, but whose? Comrade?"

CHAPTER THIRTY-SIX

"It's Lieutenant Rogers…Leighton Rogers?" the colonel asked as he glanced over his papers with bored indifference.

"Yes sir, Attached to the 27th Division, mostly New York National Guard, sir…"

"At ease lieutenant. I know General Lewis. He, Pershing and I were at the Point together…they were two classes ahead of me. The 'old Hickory' division."

"Yes sir. I hope General Jackson would approve. That elicited a grunt.

" Sir, I've been detailed to join G-2…the MID specifically. I spent several months in St. Petersburg before the Revolution and…"

"Oh? Were you attached to the embassy?"

"No sir. Bank of New York. We had a branch there but I knew many of the embassy staff. Most of them banked with us."

"So, you want to be part of Van Damen's spy corps…codes and ciphers and all that? You know President Wilson and the Army Chief of Staff hated the idea and killed it but old Van Damen's a crafty son-of-a-bitch. Got it through by going right to Secretary of War Baker. So much for chain of command. Anyway here we are in the thick of it."

"Indeed sir."

"The Brits are keen on the intelligence and the counter-espionage stuff. Truth is there are many vulnerable targets and sensitive areas here and especially in France the Huns would love to infiltrate…cause mischief. So, God knows there's work enough to be done on that score. You've been stationed in the port at Folkstone for how long?"

"Four months, Sir. Shortly after I volunteered. "

"Folkstone is a major embarkation point to the front. We pour millions into the trenches from there, thousands of toms or supplies and munitions… receive the backflow of wounded, men on leave…that sort of thing. So I know you haven't been idle."

"No sir, we've been on the jump since we arrived. What about the front zones, sir? I was hoping to…"

"France?

"Yes."

"You speak French?

"Oui, quatra ans a Dartmouth. Je ne suis pas lingueste mais competent," Rogers offered modestly.

"Well we need you French-speakers in La Havre and Calais and you can get a whiff of gunpowder if that's what you want."

"Actually I had more than enough of that in St. Petersburg. I was there when the Bolsheviks came to power, sir."

The officer looked Rogers over appraisingly. "You happen to speak Russian too by any chance?"

"Da, dostatochino malo, chtoby proti-a little, enough to get by, sir"

"Lieutenant, close the door and take a chair. There was only one chair in the bleak room other than the colonel's perched behind his olive drab field desk.

"This is strictly confidential," he said as he sat heavily. "Top secret, understand?"

"Perfectly, sir."

"President Wilson, against the advice of the War Department, is about to authorize a military intervention in Russia, in Siberia at Vladivostok and in the Baltic at Murmansk and Archangel. The official reason is to assist the Czech Legion, threatened by the fighting between the Bolsheviks and White Army forces, repatriate those men home, and guard military supplies."

"And the real reason?"

"To overthrow the communists by helping the White forces under Alexander Kolchak of the All-Russian Provisional Government seize power. It's become a bloody civil war and whoever wins it will control Russia and determine the fate of millions."

"Yes, I've been reading stories in the press and in some official cables about the power struggle but I had no idea we were about to intervene militarily."

"Only a few do. I didn't hear about it until last week. The operation will commence in July."

'That's next month!"

"The Bolsheviks control only a few thousand square miles in central Russia. They've been in power for less than a year. Its fragile...they're vulnerable. Wilson's being pressured by the Brits and French at Versailles to join them in helping to tip the scales without getting our hands too dirty. These opposition Whites are a mix of liberals, old czarist loyalists, moderate socialists who want to kick out the communists and create a social democracy...if they can."

"That's what Kerensky and the Menchiviks hoped to establish while I was in St. Petersburg before Lenin and Trotsky high-jacked the revolution," Rogers confided. Another grunt.

"What the Entente powers and Wilson really hope for is that the Whites will tear-up Brest Litovsk and start killing Germans and Austrians again," the colonel scoffed.

"G-2 is putting together a small elite detachment of Intelligence personnel to accompany the combat troops Pershing is committing...about 13,000. The 339th regiment is to go to Arkhangelsk...they're all Michigan men so they'll feel right at home in the Baltic. Amother force some 8,000 men of the 27th and 31st Divisions will sail from the Philippines and California to Vladivostok to guard the Trans-Siberian Railroad. Talk about climate-shock!"

"So it's just us the Brits and the French?"

"Hell, it's a hodge-podge of troops from seventeen countries...including the Japanese. The kicked the hell out of the Russians in '05 and I think they hope to horn-in on some territory while the Reds and White fight it out. Then there's the Czech Legion."

"Who are they again, sir?"

"80,000 of them left stranded in Russia when it left the war. They were fighting with the Russians but declared neutrality and wanted nothing more than to be evacuated back to the Western Front. They control the Trans-Siberian Railroad and have increasingly sided with the Whites which makes things dicey militarily and diplomatically," the colonel explained. Rogers was beginning to get the picture.

"So, we are sending small IP teams to Arkhengelsk and Vladivostok to keep an eye on things for G-2. Interested?"

"Do I have a choice?"

"Of place or of going at all? No, neither," he shrugged. "Pack your kit for Arkhangelsk. You'll be joining the 'Polar Bears.' And it's only 500 miles north of St. Petersburg, Perhaps you can take a side trip on a pass and see what a fucking mess the Bolsheviks have made of it. Dismissed…"

Tim pushed back from his table at the National Archives, rubbed his eyes, swigged from his plastic water bottle. Four collection boxes sat near his elbow, two yellow legal pads and assorted pens and colored highlighter lay about. This was day two. Three more to go until he needed to get back to Prescott. Classes began again in ten days…a new semester. He'd be cutting it close. Closing his eyes for a second in the quiet space of the Library of Congress, he thought about their last conversation the night before he left for DC. It wasn't an easy discussion to have or one easily forgotten.

"I think it's something I really need to do, Abby. The items we found are gone and as much as I was captivated by them I say good riddance. They caused us nothing but grief to put it mildly. I'm pretty sure you feel the same way."

"'Mildly' doesn't cover it, Tim. You have no idea how this has seriously messed with me. I know it's not your fault…no one's accountable. We had no earthly idea that stuff was hidden in the wall. I get all that. It was exciting. I mean who does that happen to? It's what's happened after that. Your trip to St. Petersburg, being followed by the KGB, being targeted by the Russian mafia, our nearly being killed at the cabin, having to involve John…that's enough to piss-off anyone and, Tim, I'm a whole lot of both."

"Abby, I'm sorry. I know you were. Hell, I am too. You know that. But the danger's over. If anything, Bakakov and Andre should be worried. They have the artifacts and it's obvious that we were not involved in the switch. I would imagine that Vytali is taking the heat for being duped …perhaps as in 'terminal heat,' the way those criminal syndicates operate. They have no reason to come after us. Besides I'm pretty sure this is now a power play between the Kremlin, the Church and the criminal syndicates in Russia. We have nothing they want. We're not on anyone's radar anymore."

"But it's not over, Tim. Now it's your obsession with that military insignia and how those artifacts found their way to way to Show Low and Justin's cabin. Who knows where that's going to lead or what hornet's nest it might poke. Don't you see? This is the next thing and there will no doubt be another one after it. It's what you do…your nature, your profession…your curiosity.

Well, you know what they say about that cat. I'm not faulting you for any of that. It's who you are. I just saying that I don't know if it's something I can live with…always wondering when the next ax is going to fall or however you want to put it." She was uncomfortably insightful.

"Tim, I've never been without fear in my entire life. My father damaged me in ways I've never really confronted and I'm just now coming to terms with that. He terrorized me. It became my 'normal.' My mom was my rock even as absentee as she was at times for reasons we both understand now. But she was there in intangible ways…just the idea of her. Then my dad murdered her and Kyle died as sort of collateral damage. My only safe place was my job at McDonalds…how pathetic is that! Do you have any idea what that was like?" All he could do was acknowledge her distress.

"But there was also your classroom. It was a refuge, a place where I was forced to think about something other than my shitty life. You, Tim, were a constant…someone I could trust…a man I could trust. I love history but your classroom for me was also about the present… for at least an hour a day it was a shelter from the fucked-up mess that was my reality."

. What could he say? She was right, certainly from her perspective…right about his passion. He'd never thought of himself as obsessive but perhaps she was right about that too. And even as he allowed that thought to creep-in he knew she was. He'd always thrived on the thrill of the unknown and discovery, finding the hidden and unexpected. It was why he loved research so much…he was the detective who solved the mystery.

He was Sherlock in tweedy coat and elbow suede always on the case. It was a high-octane high. How could he expect her to share his zeal? Feeling the way she did could he simply expect her to share his life…at least the way he was living it? Did he have to change…could or would he to save their relationship if that's what it took? Maybe one clue was that here he was sitting in the Library of Congress 3,000 miles from Prescott with an empty hotel room to go back to that night, and with a new wife at hone…alone and probably not missing him all that much. That insight cut like a dull knife.

With Karen it had been easy. They were both academics with tenured, mid-career faculty positions comfortable in their routines and the world of intellectual, scholarly discourse. And they were nearly the same age with similar experiences and easy, middle class backgrounds. That all counted for more that Tim had realized. Abby, although smart as a whip, intuitive and with an inner strength he truly admired, was nearly twenty years younger, her life trajectory anything but 'comfortabele'. He couldn't simply dismiss that as irrelevant. He'd known it was always a risk. Had his intoxication with her so clouded his judgment he was now paying the price for his hiatus from what was practical and sober? Or was she worth the risk, taking the chance that it could work? Anyway he looked at it he had a lot of reflecting to do. He figured they both did....

Eagerly he reached for Wine of Fury, Leighton's memoir of his Russian experience, and resumed reading in the chapter focused on 1917-1919. He was using the memoir for its narrative and first-person observations, augmenting that with archival documents from the relevant record groups and files that he'd referenced as primary source material. Correspondence of the principle British and American officers, diary entries of soldiers, official communications of the Allied High Commission at Archangel, and other documents. The book wasn't nearly as valuable as the typescript Tim located by chance titled, 'Czar, Revolution, Bolsheviks based on his never published diaries. It proved to be a gold mine.

He'd already refreshed his memory on the details of the American intervention from several solidly-sourced secondary monographs. Together he hoped they would allow him to recreate Leighton's experience with the IP and offer clues explaining how he came into possession of the artifacts. So far he'd been able to determine that he was released from his Intelligence Police duties in Britain to join the Siberian expeditionary force because he spoke Russian and had been in St. Petersburg for the Bolshevik coming-out party.

So far a fairly clear picture was coming into focus and he was encouraged that he was on the right track. Still, he knew the pitfalls and disappointment of over exuberant expectations. One clue at a time or in their absence extrapolate....otherwise known as 'best guess'! Still, there was a well-demarcated line between fact and fiction. Historians didn't simply make shit up. But they often did venture context and logical inference based on fragmentary and suggestive evidence...venturing the possible and hypothetical. It wasn't counterfactual so much as 'extrafactual'...like Daniel Defoe did so brilliantly in The Journal of the Plague Year published in 1722, a wholly and brilliantly fictionalized 'eyewitness' account' of the Plague of 1655. Thus Tim determined he would reconstruct a partially imagined past merged with the hard evidence he had...

Half the forces in Northern Russia were British under the overall command of British Generals Knox, Pool, and Ironside, while General William Graves commanded the 'Polar Bears.' Leighton was assigned to Grave's staff in Archangel where he arrived shortly after the Armistice in France in November 1918. For Allied troops in bitterly cold North Russia things were just heating-up.

The first good clue was Leighton's reference to their steaming into Kola Bay in the Barents Sea onboard the American cruiser USS Olympia. At their first stop in Murmansk, attending a reception of Allied military and evacuated Americans, he met Ambassador Francis on his way to England. Along with sailors from the Olympia Rogers was one of the first Americans to set foot in Northern Russia. Francis and Rogers had become acquainted in St. Petersburg as the bank handled the embassy's finances so they were on a first name basis. That fortuitous meeting resulted in the ambassador taking him aside and sharing a confidence. Tim tried to write a narrative of how it must have gone.

"Look here Leighton, I have a favor to ask of you."

"If I can, of course. But if I may sir, you don't look well, he felt compelled to observe."

"Francis waved that off but Leighton soon learned it was a severs gall bladder infection that would one day kill him.

"Are you familiar with the name Speranski?"

"I don't know of anyone by that surname but I believe there is a royal connection."

"Correct young man and not just any connection. Prince Mikhail Cantacuzene was born into a branch of the Russian Royal family. Rose to the rank of full general of cavalry and was an aid de camp to Czar Nicholas II. Brave and loyal to the monarchy to a fault. After the Revolution the Bolsheviks wanted to execute him but he and his wife escaped from St. Petersburg, she with her jewels sewn into her clothes, as I understand it. Imagine!" It is the princess that I am interceding for. Do you have any idea who his wife is?"

"Not a clue, I'm afraid."

"Princess Cantucazene is the granddaughter of Ulysses S. Grant…yes the former president…married herself a Russian Prince like a lot of American women did before the war. Now that's what I call social-climbing!" he rolled his eyes. They met in Rome and married in Newport. Quite the society wedding!" A narrative began to take shape.

"They had a home in Ukraine but spent most of their time in Petrograd. They were there when we were as the revolution overthrew the Provisional Government. The Prince was still recovering from a bad war wound. As I said they barely escaped. Soon they will be taking ship for Finland and then back to the states to reclaim their American citizenship." Leighton no doubt wondered where this was going.

"They of course had to leave everything behind in St. Petersburg. Commies must have had a field day ransacking and pillaging. I haven't spoken to Julia…Julia Dent is her American name, in days. The both of them have been deeply despondent since the assassination of the czar and his brother Grand Duke Michael Alexandrovich, Nicholas' younger brother." Tim took another note of all these Romanov familial connections with the Cantucazenes. He was now beginning to see a glimmer of a connection.

"Pool moved the Brits south to blunt Bolshevik expansion of their territory but it won't be easy. We had a very sharp fight last week, ironically the day the Armistice was signed…Brits and Scots and some Americans mixed it up with Trotsky's Reds. Graves has his hands full in Vladivostok with the Czechs and Kolchak's Whites. It's going to get very dicey, I'm afraid. I already hear there's opposition building in Congress and Wilson seems erratic and distracted.

"Nicholas, as you know, lived in Alexander Palace thirty miles south of St Petersburg in Tsarskoe Selo…enormous place. The Russians do everything enormously. But what I'm asking you to do if you can is to slip back into St. Petersburg and help the Cantucazenes."

"I thought you said their home was ruined by the Bolsheviks?"

"I did and it was. But no, I'm talking about the residence of another member of the royal family…Grand Duke Alexi Alexandrovich. His palace is on the little island in central St. Petersburg encircled by the Moyka River. As you may know he was Nicholas IIs nephew and by all accounts the czar was very fond of him."

Reading Leighton's diary entries, seeing the name of Czar Nicholas, the Grand Duke who's revolver he and Abby had discovered, and having it connected to Grant's granddaughter, sent Tim's head spinning as he recreated these revelations into some sort of order and coherence that he hoped he could add to and attach hard facts to. His notes now filled two legal pads. He began his third.

"My Russian friends tell me," Francis continued, "that it was spared the worst of the mayhem because he was never in the direct line of Romanov succession and he was generally very popular until the disastrous war with Japan in 1904 and the Baltic Fleet was sunk. He died in Paris four years later. Princess Cantucazene confided in me a secret that before they fled St. Petersburg they left something at Alexi's palace for safe-keeping they couldn't possible take with them...far safer than the home of one of the czar's closest military advisors. And they were searched."

"What did they leave?"

"Ah, that they did not reveal to me but they were adamant that it is something of how did Julia put it…surpassing value," he managed to say but with obvious effort. I must lie down for a while now but if you can do this it would be an immense favor…and perhaps far more than that."

"Sir, I'll do what I can…"

Tim could imagine the ever-dutiful Jennings helping the ambassador retire leaving Rogers stunned and at a loss for words. Leighton never saw Francis again as the ambassador died not long after returning to Missouri. Nor was he able to make good on his promise, at least not immediately as the military and security situation in the Baltic grew more and more precarious. An attack on a "Polar Bear' position in January 1919 killed half the platoon in a battle fought at 45-degrees below zero some 200 miles south of Archangel along the Volga. These attacks, mounting casualties and absence of convincing rationale prompted Congress to end the intervention. Only Wilson's determination to persist and White victories blocked withdrawal. The president's stroke and the collapse of Kolchak's offensives finally resulted in a change of policy. In January 1920 the

United States withdrew its forces from Russia in what nearly everyone conceded was failed and misguided military adventurism.

But for Leighton Rogers,as Tim pieced together, an opportunity presented itself that allowed him to make good on his promise before America quit Lenin's Socialist paradise. That opportunity came in August 1919.

CHAPTER THIRTY- SEVEN

British Rear-Admiral Walter Cowan steered his small battle fleet little, little more than a squadron really, of destroyers, cruisers, and gunboats into Kronstadt harbor on the outskirts of St. Petersburg now officially Petrograd repurposed to serve Bolshevik propaganda, engaging targets as he closed. Ranges still exceeded 12,000 yards. Deadly mines bobbed in the water like spiny tarantulas. His Latvian and Estonian allies in this and preceeding operations had proved stalwart fighters. In their hatred of Bolsheviks and desire for independence they knew no limits.

Fast 40-foot long lightly armed coastal motor boats harassed the enemy on shore. It was exceedingly foggy with ice crystals giving everything a gauzy visual texture. From one such boat, Lieutenant Leighton Rogers leapt into the frigid knee-deep water of Kronstadt Bay and waded ashore near the mouth of the Neva, dressed as an average Russian laborer. His heart was pounding, his senses on high alert. Even on this remote part of the estuary he had to be careful.

It wasn't long past a cracking cold dawn and there was no sign of anyone. Then without warning from out of the mist to his left came the challenge: "Kto pnkhoidt! Identifitfirovat' sebya ili byt' zastrelennym!" Leighton new exactly what this was.

"Drug, drug. Grazhdani Sankt peterburg. Lovlya ryby," he held up the fishing pole prepared for such a moment, Tim imagined plausibly.

From ten feet way a young man approached his bayoneted 1898 Moson Nagant thrust out in front of him. He looked him over suspicion creasing his face. "It's very early and cold to choose fishing," he observed dubiously.

"It's to feed my family. We have virtually nothing, hardly any bread. The children are starving. It's not vybor comrade, yego neobkhodimost…or we starve. We are very poor."

"Where do you live?"

Leighton dug deep to remember the city. "We live on Vasilyevsky Island just across from the Winter Palace we liberated," he spat for emphasis. "I work at the Putilov industrial plant…machinist.

"Ty vi armiya? The soldier indicated his coat and cap.

"Net, moy mertitvyy brat…dlya tyepla," he explained that he wore his dead brother's clothes for warmth and memory.

Seemingly satisfied the soldier lowered his rifle but did not stand aside: "Ty ne otsyuda-you are not from around here.

"Ya s kavkaza…I am from the Caucasus.

"Byt na vashem puti," he indicated with a sweep of his weapon. "Be on your way."

Within minutes, heart still pounding, he was safely within the city snugged deeply into his Red Army overcoat provided by Brits, a brown wool Ushanka pulled down around his ears. Sheepskin gloves kept his hands from frostbite. Wisps of frost rose at every breath. St. Petersburg- he would never call it Petrograd, seemed to be snuggled-in as well. A few pedestrians were about, small groups of soldiers and civilians huddled around street-corner fires. Here and there on Nevsky Prospekt a tram trundled by but otherwise there was little sign of organized military presence…no armored cars or Cossacks like he'd seen months before. People were hunkered-down enduring another brutal winter.

With sudden recognition he realized he was walking across from the National City Bank-the former Turkish embassy on Palace Embankment, the day the first spontaneous riots had broken out in October. In his pockets were stuffed nine million rubles in short term Treasury Notes he'd set out to deposit in the Volga-Kama Bank. He'd barely escaped a bad fate. He shook-off the memory as he trudged on through the few inches of snow that had fallen the previous night.

The fixed bridges connecting Nevsky Prospekt with the Ekaterininsky Canal and the Moika and Fontanka Rivers he last seen protected with troops from the Volynsky Regiment and machine guns were now eerily empty. He'd heard rumors he believed of the scores of men lined-up along the Moyka Canal and summarily shot in the head by Red Guards, tumbling dead into the river. It was said that for hours the bodies floated down the canal for all of its five mile length. Now all seemed like a tranquil Savrasov still-life. Leighton's diary entries were riveting in their detail.

A mile further and he came to what he'd been told to look for…the turret spires of Alexeevsky Palace perched on the Embankment on the other side of the Moyka with its unique contrasting Revivalist facades. Crossing over the wide Blue bridge…all bridges over the Moyka were painted distinctive colors, from Ulitsa Glinka he entered the seemingly deserted grounds of the palace. It was immense with spacious park-like grounds, now bleak in winter's grip. The place looked as dead as its departed former resident.

Alexi never witnessed the collapse of Imperial Russia and the assassination of his Uncle and his entire family but he was no stranger to revolution. Mutinies, worker strikes, peasant revolts, and anti-Romanov rule rocked many parts of Russia in 1905. The assassination of Alexi's brother Sergi sent him reeling emotionally and convinced him to leave Russia for good, relocating to Paris where he'd purchased a mansion in 1898 on Avenue Gabriel. There he died of pneumonia nine years before the chaos of 1917, leaving Alexeevsky Palace to the people of the city and its caretakers, Leighton presumed with all the city's rich driven into exile.

Now here it sat- all 20,000 square feet of it the main structure and wings, four story guest house, stables, workshops, and greenhouses fronting on the Moyka Embankment separated from the promenade by a tall wrought iron fence. He stood there staring up at the Grand Duke's golden Imperial coat of arms. Curiously the palace was tucked into adjoining working class neighborhood and factories. On the palace's eastern corner a nearly five story windowed-tower rose like something from medieval France complete with pointed cupola.

That was Leighton's objective. That's where the Cantucazene's, according to Ambassador Francis, had secreted whatever it was he was supposed to retrieve. Light was now leaking over the city and the Gulf of Finland which stretched to the West out into the Baltic Sea like a barely rippling sheet of glass.

For the first time Leighton saw signs that the palace was not abandoned after all. A light previously blocked by a stable cast a worm yellowish glow onto the snow. There was no other light to be seen. Was everyone else still asleep...an early riser...a night watchman?

From the stable a horse nickered. Not for the first time he thought he was crazy to be doing this. It could get him shot. Chance and randomness...chaos of the unknowable and unpredictable determined what happened. Which flower will the bee land on? He was leaving tracks in the snow. Would anyone see them? Plans and what actually happens is like a break shot in billiards when the cue ball slams the stack...instant order to chaos, he ruminated. He took a deep breath.

Leighton reached the tower unobserved. No one yelled out...raised an alarm. There was no apparent ground floor entry but he'd been told there wasn't. The Cantucazene's however had revealed that he would find a small service entry door at the back of the tower used by servants and as an emergency exit in case of fire. It accessed the main structure through a narrow interior passage that exited into the main stairway through a door. Barely ten feet into the dark passage he came to it, depressed the handle and felt it give inward. A dimly-lighted spiral stairway led upward. It was deathly silent. Slowly he began his ascent.

As Leighton did he reflected on how worse it might be. Whatever object was here could well have been interred with the Grand Duke in the Romanov mausoleum located in the Peter and Paul fortress which would have made all of this quite impossible.

Alexi was its first resident and literally out of reach in his protected vault in the middle of a citadel!

Reaching the third floor, nearly every wooden tread producing an alarmingly loud squeak, he entered a circular well-appointed room of 18th-century Louis XIV décor. Sure enough on the far wall was a framed Matthew Brady photograph of the Grand Duke and President Grant shaking hands at the White House, the much younger Duke's forked mutton chops and Grant's now salt and pepper beard a contrast in age and experience…and the wages of responsibility, Leighton no doubt thought.

As Tim gradually pieced together the narrative from the official records and Leighton's diary entries the picture in his mind was gaining some shape and coherence. Leighton was certainly not risk-averse and impressively-experienced for a young man. He knew from his research that Leighton and Alexi shared that in common, although along very different career paths. Tim reflected on that for a moment.

Alexie's career had been in the Imperial Russian Navy and a successful one until the disaster of 1905. American Admiral David Farragut had led a squadron into St. Petersburg in part to acknowledge Russia's at least symbolic support of the Lincoln government during the Civil War. Russia reciprocated in November 1871 dispatching its own squadron and diplomatic mission to New York led by the Grand Duke, then barley 21-years old.

That was followed by a months-long tour of America beginning with the White House meeting the president, wife Julia and most of the Cabinet, a subdued affair because of a lingering unrelated point of friction between the two nations. East Coast travels included the Naval Academy and major cities and the visit to the Smith and Wesson factory in Philadelphia. Then it was on to Canada, the Mid-West and finally to Nebraska for the buffalo hunt with Cody, Custer, and Sheridan.

Further travels took him to several southern states, then on to Japan and China, before returning to Vladivostok, home port of Russia's Pacific Fleet and finally to St. Petersburg via the Trans-Siberian Railroad. In all eighteen-months of travels had heavily influenced the Grand Duke on the need for major naval reforms and modernization which he spent the following thirty years championing, appointed Admiral-General in 1883. Unfortunately these reforms availed Admiral Rozhestvensky little against Admiral Togo and the Japanese at Tsushima Strait and Alexie's reputation never recovered…

The room smelled faintly of fine books, cigar smoke, and leather befitting a confirmed bachelor and 'ladies-man,' earning him, following the Tsushima debacle and however unfairly the epithet, 'lover of fast women and slow ships.' The room was clearly one that the Grand Duke had frequented. Now all Leighton had to do was find what Julia Dent had said would be 'hiding in plain sight.'

He had no idea of how much time he had but he wanted to get in and out as quickly as possible. Time was not his friend and it was getting lighter by the minute. His eyes searched the room until fixing on an ornate side table. He walked over to see a square rosewood box. On it in raised enameled relief was the Imperial Romanov coat of arms. 'Hiding in plain sight.' Unlatching the case, Leighton lifted the lid and stared at an astounding assortment of objects he knew immediately as a banker were enormously valuable. The exquisitely engraved revolver and a unique silver ruble intrigued him even more. He knew Russian Imperial currency and specie backwards and forwards but he couldn't remember ever seeing this particular coin in circulation. Still more intriguing. But not his concern. He reminded himself.

Tucking the case under his arm he made his way out the hidden servant's access and outside into the still frigid morning. As he neared the stable he realized how conspicuous he looked in his garb carrying an obviously expensive case. Slipping-into the stable provoked two horses to poke their heads out of stalls to look him over. He was obviously someone they didn't recognize and became somewhat agitated at his presence.

Looking around he found a well-worn heavy leather shoulder bag which on inspection carried sets of horseshoes. He removed them and shook-out the bag, slipping in the box and exiting the stable, feeling more confident about blending-in. Walking as casually as possible, head down, making no eye contact, meet with no challenges on his return through the city slowly coming to life. Now with better light he saw red flags flying everywhere with an upper rectangle of Gold Cyrillic lettering proclaiming the Russian Soviet Federative Socialist Republic. History had changed on a dime…or a ruble in this case, he enjoyed the monetary pun. What banker wouldn't.

It had been arranged for a British crew manning a Finnish S-Class torpedo boat earlier captured from the Imperial Navy to pickup Leighton from the beach not far from where he came ashore, a curve in the coastline obscuring easy observation from The Kronstadt fortress, and few Russian ships ventured out through the minefield in this chronically poor visibility.

The following day Leighton was back in Murmansk. But the Cantucazene's were gone taking ship unexpectedly as the opportunity presented itself. They dare not squander it. With them as well as the ambassador gone, Leighton had little choice but to secret away the box and its contents until he could somehow make proper arrangements. Before he did he placed one of his IP collar insignia inside the box that might later be helpful in identifying his custodianship.

Weeks later as he went about his now routine intelligence duties, with the IP it was announced that the Brits had convinced the Bank of England to underwrite a financial institution for Murmansk called the Emission Caisse…or note issue office in French, immune from Bolshevik seizure if things went badly. He deposited the box with the bank for safe-keeping before being detailed south to Arkangelesk as part of now eminent evacuation preparations.

The Bolshevik offensive against British and American forces accelerated dramatically in January 1919, driving the 'Polar Bears' north from several villages along the Vaga River. Casualties mounted as political support in Congress faltered. Troop morale plunged and mutiny became a real threat. General Graves and Secretary of War Baker recommended a pullout and through the spring the 339th prepared to evacuate Murmansk and Archangel. In mid-June Army transports evacuated the last American troops from Northern Russia. American troops would remain in Vladivostok until April 1920.

This is what the official records in the National Archives and now in the Library of Congress confirmed. Tim slid a book mark in Leighton's diary transcript and put down his pen after three hours of steady work. It reminded him of the Russian State Archives marathon in St. Petersburg that had set him firmly on his present course. It also reminded him of the Hermitage and Andre and all that had transpired so improbably since.

That, in turn, led inexorably to thoughts of Abby. They'd spoken once in a week. He'd called her. The conversation had been perfunctory and without any drama or unpleasantness, but unsatisfying in spite of that. He didn't feel the connection or the warmth they typically shared and that left him feeling empty and unsettled.

To his relief, she told him there had been no repercussions of any kind since Show Low and no contact with Bakakov whatever his role in the recent events had been, whether as orchestrator or facilitator she still had no idea…and didn't care. She had changed the locks and ordered a new security system for the house which Tim approved. Ralph and Tweeks were fine. They missed him. She didn't say that she did, an omission he tried to tell himself was an oversight failing miserably and feeling shitty about it.

She'd asked about his hotel, he had a faculty discount at the Hay-Adams, and about his progress…about this and that but it all seemed superficial. He told her DC was still in turmoil after the Mount Pleasant rioting of the previous May and residual racial tensions, and how the homicide total so far of 494 had broken all records and had the city on edge, and how the Clarence Thomas-Anita Hill confirmation hearings circus was like red meat for both parties.

He asked her about what she'd been doing and if the non-profit was sill set to restart in two weeks and what the weather had been like. It was clear from these exchanges that neither wanted to talk about the really important stuff, preferred to ignore the 'elephant'…the one filling the room and the space between them.

Better leave it unsaid, he resigned. Besides nothing ever got resolved or constructively communicated over the phone.

He said 'I love you'. She said 'me too.'

That was all still roiling through the back of Tim's mind when he resumed reading Leighton's diary again for a bit before calling it a day. It was only one word but it leapt off the page… 'disaster!'

> 'Returned to barracks about 4 p.m. Letter from the Emission Cassie dated
> a week ago. Safe deposit box gone! Emergency evacuation of all financial personnel and all private accounts transferred to London, Bank of England.'

Leighton inquired immediately of the British Royal Navy officer he'd become acquainted with about how the accounts had been gotten safely out of the war zone. It had been done by L-Class submarine and specifically by HMS L-55 based at Tallinn in Estonia as part of the Baltic Battle Squadron. She was less than a year old with a crew of 44. L-55 was one of the last Allied naval ships to leave following the departure of the Americans under Admiral Newton McCully. Jr.

Leighton's relief lasted less than 24 hours. Having an off duty beer with his British Intelligence counterpart he learned the worst. The L-55 had been sunk in Caporski Bay in the Gulf of Finland when she was attacked by two Bolshevik minelayer-destroyers and sunk by gunfire with the loss of all hands. She now rested on the sea bottom 234 feet under the surface…and so did Alexie Alexandrovich's presentation revolver and the Constantine Ruble…!

Tim sat motionless for a time struggling to wrap his head around this totally unexpected revelation. What now? The explanation of how the artifacts found their way from a sunken submarine in the Gulf of Finland to Show Low abruptly became far more complicated and defiant of any simple narrative he could imagine. It was maddening in the extreme but it was also fascinating because he knew there was an answer, an explanation out there somewhere. Eagerly he turned the page....

CHAPTER THIRTY-EIGHT

"Leighton, this is Edward Stettntius, Chairman of the War Resources Board, and Harry Hopkins, President Roosevelt's top advisor. Gentleman- Leighton Rogers, executive of Bell Aircraft Corporation and formerly President of the Aeronautics Chamber of Commerce of America. They shook all around and took chairs in Hopkins' office in the White House. Leighton sat across from general 'Hap' Arnold, Army Air Forces Chief of Staff who'd done the introductions. It was early November, 1941

"As you know a few months ago the president signed the bill creating Lend-Lease, our life-line to Britain to keep her in the war. Last month he extended the program to the USSR. Both Churchill and Stalin, as Harry can attest after recently meeting with both, are in dire straits and eager for the aid. So in the case of Bell Aircraft we're going to figure out how best to do that…"

After his military discharge, Leighton returned to New York. His banking and military service overseas brought him to the attention of the US Department of Commerce keen on expanding American trade in a public-private effort driven by profit, political leverage and diplomacy. He advanced rapidly becoming Trade Commissioner of the Aeronautics Division during the mid-1920s, and then serving as President of the quasi-governmental Aeronautics Chamber of Commerce of America throughout the Depression. He traveled widely leading missions to Japan, China and Europe. During the war his services and expertise were attractive to fellow New Yorker Larry Bell of Bell Aircraft who made him an executive for production and contracts. It was why he found himself in Harry Hopkins' office that November.

The Soviets were in desperate need of fighter aircraft and Bell Aircraft was awarded a government contract to produce the P-39 Air Cobra for Lend-Lease export to the allies including the USSR, and because of his military background and language proficiency Leighton was the obvious choice for facilitating the contract. By war's end Bell exported over 9,000 P-39s, 2,500 of which saw service in the skies over the Soviet Union.

Instead of being sent east over the Atlantic and through the Baltic to Murmansk and Archangel, the fighters were flown by women Air Corps Service pilots from Buffalo, New York to Fairbanks and Nome, Alaska over a route known as the ALSIB. From Nome Russian pilots flew them across the Bering Strait to Siberia and from there to the combat theater. For Leighton it was nostalgic in ways he hadn't quite anticipated and in March 1945 it became more than reminiscence.

Leighton and a small team were sent on a top secret mission to the Soviet Union for the Army Air Corps in connection with what was called a 'Operation Frantic' to establish US airfields for heavy bombers and fighter escorts in Russia beginning in late 1944. Three airfields in Ukraine were operational by the end of the war. Leighton and his team flew from Mehrabab in Iran to the Poltava base. Russian aircrews and mechanics were also based there and Leighton made acquaintances easily. It was almost like twenty-five years had vanished.

One night at a makeshift officer's club enjoying drinks with some of his team and Russian officers he'd gotten-on with, he shared details of his Murmansk IP service. A colonel about Leighton's age offered a boozy confession that he's supported the Menchiviks and Kolchak's Whites, careful not to be overheard by his Stalinist counterparts.

The conversation included Leighton's surreptitious foray into St. Petersburg on behest of Ambassador Francis. He'd told the story many times at cocktail parties and to various associates over the years, trying not to embellish things too much but always enjoying revisiting what had seemed so all-important and adventurous in his youth.

"So, I find these artifacts and give them to a bank set-up in Murmansk for safe-keeping," he explained, "only to learn that in my absence on a mission all of the bank's assets had been evacuated by a Royal Navy submarine, the L-55, for England. But that's not the worst. The damn thing was torpedoed in the Gulf of Finland and sunk to the bottom, all hands and my charge with it."

His Russian counterpart was silent for a moment, contemplative. "Podvodnya lodka- a submarine you say, HMS L-55… this was late 1919?" Leighton confirmed it was. "Before the war, in the early thirties, I worked for an undersea cable laying company in Arkhangelsk. I remember because it was big deal," he downed another shot of vodka.

"What was?"

"Our Navy located that boat and raised it in 1928 pretty much intact and partly sealed as I recall because they recovered the bodies of the crew. We refused to allow the Brits to enter the Baltic to retrieve their dead and personal effects so we prevailed upon a British merchantman to convey the crews remains back to England." Leighton jumped-up from his stool. "what?!"

The Colonel repeated his revelation. "Da, my spasayam podvodnya lodka."

"You salvaged it?!"

"Da, it was repaired and re-commissioned in 1931. As I remember we christened it 'Bezbozhnik'…Aethiest!" he roared.

Thunderstruck. Never in his wildest imagination could Leighton have come up with this scenario. The liquor flowed well into the wee hours and his head buzzed with more than the alcohol when he finally gave it up for bed. For the rest of his mission at Poltava he could think of little else other than how he might be able to follow-up this truly amazing turn of events. Tim could only imagine the exhilaration Leighton must have felt…and the anticipation.

The answer came when Bell authorized him to leave the mission in Tehran and fly to London for a two day stop-over before returning to New York. At the National Maritime Museum at Greenwich, Leighton confirmed the story and other details, how the merchantman, Turo, transferred the remains of the crew to the Light Cruiser HMS Champion, and they were subsequently buried at Hasler Royal Navy Cemetery with full honors.

With a deep breath and nerves sizzling he walked into the Bank of England Museum on Bartholomew Lane literally on a wing and a prayer. That seemed appropriate considering his career choices in aviation. The middle aged woman looked-up through glasses as he entered, smiled warmly. May I help you?"

He'd rehearsed this over the past few weeks. "Yes, well…I hope so. I'm interested in a presentation cherry wood box that the bank may have acquired at the end of the Great War. It has a Romanov crest on its top."

"You don't say. Come with me…."

CHAPTER THIRTY-NINE

She led him to a small alcove in the stone building still protected by piled sand bags. As he walked-in he could see an anti-aircraft gun positioned at an intersection. German raids, though now far more infrequent and largely now by V-1 and V-II rockets, were still a reminder of the danger. Floating lazily overhead on its tether a barrage balloon hung like a fat grey sausage. The room was clearly dedicated to the Great War and the Bank of London's role in its massive financing and supporting the war effort, Leighton surely registered.

She took him to a tall wood and glass cabinet. He stopped abruptly. On the third shelf Alexi's presentation box appeared just like he remembered it, seemingly undamaged for having sat on the bottom of the Gulf of Finland for nearly twenty years. "I presume this is what you were referring to?"

"Yes," he managed haltingly.

"May I inquire as to your interest in the Romanov box as we call it?"

What to say? "Are you familiar with how that all happened?"

"Yes, generally. It is quite a story. How the original survived its harrowing journey from Murmansk to London is truly a miracle." He blanched.

"The original?"

"Why yes. That box is a duplicate…an exact facsimile of the original. It was commissioned not long after the genuine Romanov box arrived with those poor souls. It was protected in a watertight locked canvass valise and amazingly enough unmolested by the Bosheviks. We suspect they were more interested in keeping on the good side of the Bank of England given their financial challenges and didn't touch any of the gold, silver or bank notes. All the ledgers balanced.

"That is quite remarkable under the circumstances," Leighton agreed.

"I was told by my predecessor that several months after the repatriation, a barrister…a lawyer arrived with papers proving ownership and the Bank released the box unopened. We really have no idea what was in it," she apologized. It is such a compelling story the Bank had a duplicate box made for display in this exhibit," she explained.

"Do you mind if I sit?" Leighton indicated the bench seat collapsing heavily into it with a sigh. This was a turn of events he hadn't at all expected. But then realized how far-fetched it was for him to think it would be so simple…so convenient. "Do you…does the Bank have any idea, any record of who claimed the box?"

"Again I was told that the claimant was anonymous and the entire thing was arranged by the legal representative of the party. We do know the barrister was British but there was the sense that he had been hired by someone else," she offered knowingly. "A month or so after we took possession an American officer, a general I think, came into the central Bank of London office and met privately with Sir Bryen Cokyane the Bank's Governor at the time. All very unusual that," she pronounced. "The Bank surrendered the box and that was the last we saw of it. May I ask what explains your interest?"

What harm would it do to tell her at least part of the story, he decided, and so he did, leaving unmentioned certain names and details, focusing on his Army Intelligence Police work. "There was a lot of counterfeiting and black market stuff going on, rumors of this and that, and one of them was about that box and some connection with the Bank. Just here in London on a visit and thought I'd pop-in and see if there might be any truth to the story."

"Well then now you know it but it's not the one you was expecting, eh?"

"No not precisely," he understated, "but fascinating all the same. Thank you and good day," he offered as he welcomed the cool, damp London air. Astoundingly the box had in fact survived and was now in the possession of someone who must have been connected to the American intervention, St. Petersburg and Murmansk. But who could that be? Later sitting on a bench near Trafalgar Square his memory sparked on Ambassador Francis and what he had told him about the Cantucazene's and specifically Julia Dent…the Princess-Ulysses S. Grant's granddaughter…

Out of uniform now for the second time and having spent two world wars in government service, Leighton Rogers contemplated his future over a beer at the Tombs in Georgetown. He figured he might as well stick with aviation consulting. Money was good, his expertise was sought-after, his reputation solid as they come. Why not? 1954 was starting to look like a very good year. America was on the move. Everyone liked 'Ike'…well almost everyone and he certainly admired the former Allied Commander and President elected two years before. Hard to go wrong with Republicans in charge, he approved.

But he was not in town on aviation business. He was here to meet someone. It would be a reunion of sorts. In another hour he was to meet the princess, Julia Dent Cantacuzene Speransky herself at her Victorian not far from the University on 33d Street NW. He wanted to explain in person what had happened to Grand Duke Alexi's box that ambassador Francis had charged him with retrieving and returning safely to her and the Prince. He felt he owed her that…a loose end to tie-up. An obligation to be settled from long ago.

He'd read that she and the prince had parted ways a while back…in 1934 and she'd remarried. The same article indicated that her health was somewhat diminished, including partial blindness, but for someone born in 1876, 78 was a long life and one, he had no doubt, well-lived. He'd certainly never met anyone born in the White House much less a princess but by all accounts she was a gracious woman and an accomplished one at that quite apart from her royalty, writing numerous articles and published essays. In fact they did have that in common. Like Leighton she'd published books on her life in Russia and St. Petersburg society. No doubt her Russian was better than his.

"Mr. Rogers, so pleased to meet you," she offered graciously extending her hand.

"And I you ah," he hadn't even thought about how to address her he realized suddenly..."princess."

"Julia, please. That was a life-time ago in so many ways I hardly recognize myself. So, you were in St. Petersburg in 1917, I understand. Working for the Bank of New York?"

"Yes, I was a banker back then…barely out of college, before enlisting in the AEF."

"Yes, I know, I read your book 'Wine of Fury,' You captured the moment very well, and your service in the Intelligence Police and subsequent career, speak well of you. As you can see my eyes aren't what they used to be but I can see extremely well in my memory…my mind's eye. My memories of St. Petersburg that fall and winter remain vivid. Dear Mikhail and me and all the other bon-vivants without a clue of what was about to happen…not really…her voice trailed off.

"Julia, do you remember American Ambassador Francis?"

"Oh, yes indeed, I do. David was a difficult man, quite ignorant of Russia but well-meaning. We entertained a lot, lavishly you know- our Russian friends, the Brits, French, titled aristocrats, important Americans from the colony. One week it would be this townhouse, the next someone's suite at a favorite hotel… and yes sometimes at the embassies. A friend, Madame Matilda de Cram tried to teach Francis Russian. He was an indifferent student," she laughed. "His 'man' Jordan became quite proficient. One never knows…" her face submerged into the moment and her countenance became progressively introspective, Leighton noted.

"I urged Francis to get out of St. Petrograd as the July Days raged on into that fall and certainly after the October Revolution but he adamantly refused, saying it was his duty, insisting on keeping the embassy open and functioning as everything else around us disintegrated…when things became so dreadfully desperate. I never thought much of Kerensky but he was all we had. We placed all our hopes on the Mensheviks and then on the Whites to trounce that Red rabble…Communist flame-throwers, but alas it was not to be. We raised a lot of money for the White cause but for naught. All of that is gone now. You know I was watching Walter Cronkite the other day-you just know when you can trust what some people are saying…he was talking about 'witnessing history.' I always thought that was a rather sterile, abstract way of putting it," she digressed. "We live through history's great momenta…we are participants not simply onlookers. We are all swept-up in it in one way or another. Isn't that so, Mr. Rogers?"

Leighton hesitated interrupting her reminiscence but diplomatically redirected her to his purpose. "Julia do you remember what you asked Ambassador Francis to retrieve for you from St. Petersburg while we were in Arkhanglesk? "

A smile crept across her face. "I was wondering when you were going to get to it. Of course I remember. Mikhail was especially keen on saving some Romanov momentos and having some hard currency we would need…besides my jewels! There were some gold rubles, bank notes, a very rare coin and a most handsome revolver that I believe belonged to cousin Alexi, presented to him at my grandfather's request. It was also a ploy to win a lucrative contract with the Czarist government," she barked a laugh. And, Mr. Rogers you failed us," her eyes bored into his.

"I…I slipped into the city and found the box where you said I would find it, and I returned to Murmansk with it only to find that you and the Prince and Ambassador Francis had been evacuated. So I did the only thing I could at the time given my military duties. I placed it in the Bank of London's care when it withdrew its assets from the war zone."

"The submarine that the Bolsheviks sunk," she replied.

"Yes, that was an unforeseen mishap."

"Mishap? It was a damn sight more than that!" she snapped. But in softer tones she said: "It was not your fault, heaven knows, Mr.

Rogers. What do they call it…'the fog of war?' We cannot know how things play-out before they do can we? So, you have my forgiveness for what it's worth. And besides it turned-up didn't it," she offered brightly and somewhat mischievously, Leighton thought.

"That's what I learned in London after the war, yes, and I am pleased it was returned safely to you." He was about to ask when she preempted the question.

"Mikhail had many financial dealings with the Bank of London. He knew Governor Cockyane well. He also had contacts in the Admiralty. We didn't know what to think about you or what might have happened to our possessions, her inference was clear, but Mikhail made inquiries and that's how we learned of L-55. It was then simply a matter of arrangements between him and the Bank."

"A British barrister, I was told?"

"Yes, a legal acquaintance who proved most helpful in his discretion."

"So you have had the box safely here with you all these years?" Leighton's fingers were a-tingle.

"Sadly, no."

"I beg your pardon?"

"I'm afraid it's a family matter," she was clearly uncomfortable. He waited.

"After Mikhail and I divorced I never remarried. That was in 1934. I have a son and two daughters by the Prince- Mikhail, Barbara, and Zinaida…all four years apart. Mikhail was born in July 1900. All lovely children a mother can be proud of. That means that I have six grandchildren and…my goodness I've lost count, but I think twenty-four grandchildren. There's bound to be one that goes astray."

"He hesitated. "Astray?"

"My son Mikhail, obviously named for his father, had a boy, always rebellious and contrary that one. He could never seem to live-up to the family name…our heritage. I confess to being judgmental." She didn't apologize. "We never saw him after they moved north to Chicago and the marriage ended. The mother died when he was young. It was all very ugly. Michael was despondent, became reclusive, especially after his father and I divorced and then all that with his wife." Leighton didn't press.

"We never learned what happened to the child. Trouble seemed to attach to him. We only saw him once on a brief summer visit in Sarasota. The Prince is still there tending to the business and his properties…remarried. Skeletons love closets. Every family has them," she ruminated. Leighton was trying to follow the family saga when it struck him.

"I don't want to be rude but do you mean…are you implying…"

"The Alexandrovich artifacts? We don't know who or when. The family has no idea what happened to the box or to its contents. It was kept in a locked display cabinet in the Sparansky's office and it simply vanished before the divorce was final."

Leighton balked. Forgive me but I'm surprised your husband didn't wish to have the Romanov artifacts?" he tried to put it delicately.

"Oh, he meant to. I agreed he should have them. We'd just separated and he was going to have it shipped to his farm near Chicago with other heirlooms and possessions. He accused me of absconding with them but that's preposterous." What do I need with an old gun and a bunch of rubles? Stunned, Leighton fought for words. After all of it…all of his harrowing experiences, for it to come to this struck him as so ludicrous he began to laugh, much to Julia's dismay.

In fact he was still laughing as he checked out of his hotel, the Hay-Adams, for the four-hour drive north to New York. Princess Cantacuzene was certainly right about the 'fog of war'…but there was also the 'fog of life' as we live it, Leighton reflected as he headed north on Route 41, never knowing what's around the corner until we're in the thick of it. Moving in any direction can be a risk. But what's the alternative?

Sitting back in his chair Tim couldn't help but reflect on his own circumstances and life's obscurities. He was taking his own risks but like Leighton…what real choice did he have?

CHAPTER FORTY

Tim thought about that for a long time as the afternoon sun dipped below the Capital Building. As Leighton had surmised, there was no alternative. Hell, life was all risk and fickle. Only one inevitable certainty. Everyone knows the end of that story.

He pushed back from his chair, slipping legal pads and pens into his briefcase. He was done. After four 10-hour days of research at the Library of Congress and the National Archives he now knew the story…or as much of it as he was going to find here. A good deal of the fog clinging and obscuring what had happened all those years ago had dissipated. There remained only this one final piece, the one lose-end to tie together, if he could find it. But to do that, he would have to go home to Prescott and to Abby. And he realized, uncomfortably, he almost dreaded the prospect. In having solved so much of the mystery surrounding Grand Duke Alexie Alexandrovich's artifacts, he'd uncovered, however unintentionally, truths about his relationship with Abby. And those verities bothered the hell out of him. Where would confronting them lead?

He'd called her from the Hay-Adams to tell her he'd finished all the research he could do. He shared with her what he'd discovered and told her that he was on the way home. She was cheerful, sounded like the 'old Abby', not the self-preoccupied woman she'd been only days before…glum, moody. Introspective. Relief…a reassurance, he seized on the thin reed of wishful thinking. If it were only so, he hoped.

She'd gotten over whatever had so stressed her out. Everything could get back to 'normal'. But what was that exactly? Was it the previous normal that they'd lived…and endured battered and bruised to be sure, but survived the past three years? Or was it something different now…something unfamiliar. Uncharted territory between them? Unbidden came mental flashes of 'Toe-Poppers' and 'Bouncing Bettys' in Nam. He tried to shake that off- physically heaving his shoulders.

As he struggled with that on the flight to Phoenix he vowed to do whatever was necessary to give her the life she wanted and needed. And he understood, finally, that it was not the lives they'd been living. Abby was right: neither of them was at fault but that didn't matter. There's had become a kind of co-dependency, he tried to explain it to himself. Those, always had consequences. How could they not? He thought of all he'd learned from Leighton's diary and from archival sources, of all the big and little choices that players in the human drama surrounding the events of 1917 had made that literally shaped history in big and small ways…leads and extras in a life and death drama.

His thought seized on Shakespeare's As you Like It, Act II, Scene VII, where Jaques says to Duke Senior, 'All the world is a stage and all the men and women merely players, they have their exits and their entrances…' Contemplating his nearly 50 years, he'd just as soon forget the rest of the Bard's brutal summation of our 'seven ages.' Yet ever intuitive and observant, the man from Stratford-upon-Avon was on to something. We enjoy a finite time on earth to get it right as much as anyone has a right to expect anyway. He needed to make it right with her and he vowed he would try and do his best to deliver on the promise to himself. He owed her that.

He's closed his eyes about mid-flight as the sound of jet-wash lulled him. It was an early morning flight from Dulles, TWA L-1011 Tri-Star non-stop. His window seat put him just behind the right wing and engine. Thank God the center seat was empty. What seemed like endless patchwork farm land scrolled 35,000-feet below him. Scrolling through his thoughts too were the revelations his research had uncovered.

After his interview with Julia in Georgetown, Tim began to explore some 'what if' questions regarding her son, Mikhail's, 'ne'er do-well' son. For example what if he'd found his way to Show Low with the box? If he could establish that, it would increase probability significantly. He would never have used a name like Cantacuzene: too memorable and obvious. But what if he used an alias, something forgettable, unassuming? Mikhail's son, the wayward son, would have been in his 20s in the 1960s. Tim chose that date-range because his cousin, Justin, acquired the cabin in 1973 so the pouch containing the artifacts had to have been hidden away sometime around then or before if Tim's scenario was accurate…and that was simply a guess. The main challenge however was that Julia had not mentioned her grandson's given name.

That aside for the moment, where would a young guy deserting his family and heritage, presumably with few resources, seek refuge? And why would it be Arizona rather than anywhere else? Arizona had obvious attractions but there would need to be something more tangible…a friend…a relative?

As always first things first. His last day in DC he'd spent in the genealogical archive at the Library of Congress and searching the obituaries in the NY Times, Newport, RI, and the Sarasota Herald Tribune. Without a name he'd get nowhere. He quickly found record of Julia's son Prince Michael and his wife Clarissa Curtis. Michael had graduated from Harvard and went into real estate in Chicago before buying the farm in Wadsworth. He died in 1972. Clarissa was from a prominent Boston family and for whatever reason left Michael and they divorced in 1934. Tragically Clarissa took her own life in New York four years later. She was just 34. Then Tim found what he was looking for. Together they had two children, a girl and a boy…Rodion. He was 6 years old when his mother died.

That was not a common name to be sure. Something Julia had said didn't fit the picture he was beginning to see however. Perhaps she was biased for whatever reason and mistaken about the boy? If that was so, then perhaps Tim was on the wrong track? He'd learned by experience that it was easy to make erroneous assumptions based on fragmentary evidence or faulty memory. When she died in 1975 she was after all 99 years old…79 when Leighton had interviewed her.

It didn't take long for Tim to confirm his suspicion but it was nothing he was prepared for. Rodion Cantacuzene was born in Chicago in October 1928. Far from a nomadic lost soul and perhaps worse, Radion graduated from Annapolis, Class of '52, served in Korea as a newly minted ensign, and retired as a captain in the United States Navy! One line in his military service biography made Tim actually gasp. Then Commander Rodion served in Vietnam at the same time Tim had! He knew he'd remember a name like that so he was certain they'd never crossed paths but the correspondence struck him as more than incidental somehow.

But it was the last line that put an exclamation point on everything he'd done over the past two months. Retired Commander Rodion Cantucazene lived in Royal, Arizona, half-way between Prescott and Show Low. He was still alive! Here, Tim was certain, must be the final, conclusive clue…the last piece of the puzzle! He made the phone call. A man answered.

The Commander, now 68, after some hesitation agreed to meet him and Tim drove nearly non-stop from Phoenix. They greeted one another at the golf course clubhouse over drinks. Small talk, reminiscing about Nam and military service, and their respective careers, steering clear of the political minefields, finally led them to why Tim asked for the meeting. Over the next fifteen minutes Tim spun out the narrative and how he was involved. Rodion's command-stare was intimidating but not unfriendly. He was tall and a still ramrod straight albeit gray-haired naval officer, complexion ruddy, eyes intelligent and probing. Tim sat back with an arm's wide, palms up gesture as he finished. "So, that's why I'm here. I'm trying to understand how in the hell those artifacts ended-up hidden in my cabin in Show Low?

"That is quite a tale," Rodion confessed. I'm impressed with your detective work. Are all historians so dogged in their pursuit of the truth?"

"I suppose no more than men with rank always make good officers."

"God knows that's true enough. I've known some of them."

"Me too."

"So you're telling me that Alexie's artifacts are now back in Russia?"

"As far as I know. They're either in the possession of the Kremlin itself, the Orthodox Church or the Hermitage Museum. At least the gangsters didn't get their hands on them.

"In my experience, gangsters can be found everywhere… some disguised as politicians."

Tim had to laugh at that observation. "So true and no country has a monopoly on virtue. Power is power and corruption is its life-blood."

"Ah, I know all about that," they clinked beer bottles. For a time they sat quietly, Tim's thoughts flying to Abby as a cloud briefly scudded across the sun. She was so tantalizingly close, Prescott barely fifty-miles southwest of them. But he had to finish this, End the chapter…close the door.

"Ironic huh? How's that for full-circle. My great, great grandfather's artifacts begin their surreptitious journey in Russia and it's their final destination as well," he shook his head in wonderment.

"Stretches the imagination some doesn't it," Tim agreed.

"All right Tim, here's the part of the story you don't know yet.

"In Vietnam I wasn't on the Ticonderoga or the New Jersey as I'd hope to be. Instead I had a shore detail as the naval attache to the embassy in Saigon on Ham Nghi. Riverine ops in the Delta against the VC primarily...coordinating with the AVRAN…swift boats…insertions. Zumwalt's 'brown water' strategy."

"I remember…Operation Marauder in '66. I was with the 173rd…us and the Aussies. That was a ball-buster but we kicked hell out of the 267th Main Force." The silence of unspoken memories. Two guys who'd never met before…veterans sharing their stories as only veterans can.

"It was the week after Tet in '68 that I received a letter from my father and with it a note from Speranski. The Prince died in '55…was still living in Sarasota.

"I know. I came across the memoir of an acquaintance of your family who visited your grandmother, the princess, in DC the year before your grandfather died. It's how I put together how you might be the key to the mystery."

As you probably know she died in '75. I never saw her again after my one visit when I was 5-6…I can't remember. All I do remember is a very handsome older woman, the ocean and miles of orange groves. I can still smell it. Anyway, the prince informed me…from him it was like a military command, that he wanted me to have the Romanov artifacts he was given by Czar Nicholas in gratitude for my grandfather's service. He said his son Michael had no interest in history or those 'old relics' as he called them. And the girls didn't either. History for them was about things best forgotten...memories best allowed to decompose."

"My students either love history or more often hate it," Tim laughed, "so I can relate."

"Apparently without telling my grandmother or anyone else, Rodion continued, "he just packed-up the box and sent it to me. He was getting up in years and I think he may have been losing it a bit…was prone to making impulsive, off-the-wall decisions."

"To Saigon? He sent the artifacts to the embassy?"

"The package arrived two weeks later. I hadn't seen the box or those artifacts since that visit to grandma when I was a kid. I remembered the gold coins and that large revolver. There was a collar insignia I immediately recognized as military but I never pursued it."

"I did."

"Of course you did. And? Tim explained. "I'll be damned."

"So what happened?"

"It sat in my office for the rest of the war. When the embassy evacuated that last day in April '75- Operation Frequent Wind, everything was chaos and totally FUBAR with the NVA just outside the city. In the end we had just minutes to evac. My quarters were in the consular compound and at some point the Marines closed it off for security reasons… the throngs of panicked Vietnamese trying to book-it out of Dodge threatened to overrun the Annex. Everything was locked down before I could grab all my gear…or the artifacts. I was in the third-to-last CH-53. All I had were my fatigues and sidearm. Had to leave everything else behind and I figured the North Vietnamese would grab it. Ironic don't you think when you consider who their principal ally was during the war."

"But that's not what happened obviously."

"No, it wasn't. I had an interpreter. His name was Lon, a great kid…loved America. I couldn't get him out," and Tim looked away as Rodion's voice cracked and his eyes turned glassy. I don't know what happened to him but I suspect he was killed with thousands of other Vietnamese who collaborated with Americans. But I do now that whatever happened to him, he somehow got into my quarters and threw everything he could into a trunk. That trunk went by sea to Malaysia to Guam and finally to Florida...carried to safety by Boat People who'd been abandoned…sold out by us. Doesn't that take the cake. It was a miracle that it survived. If only it could talk. What a story it could tell!"

"Florida…how the hell did it go to Florida?"

"I'm not sure. Dad and Grandpa were dead by then of course but I had a couple of cousins, one actually lived in Florida. I didn't know where at the time. Paul was his name. I never met him. But I did receive a letter from him when I first deployed. Maybe Lon found that letter in my quarters and wrote the address on the trunk As I recall it was an FPO. He was still in the service. Paul's a few years older than me. From what I remember grandma telling me that branch of the family was bad news among the Romanovs…"

"Wait. Paul was a Romanov and in the military?!"

Yes. Lt. Colonel Paul Dmitriievich Romanovsky-llyinsky. He was the son of Grand Duke Paul Alexandrovich, Czar Nicholas II's cousin, Czar Alexander II's great-grandson. According to grandma, the father was involved in the assassination of that crazy monk Rasputin and banished from Russia during the war. He was serving in

Persia when the czar's family was murdered…the only Romanov to survive. Cousin Paul was born in London where they lived in exile. The father ended-up marrying into a wealthy family in Cincinnati and they became US citizens. Paul joined the Marines and served in Korea as a combat photographer. That's all I know."

"So he was in direct line of succession?"

"Yes, from what I understand. But following my family's lineage is not for the faint of heart!" he laughed easily. The genealogical charts are like a Kandinsky Composition!"

"So you have no idea what happened to the artifacts after they reached Florida?"

"No. I don't. I tried like hell to track it down…follow the trail. I felt a family obligation. But all I could do was get post office confirmation that the trunk was delivered. Sorry I can't tell you more, Tim. Maybe you'll have better luck. Hell, you're the archaeologist."

"Archaeologist?"

"You dig up stuff, right?"

"In a manner of speaking."

"OK how about 'sleuth.' If anyone can solve the mystery, I'll wager you're the guy to do it."

Tim had taken a motel room for the night. Tomorrow he'd dive up to Show Low to follow-up on what he's learned from Rodion. He'd call Abby from there to tell her he'd be home in a day or two. The new semester was now only a week away. As is, he was cutting it close but he knew himself well enough to know that if he didn't put this all to bed, it would pester like an itch he couldn't scratch.

He finally drifted off into an uneasy sleep and troubled dreams. He awoke to the sound of rain, the sky heavy with the dark clouds of a storm front advancing with a fury that threatened to take no prisoners.

CHAPTER FORTY-ONE

The door of the Slow Low Historical Museum stood open as the early morning shower had blown away to the east and heat began to reassert itself. Driving through the town again so soon after their ordeal provoked a flood of emotions and visual flashbacks. He thought of Abby. He thought of John Clarke. Unable to resist, he drove by the cabin...what remained of it. Charred ruins drapped in yellow caution tape, adorned with red and black 'keep out' sign. Temptation called but he resisted the urge to get out...explore. To what end?

No sooner had he turned his rental back towards town than the familiar sedan braked to a stop in front of him. "Ed, how are you doing? He greeted the community service 'cop.'

"I should ask you the same damn thing," Ed bristled. "What the hell happened here that night?" he demanded to know. Christ, this was the last thing Tim needed. Coming out here was a mistake.

"Propane explosion. Police and fire confirmed it. Abby and I were on the back deck getting some air when it happened otherwise…Anyway, Ed, the insurance company is handling it. I was passing through town and just thought I'd check it out."

Ed eyed him severely. "There's something out of kilter on this whole deal, Tim. Those 'friends' of yours…" Tim cut him off.

"Look, Ed, I appreciate your diligence but there's nothing about this that's 'off kilter." It was a nasty accident that could have been much worse. That's all."

Ed didn't look convinced, Tim thought but he didn't want to open any other doors. Ed, how long have you lived here now?" Tim changed the subject but it wasn't a throw-away question.

"Since 1969…why?"

"Do you remember seeing Justin here at the cabin in the mid-70s?"

"I worked concessions at the lake back then. This was Hippie central. Communes all over the damn place. Lot of drug use. It was pretty wild but mostly harmless, as I remember. I can't say if the cabin was used much. Why?"

"You know insurance companies. They want as much of a history for their file as they can get…Just wondering if Justin was around then much."

"There was one crazy incident in '75 that anyone who lived around here knew about. Some guy over in Snowflake just down the road swore he was abducted by aliens. The White Mountain Independent carried a big story about it. I remember the front page photo of the guy- his name was Walton, and the headline, 'UFO Passenger.' Most everyone in town had a good laugh…thought the guy'd had a bad trip or something. But there were others who really bought into it. Hell, they even made a damn move about it in '78 called 'Fire in the Sky'!"

"I never knew about that, Ed. Very interesting." Tim waved good-by his mind working on this new twist. As amazing as was the journey of the Romanov relics he was pretty sure it didn't include alien abductions... 'Abduction'. The word struck a chord driven in part by his and Abby's recent experiences. Could it also play another role?

Tim stepped into the Historical Society Museum, a large well-maintained old Victorian. He knew the story of Cooley and Clark and their famous card game that gave the town its name. Admittedly a great story, town mythology wasn't what he was hoping to learn. As he looked about the place he couldn't help thinking about John and his little museum in Glasgow.

"Hi," he approached the young woman, no doubt a student volunteer, he guessed. "I was wondering if you have any Russian artifacts from the town's past?"

She hesitated. “I’m pretty sure there was a small Russian community near here, farmers mostly, in the 1880s. McNary was the town everyone hereabouts went to for work and supplies. It was a big lumber town 20 miles south on the Fort Apache reservation. I think there were maybe some Russians there,” she offered helpfully. Hardly definitive, Tim thought but interesting.

He strolled on through the various parlors and dens and vestibules, turning a corner and entering another ‘themed’ room, allowing his mind to wander. In minutes he found himself on the third floor of three rooms. He chose one. There he stopped suddenly as if he’d walked into a wall. On an old book stand in a corner sat an elegant wood box. It looked like Cherry wood, Tim thought. There was some kind on design the lid. As he walked closer the decoration became more distinct. It was a double-headed eagle set on a royal crest!

He examined it from every angle to make sure. There was no mistake…no uncertainty about what he was looking at. He all but ran back to the reception room. He was alone in the museum except for an older couple looking through some brochures in an adjacent room. “Excuse me miss…where did you get that presentation case in the glass cabinet upstairs?”

She put down her paperback with little disguised annoyance and walked with Tim upstairs. ‘This one,” Tim hardly needed to indicate as it was the only one on display but he was too excited to think clearly. He was about to ask another question when he stopped short. Normally hyper-observant he’d overlooked something. For the first time Tim noticed the printed card on the glass shelf. It read: ‘Austrian c. 1937. Bequest in honor of early Show Low pioneers, Olga and Dimitri Romanovsky, 1886.’ Sorry, here it is,” he apologized. She left him with a look.

Tim studied the coat of arms more closely now. There was something different about it.Then he remembered his European history. The Austrian crest of that date was during the four years between 1934 and German annexation in 1938 just before WWII, when it was redesigned briefly from a single to a… double-headed eagle! But the crest he was looking at, he was now certain, was not Austrian at all. It was Russian! He could see how a curator or even the donor might misidentify it as the crests looked very similar.

He took the stairs two-at-a-time quickly, in seconds again in the lobby breathing heavily. "Sorry to interrupt your reading," he couldn't resist, "but is here any chance you have some information on the donor? I'm family," he lied.

She excused herself returning a few minutes later with a file box. Fingering through cards she finally pulled one free. "Says here the donor's name is a 'J. S. Romanovsky.' Tim looked at her with incredulous intensity as the final piece fell into place... He wasn't lying about family after all. J.S....Justin Sasha. That was his cousin's first and middle name! But the real kicker was that Tim only knew him by his last name...'Romans' not Romanovsky. Why the obfuscation... Intentional deception? What he did know was that the presentation box in the museum almost certainly was the same one that Leighton Rogers had rescued from St. Petersburg in 1919 that had belonged to Prince Cantucazene and Grand Duke Akexi Alexandrovich...that Rodion had received in Vietnam from his grandfather...that very box that must have been sent to a distant cousin in Florida as Saigon fell! It was nearly full circle now. He had one remaining link in the chain of custody...one last bit of narrative in the saga to write.

But before he could do that he realized he must do one more thing to be certain. Making his way back to the third floor, finding himself alone, Tim removed the box from its stand. It was heavy and beautifully made. The silver hasp on the lid moved easily, the top lifting without protest. The box was empty except for some built-in compartments lined in red velvet, its contents removed...just as he'd hoped to find. Finally he looked in the upper middle of the lid and there it was... a monogram as Leighton said in his diary transcript would be there. Two letters in gold thread: AA...Alexei Alexandrovich...

CHAPTER FORTY-TWO

"Riodon, it's Tim. I'm sorry to bother you but I don't know who else could possibly help me." It was later that afternoon. Tim sat in his motel room off Deuce of Clubs. Another thunder storm was rolling through and a heavy downpour pittered his window. Thunder cracked.

"Not at all, Tim. I enjoyed our talk yesterday. What's up?"

"I just came across some information that surprised the hell out of me and I thought you might be able to help me understand it."

"Do my Navy best," Riodon replied.

"You remember the cabin I told you about…the one in Show Low?"

"I do. I enjoy Show Low when I get over there now and then. Pretty area."

"For years it belonged to a cousin of mine. We'd get together once in a while…beers, BBQ. He died suddenly a couple of years ago and it surprised the hell out of me when I learned he'd left it to me in his will."

"Thoughtful of him."

"It was. We were never best buddies and actually differed quite a bit in our politics so, yes, it was a surprise. But I've just uncovered another one…a big one, I think. I always thought his last name was Romans, Justin Romans. But he had a Russian-sounding middle name...Sasha. Well, hold on to your shoulder boards. I did some exploring at the museum here this morning and I made two huge discoveries."

"Go on."

"Hope you're sitting down. I found the box…Alexi's presentation box. It was sitting in a nondescript book stand on display in the Museum. It was misidentified as Austrian. I opened it. It was compartmentalized and lined in red velvet. At the top of the inside lid were the monogramed initials 'AA'. In Leighton's diary transcript he identifies the same lettering."

Time heard a deep exhale. "I don't believe it. That is Alexi's presentation case. The Prince showed it to me the time I visited the compound in Sarasota. I remember that vividly. You said there was something else?"

"Yes, I discovered that the donor was my cousin in honor of his grandparents who lived in Show Low in the 1880s. Their name was Olga and Dimitri Romanovsky. My cousin's last name wasn't Romans…it was Romanovsky! Why he misrepresented that I have no idea. But what's indisputable is that your family's heirlooms ended-up here in Show Low sometime in the late 60's or early '70s. Justin must have removed the relics, hid them in the cabin and gave the case to the museum."

Tim listened to silence for a long moment. Finally…."Tim, you really know how to blow-up a guys day." Another heavy sigh. We have many secrets in our extended, complicated family. This must be one of them…another one I had no inkling of. My distant cousin Paul must be related somehow to your cousin Justin."

"But why would he send the relics to him up here in Arizona?"

"Professor, ironically enough I think you already know the answer."

"And that would be?" Sitting there phone to ear he couldn't imagine.

"I think it's what ties all of this together or at least links Florida and Arizona…crime. From what you described you and your wife barely escaped the Russian mafia's efforts to seize the relics for their own illegal purposes, the contract issued once the existence of the artifacts became known to the criminal syndicates who could make use of them for their own purposes. Tim, I think it was your digging and poking around that accomplished that. Probably not what you want to hear, I'm guessing." Now it was Tim's turn to be at a loss for words. Riodon was undoubtedly right.

"As for Florida it used to be the exclusive playground of the Italian-Sicilian mafia guys
from New York beginning in the 1920s and 30s…especially Miami and Palm Beach. But that's changed from what I read and hear. Now increasingly it's Russian, Ukranian and Armenian crime syndicates who've moved in to claim territory. I don't know this for certain but could it be that these same criminal elements somehow traced that trunk to Florida and targeted Paul? For all anyone knows they could have had someone in the postal service. They are insidious and tenacious in their reach."

"So you're saying that Paul felt endangered and in order to protect the Romanov legacy sent the trunk up here to a distant cousin…Justin…my cousin?!"

"Paul's high profile and everyone knows his lineage. I didn't mention that he's mayor of Palm Beach and was just elected to a second term. They love him down there. He's surely known to the syndicates… especially a gangster named Simchuck. There's a section of the city known as 'Little Moscow,' for Christ's sake. I even heard that in the midst of the Soviet collapse, Russian royalists asked Paul to proclaim himself czar and return home, reinstating the Romanov dynasty! Back then the gangsters would have loved to get their hands on him, or the artifacts, just for the ransom. Then he said the last thing Tim expected.

" I think if you continue to dig, you'll find that along with changing his last name he changed his first. It's not 'Justin'. It's Justinin…Justinin Romanovsky."

For Tim it was like hearing an audible click…a key turning in a lock. He knew in his gut that Riodon must be right…that this was the explanation…confirmation that the mystery had finally been solved. It was an epiphany and a release. His emotional tension ebbed and for long moments he sat in subdued solitude, contemplating his journey and that of all those whose lives had been touched, from Leighton Rogers' experiences through revolution and two world wars to his own more than eighty years later, linked together however improbably by the he reflected now by the amazing odyssey of Alexie Alexandrovich's relics from St. Petersburg, Russia to Show Low, Arizona

Prescott was barely four hours away. He could be there by late afternoon. He packed quickly, stopping only to call Abby. She wasn't home…again. That bothered him in the pit of his stomach. But she was probably just out for a walk with Ralph, or at the market. As he drove south she was all he could think about…

CHAPTER FORTY-THREE

The day Tim left for DC had been difficult. God she was so conflicted, torn between loving being with him, loving the life they were building together, and the unrelenting stress that had been seeping into their relationship for the past two years until she felt like she was drowning. One thing she had no doubt about was that she had to deal with it…had to reconcile the two opposites pulling at her. Question was how to do it if it could be done at all?

It was in that frame of mind that she'd spent the past week occupying herself with things she enjoyed…shopping, gardening, taking Ralph for long walks, sitting out on the veranda watching the sun set to its brilliant vanishing point…some calling it the 'green flash.' And enjoying more than a little wine. All of it as therapy did wonders, she happily approved as one day folded into another.

They'd spoken twice. It seemed that he was making substantial progress in his quest to understand everything that had happened since 1917, events triggered by their finding those damn czarist relics. She'd suffered through one terrible nightmare about their ordeal at the cabin and being burned alive. It seemed like ever since their discovery there had been a miasma of bad shit attached to it. She knew it was stupid but it almost seemed like the relics were haunted or possessed. She thought of Rasputin and laughed…nervously.

Now he was on his way home. He'd left a message on the machine…told her that he'd taken

a side trip to Show Low and now knew the whole story...had solved the mystery. She was happy for him and part of her, too, enjoyed the satisfaction that came with knowing the rest of the story…part of her story after all. 'I can't wait to tell you,' he'd all but exploded with excitement. He said he missed her terribly, apologized…again. Said he loved her. He wanted to go out to dinner and celebrate. That was two hours ago. He'd be home in another two

"You're such a good boy, Ralph," she scratched his belly, legs askew, tail wagging, Abby reflecting on all they'd been through together and how he'd never shrunk from danger or his fierce defense of her. Tweeks came down off her perch on the sofa to rub against her leg with a soft meow. Cats were not loyal but they were intuitive, attuned creatures. "Be good to Ralph," Abby instructed, appreciating how challenging that would be, both pushing each other's buttons with relish. Looking around that house, surveying their home, she saw so much that was so comforting in its familiarity…a place full of memory and promise of endless days scrolling into the future, the past ever receding but never far from view, what lay ahead inscrutably opaque as it must always remain…

Tim pulled his rental into the driveway parking next to his truck. Abby's car must be in the garage where she usually parked. His hands tingled with anticipation. Grabbing his overnight, leaving the rest until later, he strode into the living room with a theatrical 'Hey, I'm home. The only answer he got was from Ralph who jumped-up on him tail wagging furiously, making happy little noises. Even Tweeks meowed a greeting.

The house was quiet…too quiet. He could hear the sound of the kitchen clock and the hiss of the air conditioning. "Abby…Abby?" he called out. No Answer. No throwing herself into his arms as he'd prayed she would. No smell of her hair and lightly applied scent of CK-1 he loved.

The entire drive from Slow Low had been a torture of what ifs and recriminations. Where the hell was she? Suddenly cold dread gripped his stomach. The gnawing fears that he could not deflect that troubled him all the way home were it staggered him- a premonition.

He looked around in vain as if he expected so see her belatedly responding to his voice. Folding herself into him, gazing up into his eyes, hers bright with promise and love. He tore into their bedroom sliding back the wardrobe door. Her side was barren. Then the drawers of her chest-empty. Abby wasn't gone…

It was then that he saw a white envelope on the kitchen breakfast bar. He froze. An emotional abyss opened under him and he was free-falling into it. The bottom fell out of his world. Nothing was ever guaranteed; nothing promised to us and certainly not the future. It was, it struck him, its own shadow land of unknowns and uncertainty where nothing and no one could or must ever be taken for granted.

Both animals were staring at him, accusatorily he imagined. With a deep, shuddering breath he walked to the breakfast bar. Pulling back a stool with grating protest he sat heavily, opened the sealed letter, took another breath…

And began to read.

EPILOGUE

Shadow Lands of memory is a work of fiction but it is also a book that blends fact with fiction. With the exception of the fictional characters- Tim Strange, Abby, Justin, Father Bakakov, Andre, Vytali, Duncan, and others who interact with the protagonist in Prescott, all the other are people who lived and were important actors in the drams of the Russian Revolution on 1917 in St. Petersburg. They are represented as accurately as possible from diary entries, public statements, memoirs and published materials.

Most notable is Leighton Rogers whose amazing life, memoir, 'Wine of Fury' and archival materials depict his actual experiences and memories of the world-changing events of 1917. While I have taken license with some of this material, the vast majority of the events depicted actually happened as described, while the people he interacted with were in fact and name key actors in his experiences.

www.ingramcontent.com/pod-product-compliance
Lightning Source LLC
Chambersburg PA
CBHW031726170626
46808CB00005B/1905

9781649455420